The driver was invisible behind the rapid swish of windshield wipers and the spit of snow from the van's wheels. But as I felt the jolt on my bumper, the intention was clear. The Bronco was trying to run me off the road.

I turned my eyes back a second too late. I bounced over a snow drift and landed hard on my front tires, the back tires skidding violently to the right. A second later, I felt another impact that rattled my jaw. The car spun one hundred and eighty degrees, sideswiped a young birch, then shot over the shoulder. With a jolt, I smacked into a snow-filled ditch, the shoulder harness whipping me back with a snap.

My head wrenched forward, glancing off the steering wheel. In shock, I stayed like that for a moment. Then I rapidly released my seat belt, fumbled for the lock, and fell into the snow. I didn't have to turn around to know the Bronco had stopped as well. The rushing silence was horrifyingly articulate. I plunged ahead into the woods, the snow blinding me. There was nowhere to run. Already, the snow was calf high. Despite my bravado, I knew I wasn't strong enough to outrun my pursuer. The chill had penetrated my bones again and I felt as if an ice pick were cracking through my scalp.

The ground sloped suddenly and my toe caught on an unseen root. Tumbling headfirst, I rolled forward in a whitewashed hush. When I landed, I spit blood onto my parka. Then I gave up. I turned around, ready to greet whoever had chased me here.

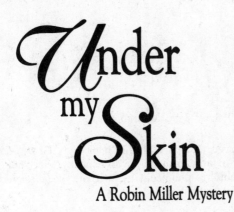

Under my Skin

A Robin Miller Mystery

BY JAYE MAIMAN

The Naiad Press, Inc.
1997

Printed in the United States of America on acid-free paper
First Edition
Second Printing 1995
Third Printing April, 1997

Edited by Katherine V. Forrest and Christine Cassidy
Cover design by Pat Tong and Bonnie Liss
    (Phoenix Graphics)
Typeset by Sandi Stancil

Library of Congress Cataloging-in-Publication Data

Maiman, Jaye, 1957–
    Under my skin : a Robin Miller mystery / by Jaye Maiman.
        p.   cm.
    ISBN 1-56280-049-3 (paper)
    1. Miller, Robin (Fictitious character)—Fiction.   2. Women
detectives—United States—Fiction.   3. Lesbians—United
States—Fiction.   I. Title.
PS3563.A38266U53   1993
813'.54—dc20
                                                                93-24909
                                                                    CIP

Dedicated to My Families —

Ira & Sylvia, Ann & Steve
Elaine & Ann-Marie, Pauline & Risa
Sharon, Michael, and the Iz-man

and

Rhea
for the gift of rhapsody

Acknowledgments

Writing is a solitary occupation that would not be possible without collaboration. Concocting events, creating characters, imagining locations, and battling elbow and wrist fatigue all require the ministration of some very special people. I owe a huge debt of gratitude to Elaine, Annie, Anna, and Lisa and my many other friends in the real "Telham Village" for inviting me into their homes, teaching me about the Poconos, and entreating me to "just think" until I fell as much in love with their community as they were. Thanks also go to my editing goddesses Katherine V. Forrest and Christi Cassidy and to the other wonderful women of Naiad. Finally, special thanks go to Maureen and Victoria for being close by when I discovered my deer, Jill and Joan for telling me the truth at just the right time, Gary K. for his religious instruction, and Gary S. for providing me with some much-needed medical expertise. (Sorry, Gar, I won't list you as coauthor.) Finally, my love and gratitude go to Rhea for her patience, courage, criticism, confidence, humor, and massages. Thank you for bringing me home and making me believe when all I wanted was a hot fudge sundae and a Yoo-Hoo.

About the Author

Jaye Maiman has written five other Robin Miller mysteries: *I Left My Heart*, the Lambda Award-winning *Crazy for Loving, Someone to Watch, Baby It's Cold* and *Old Black Magic*. She was born in Brooklyn, New York, and raised in a Coney Island housing project where she spent Tuesday nights consuming blueberry cheese knishes and watching fireworks from a beachside boardwalk. She now lives in Park Slope, Brooklyn, with her two puppy cats and her partner, playmate, editor, co-neurotic, and magic-maker Rhea.

Chapter 1

Thick clouds blotted out the moon. I flipped up the collar of my wool blazer and shivered. The road to Robert and Allan's house was longer and steeper than I had remembered, and the night air here in the Pocono mountains of Pennsylvania stung with the promise of a bitter winter. Sucking in the scent of rustling pine trees and wood-burning stoves, I paused for a moment then bent into the wind.

The night wrapped around my city eyes like a blindfold. I squinted, anxious for even a faint glimmer of light to tell me I was closing in. Instead, all I could make out was the shape of an unidentifiable animal slinking into the bushes on the side of the road. My breath spat steam as I quickened my pace.

When my teeth started chattering I began to wonder how much of my chill was due to the temperature and how much due to the phone call I had received before leaving the log-framed cabin I was renting for the month. The conversation filled my head like hot air expanding in a too tight balloon.

K.T. Bellflower was headed here. Two nights early. Or six months late, depending on how you looked at it.

The first and only time we kissed, I had succumbed to instant meltdown: weak knees, pounding heart, and that deep ache between my legs clenching hard. We'd been on Fire Island when it happened, on a boardwalk leading to one of the world's most exquisite beaches. And when our lips touched, I knew a tidal wave was coming for me. The only thing that saved me from the undertow was fear. And common sense.

In the past two and a half years, two of my lovers have been murdered. It's a track record that frankly scares the crap out of me. Understandably, I have one hell of a black-widow complex.

After that limb-shivering kiss, my internal alarm system shifted into high gear. I backed off and mumbled something about "not being ready" — one of those dumb phrases we all resort to when we feel like sprinting back to safe ground. But I wasn't scared or dumb enough to reject K.T. totally. We spent the day walking through the Sunken Forest, our hands sealed together like Velcro.

As it turned out, she left the country two days later.

K.T.'s a famous chef, with her own cooking show on PBS. For the past six months, she's been a guest instructor at the LeClerc's Culinary Academy in Paris. Me, I've been in therapy trying to figure out why intimacy seems so incredibly appealing when I'm single yet makes me want to puke small, angular stones whenever an available woman comes along. My therapist, Vivian Mauer, tells me that when I find the answer I'll also know why I turned my back on a lucrative career as a romance writer to become a private detective. I figure by then I'll also know the true stories behind the Big Bang and JFK's assassination.

At last, a light flickered at the top of the hill. I shoved aside memories of K.T. and began gearing up for the festivities.

Robert and Allan were staging a Bless-the-Turkeys party in anticipation of Thanksgiving, which was just five days away. Almost all of the gay couples living in the private Telham Village community were coming, plus a few straight neighbors. The bottom line was that, straight or gay, Helen Ananias and I would be the only single women in a room of fifty plus.

The realization almost propelled me back to the cabin I was renting, but the sensor lights tagged me and announced my presence with a blue-white beam. A second later a perfectly groomed English sheepdog had her bagel-sized paws planted on both of my

3

breasts. Knowing the salami-sized tongue was next, I feinted to my left.

"Don't tell me you walked!" Allan exclaimed as the screen door slammed behind him. Caitlin's snout headed unswervingly for my crotch. Life must be considerably less complicated in the canine kingdom. I stepped around her toward Allan, who was observing Caitlin's antics with the amused appreciation of a overindulgent parent. He smiled broadly when our eyes caught. "She loves you, Rob. Kiss her."

I complied reluctantly, receiving a healthy dose of wet dog breath in return, then tried to climb the stairs with eighty pounds of dog humping my right calf. Allan bounded in front of me. Slender, with short-cropped hair the color of chestnuts, he had the energy of a prepubescent male and the timing of a Catskills comedian. Dress him in drag, and he'd be a dead ringer for Doris Day. The fact that his lover Robert resembled a young Rock Hudson has often compelled me to burst into song. *Que sera sera*. I followed his tightly denimed butt into the kitchen and asked, "What's cooking?"

He pursed his lips and wiggled an eyebrow. "Triple fudge brownies. Robert will only eat them straight from the oven. Warm and gooey. C'mon, darling. If you don't move fast, you'll miss out on Joannie's artichoke dip."

I followed him into the great room, marveling once again at the impeccably designed surroundings. The wall-to-wall carpeting was the color of New Mexico sand dunes at sunset, with bleached oak furniture, a verdigris ceiling fan, and turquoise- and peach-toned *objets d'art* positioned around the multi-leveled home for the greatest visceral impact. Allan strode ahead of me, tracking crushed leaves under his lavender Nikes and tipping his battered Yankees baseball cap to one of the guests. I worked my way through the crowd with appropriate kisses and hugs and arrived at the buffet table. Eight feet of dining heaven. I almost cried when I spied the steaming cistern of mulligatawny.

Just then I heard voices rising above the party din. I speared a Carr's cracker into the artichoke dip and moved toward the commotion. I grimaced when I saw the source. Noreen Finnegan, drunk extraordinaire, was out on the front deck, brandishing one of Robert's potted geraniums at her ex-lover Helen Ananias. As the only other single person in the room, I rushed to her defense. Who says gallantry is dead?

"Put the flowers down," I declared with the confidence of a woman with over two years of tae kwon do under her belt. I met Noreen's fiery glance and held it till she backed down. Helen skulked away silently. "What's the problem, Noreen?" I slid the glass door behind me till it closed with a snap.

She shook her head and walked down two steps to the lower deck. I followed her, then jerked back as she halted abruptly. I took a whiff, expecting her usual acrid whiskey breath, then cocked an eyebrow. Damned if she didn't smell sober.

"Helen won't accept my apologies." The petulant tone was incongruous with her appearance. Almost five-ten, Noreen was imposing in a Phantom-of-the-Opera way. She had dark brown hair the color of the cheap walnut-veneered office furniture they sell in Kmart, and ice blue eyes that only emphasized the striking paleness of her skin. A ropy four-inch scar ran across her left cheek. Dressed in a tartan flannel shirt, black jeans, and cowboy boots, she was a model of butch fashion from the fifties.

She pulled a super-thin cigar from her breast pocket, bit off the tip, and spat it over the side of the deck. With distaste, I watched her light the cigar. Flat-chested and hipless, in another era Noreen would have been called a stone butch. All I know is that no one in Telham — gay or straight — wanted to be on her shit list. When she and Helen moved into the community last June, their elderly next-door neighbor made the mistake of calling Noreen *Mister* Finnegan. Twice. Three days later the poor man found a hamperful of dirty sanitary napkins on his back porch. Last I heard, his house was still on the market.

Helen called it quits barely two months later. Now she's renting a lackluster place on a cul-de-sac, and Noreen's got a brand-new lover installed in a massive split-level contemporary with an exquisite view of the Acee River.

I watched Noreen swing a leg over the rail and straddle it like a horse. The wood creaked lightly as she kicked a post with her heel. "What are you apologizing for?" I asked.

She looked at me with surprise. "All the shit that went down between us." From the little I knew about her seven-year relationship with Helen, there was enough shit to fertilize the Midwest twice over.

"Why now?"

There was a beat of hesitation, then she said, "I'm in recovery."

I recognized the terminology instantly. Alcoholics Anonymous. I tried to picture Noreen at an AA meeting, but the image wouldn't jell. "You usually apologize with a flowerpot aimed at someone's head?" I asked testily.

She shrugged and said, "Nah, she just got me pissed. But I almost went too far. Again." Her arm shot out in my direction and I jumped back involuntarily. Then I realized what she wanted. I shook her hand. "Thanks for interrupting," she added, sounding almost sincere.

I nodded and started back up the stairs. Her baritone voice stopped me. "You still a detective?" she asked.

"Yeah," I said defensively.

"I want to hire you." She swung her feet onto the deck with a thud that shook my soles. I watched her dig five twenties from her back pocket. Shoving them at me, she said, "I can't talk about it here. But take this as a deposit. We'll talk tomorrow. My place."

I palmed the money away from me. "Noreen, I can't take this from you. After we talk —"

She shoved the money into my shirt pocket. "I know what makes people tick. And keep commitments. Tomorrow. Around six."

With that, she pounded down the steps.

I took a deep breath and hoped that the brownies were waiting for me back in the kitchen. I desperately needed something sweet.

The dark chocolate melted in my mouth. I leaned against the rolled arm of the eggshell couch and

7

took another bite of the moist brownie. From across the room a curvaceous redhead with bassett hound eyes pointed at my chest with a sly smile. If it had been anyone but Carly I would have found the look titillating, but the two of us have known each other since grade school. I nodded at her playfully and she rolled her eyes, poking a finger at her own chest meaningfully. I glanced down and saw what had attracted her attention. There were four chocolate chips melting on my right breast. I brushed them into a cocktail napkin.

When I looked up again, Carly had Amy in her arms. I felt a pang of jealousy. After twelve years, they still adore each other. Painfully aware of my single status, I retreated to the bathroom. The one downstairs was occupied so I padded upstairs, grateful for the sudden quiet as I closed the door. I turned on the faucet and wet the edge of a guest towel. As I sponged the chocolate stain on my shirt, I heard tense murmuring in the hallway. A natural snoop, I pressed my ear to the door.

"She's driving me crazy. I've never met anyone so damn secretive. She's always talking about the importance of family, but whenever I get close she pushes me away. How did you manage for so long?" The voice was low and sultry. I tried to place it but couldn't.

I waited for the response. "It was like sleepwalking through a nightmare." The words were passionless. No regret. No anger. The emotional equivalent of fog. I knew the speaker instantly. Helen Ananias. "You have to wake up, honey. Before you slam into a wall like I did."

There was a muffled sob. The other woman had to be Emanuela "Manny" Diaz, Noreen's new lover.

She cleared her throat, then whispered, "She's selling the house. Don't ask me why. Madam Noreen just decided it was time for us to move. No discussion. Christ, we haven't even finished paying for the new porch. You know what she's listed the house for?" She stated a figure that lifted my eyebrows in surprise.

"She wants to sell quick. I keep telling her I can't afford to move again. Besides, I just started managing that antique store in Cresco. If I quit, who knows when I'll find another job. And if I ever needed the money, it's now. Some crackheads just moved into the damn tenement where my mother and brother live. If I cut off their support, God knows where they'll end up."

The voices grew fainter as the speakers wandered down the hall. I pressed against the door so hard I half-expected it to swing open. The last words I caught were Helen's.

"It's time someone gave Noreen a little bit of her own poison."

Within less than twenty-four hours, those words would echo in my head like the buzz of a mosquito hot for blood.

The party was in full swing by the time I descended the stairs. I watched the action from the landing. Allan was regaling a small group of long-time Telham homeowners with another believe-it-or-not story about Bobby Gardener, a seventeen-year-old punk whose favorite summer sport consisted of dumping potted plants and beach chairs into the community pool. The laughter seemed forced.

Bobby was a Telham native long before the New York, New Jersey, and Philadelphia crowd discovered a little bit of heaven in the Pocono mountains. In the past seven years, the makeup of the community had changed substantially. Now, twenty-five of Telham's one hundred homes were gay-owned. Most of the couples were urban refugees. Still, the community was a rare example of tolerance and mutual respect. The exception was Bobby.

The pounding in my temples told me that I'd had enough festivities for one night. I spent a few minutes with Carly and Amy planning our Thanksgiving dinner, then said goodbye to Robert and Allan, who planned to spend the rest of the week in Key West.

I snuck out the side door. The air was even sharper than earlier, but now I welcomed the bite. Memories of past relationships rose up like hard waves presaging a winter storm. Cathy Chapman arguing with me in a San Francisco bar because I had danced with a buck-toothed secretary from her office who was too young to remember *Lost in Space* or Ed Sullivan. Mary Oswell, precious Mary, staring at me uncertainly as we said goodbye at the airport for the last time. Two years later, she was dead and all our arguments would remain forever unresolved.

Despite the temperature, my cheeks felt hot. I was tired of hurting, tired of losing. And even more tired of being alone.

A tree branch snapped sharply. I stopped and

listened. The movement in the dark woods felt more human than animal. I called out. The sound ceased abruptly. I moved into the center of the road. Great vacation, I thought. I'd have to remember to thank my therapist for recommending a month in the country as an antidote for stress.

I jogged the rest of the way down the hill, my lungs burning from the cold. Minutes later, I turned into the circular driveway. The gravel crunched under my feet as I slowed, my heart beating hard. The lights were on in the living room. I tried to remember if I had turned them off before I left.

Then the floodlights shot on.

Shit. I walked between my new Subaru, affectionately known as "Hubba," and the midnight blue Buick Skyhawk with rental plates.

K.T. had arrived.

I stared at the cabin, acid shooting into my esophagus. The door opened, and she stepped out onto the porch. Even from a distance, I could see how exquisite she looked. A thick mane of curly, red-brown hair fluttered gently against her slender neck. She was wearing a spruce-green flannel shirt and tight-fitting jeans. What do I say to her after all these months, I wondered as I stepped forward. By then I was close enough to see the fire in her eyes. That's when I realized that there would be no words.

She folded herself into my arms, her cheek warm under my lips, the faint scent of cinnamon clinging to her skin. Our mouths met, and passion ran through my center like a shot of Schnapps. We slow-danced back into the house, our hips pressed tight together, our legs interlocked.

K.T. had started a fire in the living room. We

shimmied toward the warmth, then I pressed her onto the oversized couch and explored her mouth, its silky depths, her tender, moist lips. I pulled back for a moment and stared at her. She rested her head against a throw pillow, her eyes closed and her mouth open, waiting for me. Something exploded in me, something far more potent than simple desire.

I licked the center of her upper lip with the tip of my tongue. She shivered beneath me, and I felt myself grow wet in response. Our kisses grew deeper, more urgent, our bodies grinding together. I rubbed myself hard against her long, tight thigh, listening to her breath become more ragged, her moans deeper. She ran her tongue around my ear, then blew lightly on the spots she had moistened. Chills went through me. Over and over again, she whispered in my ear two words and only two words. *I want. I want.*

We rolled onto the floor, the ache between my legs wonderfully excruciating. I tugged her shirt out of her pants and slipped my hand against her cool skin. She arched against me, and my palm discovered the delicate hollow of her lower back. Her mouth moved to my neck, biting lightly, teasing me with pauses that elicited involuntary groans. I began my own mantra.

Yes.

Yes. To desire. To making love. To taking. To being taken.

K.T. shimmied under me till her head was at my breast. She opened my sodden shirt with a tug of her teeth, then began sucking a nipple through my bra. I flattened myself against her knee, craving the pressure. She moved against me, slow and sporadic by design. The irregularity made the tension unbearable. I could no longer hear the crackle of the wood in the fireplace, the wail of the wind against the corners of the cabin. I felt blind and dumb, with one purpose.

I lifted her half-buttoned shirt over her head, but the sleeves caught on her wrists. I left them tangled in cloth above her head and propped myself up onto my elbows to stare at her small, pale breasts. Again she arched, till I lowered my mouth onto her hard nipples. They blossomed in my mouth, swelled under the flick of my tongue. I traveled between her nipples like a drunk reveling in her taste, her texture, her curves.

Her whimpers were a dizzying symphony, an opera played only for my ears. She didn't struggle to remove her shirt, but stared at me openly, with a vulnerability and a trust that briefly disoriented me. I kissed her eyes, whispered into her ear all that I intended, and was welcomed with a moan so deep that I felt it rumble through me as if it were my own.

I removed her pants, running my tongue just below her belly button. Her thighs were full and tight. Suddenly, I wanted time to cease, wanted these exquisite seconds to last for an eternity. I slowed my pace, stroking her length with my fingertips, licking her so lightly I could feel the fine hairs of her body yielding under my tongue. She filled all my senses. The saltiness of her moist skin, her singsong whimper, the edges and curves of her sweaty limbs, the sharpness of her nails as they dug into my shoulders, and the scent of her desire.

At last, I parted her with my tongue and entered her, beginning a voyage long overdue. I sucked and licked and probed her till I carried us both far beyond the stars.

By the slant of light falling over K.T.'s belly like a lover's arm, I guessed that it had to be late afternoon. Neither of us had left the bed for longer than the time it took to run down the hall to the bathroom and back. Once I took a few extra seconds to gum some toothpaste, then I was back in her muscular arms, nuzzling her salty neck, her supple lips.

"Are we still on earth?" K.T. whispered hoarsely. Still half asleep, she rolled onto her side and smiled at me.

I traced the line of her jaw and said, "Lady, we're not even in the same galaxy." She cuddled into me, her nipples hardening against my chest. Her mouth pressed against my ear as she began murmuring descriptions of what she wanted to do to me, specifying how often and how deep. I wasn't about to argue.

Just then, off in the distance, the phone rang. I groaned and buried my head under the covers.

K.T. joined me under the sheets. "That's the fifth time. Maybe you should get it."

It took less than ten seconds to convince her that we had more pressing business at hand.

I was on the edge of tumbling into a glorious black hole when the doorbell rang. I crashed back to earth with a painful thud. "Shit." I grabbed an oversized flannel shirt from the back of the door and buttoned it as I ran down the stairs and into the living room. Whoever it was had better be wearing a bulletproof vest and one hell of a crash helmet. "Be prepared to defend your life," I shouted as the intruder rang the bell again *and* slammed the knocker.

"Cool your jets and open the damn door."

It was my friend Carly. I swung the door open and stared at her menacingly. She was pale and her bottom lip was trembling.

I grabbed her hand, pulled her inside, and closed my arms around her tightly. The scent of fear rose from her skin. I glanced up over her shoulder and saw K.T. glaring at me from the top of the stairs.

Christ.

She spun around and stormed toward the bedroom.

I half-grimaced, then moved Carly to arm's length. I would have kicked her out, but she looked like hell. "Is Amy okay?" I asked, a knot forming in my throat. Carly and Amy are an anchor in my life. If anything ever happened to either of them . . .

"It's not Amy," she said. "It's Noreen Finnegan. She died a few hours ago, and Helen's up at the house stinking of booze and wailing like a banshee. She thinks the police are going to arrest her for murder."

Chapter 2

The kitchen smelled of Dewar's and vomit. I watched with trepidation as Helen lit her cigarette, fully expecting the house to explode as soon as the match caught. Instead, she held the match with quaking hands and inhaled deeply. I watched the tip of the cigarette begin to glow and tried to ignore the fact that I was still throbbing from K.T.'s touch.

"Let's go over this again, Helen," I said. "This time, take it slower. What happened after you left the party?"

She squinted at me through the smoke. Behind

her I could see Amy frown. I knew what my favorite herbalist-slash-chiropractor was thinking. The house would stink for days.

"You saw what happened with Noreen," Helen said. She paused to remove a leaf from the sleeve of the same straw-colored wool blazer she had worn last night. But the muddy stains were new. "She was in rare form. First she tells me she wants to make amends for screwing up my life for seven years, and the next thing I know she's waving a flowerpot at me and threatening to bash in my head. Some goddamn recovery."

I nodded indulgently. Get to the part I don't know, I urged her silently.

"Last thing I needed last night was another one of her alcoholic rages," she continued.

I watched her tap ash into a lid from an empty mayonnaise jar. "You sure she was drinking?" I asked, puzzled.

"Hell, yeah. Didn't you smell her? That's what got me started. I could smell the scotch on her and it propelled me right back to the good old days of drinking, fucking, and fighting." The bitterness in her voice stung. So did the contrast in our memories. I could have sworn Noreen was sober when we spoke.

Helen sucked the cigarette greedily, then sighed. "I left shortly after you stopped her from cracking my skull. When I got home, I collapsed. It was just too much. I mean, there had to be at least sixty people at that party and I was the only one by myself. Excluding you." She pointed the cigarette at me meaningfully, and all at once I felt inexplicably guilty about having spent the night with K.T.

17

"You know what I felt like? Like a damn ship without a port. Everyone else had someplace to dock. But I was running loose. Being home alone in my lousy two-bedroom ranch just made it worse. I kept thinking of how I had signed my house over to Noreen two months after I bought it just so I could escape from her, and now she's living there with Manny like it was always hers. Christ," she exclaimed, focusing on Amy with barely concealed rancor. "Do you know she was planning to sell it for a fraction of its worth? It hasn't even been ten months since she first became obsessed with the place and made me blow my inheritance on it!"

She smashed the cigarette stub into the mayonnaise lid and strode to the glass doors separating the back deck from tne kitchen. Suddenly, her tone turned strangely calm. "So I opened my cabinet and dug out a dusty bottle of whiskey and started chugging it." She turned around and stared at me hard. "I haven't done that in over three years. I just wanted the hurt to stop, Robin. I wanted to step out of my life. Do you know what I mean?"

I nodded, remembering all the ways I'd tried to escape my own painful memories.

"I just wanted to disappear. And that's the problem." She held my gaze and said, "The booze felt so good going down. I started feeling incredibly strong, like it was time for me to tell Noreen just how I felt about her, how she had fucked up my life. And that's the last thing I remember . . . till this morning." A shudder punctuated her final words.

When she had awakened, it was a little after eight o'clock. She was curled up in Noreen's gardening shed, shivering and sick to her stomach. Her first impulse was to get warm. She knocked on the back door. When no one answered, she tried the knob. Many homeowners in the community don't bother locking their doors, so she didn't find it strange that the door opened.

"But the smell hit me right away," Helen explained. She scratched at a dried splotch of paint on the glass door. "I remember thinking, man, she really tied one on last night. See, I recognized the stench. Scotch and vomit. But there was something else. Something that made me think of the time some kid crashed his 'Vette into a deer right outside our house. A peculiar odor, somehow sweet and musky. That's when I saw her. She was lying in front of the sink, blood pooled around the back of her skull, her eyes staring up at the ceiling. Her skin was the color of putty, like on an old IBM PC. I knew she was dead."

I pinched the bridge of my nose. The headache from last night had returned. I glanced up and realized that Amy looked slightly out of focus. Maybe I need glasses, I thought. Or maybe I just didn't want the image of Noreen to be so damn vivid.

Death and I are old friends. I learned about it first-hand when I was just three years old. The gunshot still reverberates in my head. Even now I can see my sister Carol's eyes flashing wide open in the darkness of the closet, a deer caught in headlights, the cry from her five-year-old body wrapping around me like a net, the gunsmoke searing my nostrils, her blood splattering my cheeks, my upper lip.

I stood abruptly, crossed to the sink and splashed

cold water on my face. This always happens at the beginning of a case — the razor's edge of memory slicing through the years, skinning me like a hunter, leaving me raw and bloodless. Maybe this was why I turned my back on the bodice-ripping romance novels I used to write and became partners in a detective agency with a Bible-quoting ex-cop fighting demons of his own.

I crossed back to the kitchen table and picked up the notes I had been jotting, then continued. "When did you call the police?"

"I don't know. Maybe five minutes after I found her. It took me that long just to stop shaking. I called Amy first. It didn't hit me right away, you know, how it would look. But when the Starret Township's police chief pulled up in the driveway, reality came crashing in." She sat down heavily. "If Noreen *was* murdered, I could be in serious trouble." She trained those soulful eyes on me and said, "I may really need your help, Rob."

I cleared my throat and asked quietly, "Why did you automatically assume she was killed? Maybe she just passed out."

The question surprised her. "Noreen's a practiced drunk. She never passed out."

"You did."

My response flustered her. Staring at me with increasing distrust, she said, "Until last night, I hadn't had a drink in years."

"Wasn't Noreen in the program?"

She crossed her legs and smoothed down her jacket. "Sure. She was sober for a few months. Big deal. I lived with the woman for seven years. I know how she drinks. She didn't pass out."

Her certainty was disconcerting. "So you just assumed someone killed her?" I asked, the sarcasm in my voice evident. Amy shot me a warning glance over Helen's head.

"For God's sake, Robin, her head was bashed in! Besides, it's not like the woman was Miss Congeniality. I don't know anyone who didn't have reason to want to bop her good at least once. She was suing one of our neighbors for a damn fender bender she no doubt caused. She kept files on anyone who so much as sneezed in her direction. You should see the documentation she gathered on that shithead Bobby Gardener. I've never known anyone who took vengeance as seriously as Noreen. I think it was only second to booze. In her eyes, she was some holier-than-thou avenger. But she was just a mean drunk. Period."

She lit another cigarette and started pacing in front of the refrigerator. I poured myself a cup of coffee and said, "Last night Noreen talked about hiring me. Do you have any idea why she'd need a private detective?"

She shrugged, her face as tight as a drum. "She did that periodically. Most times she just wanted a background check on people. Last year it was something else. You know she was raised in foster homes? Her parents died when she was just twelve. I think it was a car accident. I never pushed for the details. Last year she hired some guy from Philly to find her lost siblings. I think he's the one who made her think about moving here in the first place. He had a cousin in real estate who knew about Telham. Anyway, the geezer died in August. Maybe she just wanted to start up the search again."

It took me a moment to catch on. "She was separated from her family after her parents died?"

Pulling her hair back from her face, the cigarette dangling from her lips, she answered warily, "It was pretty traumatic for her. But Noreen didn't talk about it much. I learned the hard way that it was one of those 'off limit' topics. All I know is there were three brothers and two sisters, or maybe the other way around."

She slumped toward me and I had to fight an impulse to cradle her. I had often fantasized about sleeping with Helen. She had salt-and-pepper hair cut in a shoulder-length bob, olive skin, cocoa-brown eyes, and full lips that curled in a perpetual pout. Her delicate features made me feel at once protective and aroused. But looking at her now, my only emotion was pity. It was as if she were crumbling before my eyes. Her shoulders started to heave, then her hands shook. Finally the sob broke free and she doubled over and wailed. Amy scampered over and gathered Helen into her arms.

I turned away and caught Carly gesturing toward the front door. The two of us stepped onto the deck and gulped the frigid air. Then she asked, "What do you think?"

Not waiting for my response, she lifted the broom from the corner of the deck and began sweeping the leaves over the side. I sat down on the top step, closed my eyes, and listened to the rhythmic shushing of the broom. In the distance, there was the faint pong-pong of guns exploding in the neighboring preserve — an ironic appellation for a piece of land on which hunters had carte blanche to chase down and slaughter defenseless game.

I was sick of confronting death, sick of cleaning up the aftermath, and sick of trying to prevent the inevitable. Death was an opponent I no longer had the strength to battle. At the moment, all I wanted was to be back at the cabin, traveling along K.T.'s long, lightly freckled legs.

I shook my head, suddenly recalling the embittered exchange I had overheard last night. Wearily, I asked, "Where's Manny?"

"At her mother's. She drove back there after the party. Guess she wasn't in the mood to face Noreen after what had happened between her and Helen. Amy's the one that finally located her. Must be hard as hell losing a lover like this." She paused and bent over. "She's sedated now. If she's not up to the drive tomorrow, Amy may go into the city and pick her up."

Carly was staring solemnly at a slug. Her gaze was so intent, her eyes almost crossed. Despite my mood, I smiled. "Love that country living, don't you?"

Carly and Amy used to live in Park Slope, Brooklyn, just across the street from my brownstone. They moved up here four years ago, but they still marvel at every annoying cicada and over-zealous gypsy moth.

She looked up, a glimmer of her customary playfulness returning. "Just imagine, Rob, one day you too can —"

"Own a home in the country," I finished the refrain for her. "I know, I know. I can't wait to discover my very own slugs."

Unexpectedly, the energy between us shifted again and I sensed that our thoughts had wandered back to the one place neither of us wanted to go.

23

Carly spoke first. "Do you think Helen could have killed Noreen during her blackout?"

I shuddered, imagining the impact required to bash in a skull. Then the professional part of me kicked in. Something was off. According to Helen, the blood was pouring out from the *back* of Noreen's head and her eyes were fixed on the ceiling. From that description, I had to deduce that she found Noreen lying on her back. A powerful blow from behind would have undoubtedly pitched her forward — which meant that the head wound most likely resulted from the fall itself. The question was, what could have caused her to heave backward with such force?

Helen is just 5'3", a full seven inches shorter than Noreen. I wondered how much strength was in her wiry arms. Probably not much. But I had to factor in years of pent-up fury. That's when I started to worry.

"It's hard to say. Let's just wait for the forensics report," I said coolly. What I was really thinking was: motive and opportunity. Helen had both in abundance.

Carly scoffed. "Forensics? Get real, Rob. This is Starret Township, remember? Douglas Marks is our coroner. You know who I mean? The funeral director who owns the chalet on Forest, around the corner from the cabin you're renting. He's the one Noreen almost decked last summer just because he was nice enough to pick up her mail when she was away for a week. Believe me, he won't be too aggrieved by her passing. And then there's our damn police chief. He makes Barney Fife seem like a veritable Rhodes scholar."

Carly was practically sweeping the paint off the deck, all the time muttering something to herself in Italian. I figured she was getting too pissed for English, and I could guess the reason why. Last year there was a series of break-ins in the community. When Police Chief Robert Crowell realized that three of the homes were owned by gay male couples, he stopped the investigation cold in its tracks. The community hired my agency and we gathered evidence that clearly pinned the break-ins on Bobby Gardener and one of his friends. Crowell refused to pick up the case. Despite what they say, justice is far from blind and the scale hardly ever balanced.

"Did you speak to Crowell yourself?" I asked.

"Barely." Carly had exchanged the broom for a bucket of birdseed. I followed her down the stairs and around the side of the house. "He took one look at Noreen's outfit, then glanced at me, Amy, and Helen. It didn't help that Helen was still obviously drunk. You could almost hear his Tinker Toy brain clicking away."

"He didn't question you?"

"Sure he did. He sneered at us and said 'You ladies been drinking?' What could we say? The kitchen smelled like a damn distillery. We told him about last night's party and he snorted like he was trying to blow his nose through his mouth. Then he nodded to himself."

I had a sinking feeling. "Did he cordon off the area? Trace the position of the body?" Carly's puzzled expression cut off my questions. Frustrated, I blurted, "What *did* he do?"

"He had two of his deputies cart her body out to

some kind of van, then he told Amy to make us all some coffee —"

"He what?"

"Well, you know, Amy has that waspy, femme look. The blonde hair, the ponytail, the paisley skirt —"

"Shit, Carly, I'm not asking for a fashion report. You all sat down in the room where she was found?"

She scooped the seed into the feeder and pursed her lips in annoyance. "We weren't being disrespectful —"

I groaned. "Ah, Carly, that's not the point. I'm thinking about evidence. The placement of objects around the room, footprints on the floor, fingerprints . . ."

"Oh." I watched her snap the lid back onto the bucket. When she finished, she looked up at me with concern. "I didn't even think about all that. I was so worried about Helen . . ."

Taking a deep breath, I asked, "Did he bother searching the house?"

Carly tapped the feeder with her index finger. "No. All he seemed interested in were the names of everyone at last night's party and our level of alcohol consumption. You should have seen his smirk when we told him that Robert and Allan flew down to Key West this morning. Amy said she heard him mutter something about sending the rest of the queers south."

Great. "Did he run sobriety tests on all of you?"

She shook her head.

I asked her a few more questions about Crowell's half-assed interrogation, then we walked back to the deck in silence. I rapidly added up everything I knew so far and I wasn't real pleased with the direction in which my instincts were driving me.

When we got back to the front of the house, Helen was stretched out in a mesh hammock, Amy standing alongside her massaging Helen's temples with some kind of liniment. I felt Carly stiffen beside me. I knew the scene was innocent, but I nevertheless understood Carly's reaction. The two of them looked a little too cozy.

I walked over and said, "It doesn't sound like you have much to worry about, Helen. From what everyone's told me, I doubt Crowell has any interest in investigating Noreen's death." Disapproval slipped into my tone. I knew my words represented good news for Helen, but they galled me. "I'd still like to check out the scene myself." As Helen's eyes narrowed in suspicion, I added quickly, "Just for extra assurance, in case this ever goes to court." The truth was my curiosity was greedier than Ivan Boesky.

Amy handed me a cracked leather key case. "I used Noreen's keys to lock up when we left."

I pocketed the case and headed for my car. I could feel Helen's gaze burning through my corduroy jacket.

The smell of whiskey hit me as soon as I opened the front door. Man, I thought, she must have bathed in the goddamn stuff. The entryway led into a great room with a cathedral ceiling dotted with skylights. Dust motes floated in the shafts of natural light transecting the room. I glanced around and knew instantly whose hand had orchestrated the room's design.

The carpeting was maroon, the furniture constructed of fine cherry wood outfitted with gleaming brass handles. The sofa and matching armchairs were upholstered in tufted black leather. A cast-iron grating covered the brick fireplace on the far side of the room, and ornately framed paintings of horses bucking, prancing, and vaulting adorned the walls. Overall, the decor was distinctively masculine and upper-class, reminding me of a musty, private men's club my ex-publisher once dragged me to.

I wondered how Helen had lasted here for as long as two months.

In the kitchen, the atmosphere was drastically different. Ice-cold contemporary. Steel counters, black-and-white tiles on the walls, gray industrial carpeting covering the floor. The only other colors in the room were shades of red. Headache-red faucets, cranberry dish towels, scarlet Venetian blinds, and a crimson stain spread out in front of the sink like a mutant amoeba.

I slipped on a pair of dishwashing gloves, then knelt down and inspected the carpet on my hands and knees. The charcoal fibers reeked. I removed a handkerchief from my back pocket, sprayed a little peppermint Binaca on the center, and tied it around my nose. Then I swept my hand around the stain, hoping to dislodge any item not immediately visible to the eye. Still fingering the carpet, I traced the faint discoloration that delineated the edges of where Noreen's body had apparently lain. I paused, puzzled.

The carpet felt damp in the area *surrounding* the

outline, but was bone dry where she had fallen. I untied the handkerchief and sniffed the floor covering like a hound dog. The stench of whiskey was concentrated along the curving line of discoloration that marked the body's position.

I stood up and surveyed the room again. There were no other bloodstains visible. The sink bore a trace of vomit, but the counter, neighboring stove top, and wall tiles were clean. No spatter marks from a powerful blow to the head, no drops from a bloody weapon. I ran a finger along the surface of the counter and walls to see if they had been recently washed. The kitchen grease on the tip of my index finger was an unambiguous answer.

My pulse was racing by then. I grabbed the wastebasket from under the sink and rummaged through the contents. I found browned apple cores, crusted coffee grinds, the remnants of an omelette, junk mail inserts, but no bottle of booze. My suspicion grew as I searched the cabinets, broom closet, buffet drawers, and even the refrigerator. I walked into the adjoining bathroom next and checked the medicine cabinet. There were expired prescriptions for everything from Seldane to Antivert, plus several herbal treatments prepared by Amy. The first shelf contained a vial of Amy's remedy for sciatica. I knew the stuff well. Just five months ago, a mean case of sciatica had ripped through my right thigh and into my back. It lasted five painful days. Amy tried to convince me to try her herbal concoction, but I had stubbornly refused. Now I remembered how Noreen finally sat me down with a sheaf of articles and convinced me to keep an open mind.

With a shiver of guilt, I acknowledged the fact that Noreen had a compassionate side few people ever saw. I wondered if anyone would truly mourn her loss. Including me.

I opened all the containers and sniffed them tentatively. Within seconds, I had a violent sinus headache. Slamming the cabinet door shut, I headed upstairs. I tried the master bedroom first. Under a cherry-wood sleigh bed I found a metal file box. From its weight, I was pretty sure it didn't contain any booze. But I had to be sure. I pulled out the silver case of picks given to me by my brother on my last birthday and snapped the lock open. Nothing but basic financial and legal documents. I scanned the files, jotted down a few key numbers and replaced the papers.

An hour later, I finished combing through the rest of the house.

There was no alcohol on the premises.

Chapter 3

I assumed a Southern accent and said, "Police Chief Crowell, please."

"One moment, please." The receptionist's voice reminded me of Julia Child's. Suddenly I found myself craving a slice of crusty French bread with a thick slab of butter. She murmured something out of range of the telephone receiver, then returned. "Can I say who's calling?"

I thumbed through the compact disks Noreen had stacked on the shelf next to the phone. "Meg Christian from the *Pocono Record*." The name sounded nice and proper. I figured Crowell's favorite song probably wasn't "Ode to a Gym Teacher."

"Can you call back tomorrow, ma'am? It's just after six, and he's kind of anxious to get going. Promised his wife that he'd pick up a turkey on the way home." She chuckled congenially. I love these small-town folks.

"Well, I understand that. Truly. I'm cooking up a storm myself, come Thursday. But I have this deadline, see." I poured it on thick, complaining about my tyrant editor and the horrific prospect of being plunged into yet another job search. A minute later, Crowell picked up the line.

"Thank you for taking the time, sir." I wanted to sound like Pat Robertson's dream female. "I'm new here on the paper and I'm just following orders myself. My boss said 'Get on the phone to the police chief' and I just hopped to it. Hope your wife won't mind. I imagine she knows you're an important man 'round here."

He had Dan Quayle's high-pitched laugh. I shuddered.

"Honey," he said. "You sure don't know my wife. Now, how can I help you?"

"John heard that someone died under rather questionable circumstances up in a community outside Canadensis. I wrote the name down somewhere. Hold on, here it is. Telham Village. What can you tell me about that, sir?"

He almost giggled this time. "Questionable, honey? Is that what the man said? Shoot. Nothing questionable about this one. Some bulldyke up in Telham drank herself to death. Simple cardiac arrest. Now, you go tell your boss to stop listening

32

to them gossipmongers and naysayers. Thanksgiving's coming. I want to read some uplifting stories. Kids from the high school are planning a real nice parade. That's the kind of story folks want to read."

I bit my lip, then said, "Couldn't agree more. My mama sure didn't raise me to be writing about drunks, but I have to make a living. Now, are you sure about this woman? Maybe someone just tried to make it look like she was drunk, you know, poured alcohol on the body *after* she fell. Something like that."

"Whoa, sweetheart. You should be writing for TV, you should. No such possibility."

"Have you determined the time of death?"

"Huh? Can't see that that matters much, but yeah, we did. Coroner guesses it was sometime between midnight and four in the morning."

"There's a kid in the community I've heard about. A real troublemaker —"

"Bobby? Nah. The boy's just high-strung. Besides, I hear that he's biking cross-country. Look, hon, I talked to her friends. They were *all* drunk as skunks. I even checked with some neighbors. Matter of fact, the coroner knows her personally. No, sweetie. She just over-imbibed. Pure and simple. Now, if you don't mind, I better be getting to that meat market before all the turkeys are dead and gone."

I hung up angrily, thinking, fat chance. The turkeys will inherit the earth.

When I returned to the cabin, K.T. was sprawled

in the overstuffed plaid couch reading *Bon Appetit*. I tossed my jacket onto the coat rack, then turned to her. The glow from the fireplace highlighted the reds in her hair. She looked up and smiled at me contentedly, and my hands started to shake. Wordlessly, I headed into the kitchen. Every burner on the stove was occupied with pots or saucepans and the air was deliciously aromatic. I peeked under the lid of the stockpot.

"Chicken kurma." K.T.'s voice drifted toward me from the doorway. I didn't turn around. She continued speaking as she approached me. I could feel myself stiffen in anticipation. "I brought the spices with me. I'm also making some curried rice." She wrapped her arms around my waist. "Maybe we need to talk."

Inexplicably, I started to quake.

She spun me toward her and stared. "What is it?" She looked frightened.

What could I say? I was terrified. More terrified of what was happening here in this house than I could ever explain to anyone — including myself.

I shook my head and extricated myself from her arms. "I don't think Noreen's death was accidental," I said.

She narrowed her eyes and shot me a look that penetrated far too deeply. I meandered around her.

"This isn't about Noreen. Christ, I'm not stupid, Robin. You're freaking out about last night, aren't you?"

Her Southern accent was more apparent when she was irritated. I wanted desperately to kiss her. Instead I snapped, "I have a surprise for you. My world doesn't revolve around K.T. Bellflower, chef extraordinaire. I spent the afternoon investigating a possible murder. Not quite as lovely a pastime as dabbling in the kitchen."

I watched the blood rush to her cheeks and waited for the explosion. She sighed deeply, wiped the back of her hand across her forehead, and smiled. "You're good at this, aren't you?" she asked, sending a shiver up my spine.

I felt naked and trapped. "What are you talking about?" I asked, looking frantically for some safe place to hide. I walked into the living room and picked up the television remote. Click. The weather channel.

A hand fell softly on my shoulder. "You've been running from me for six months. Every time we talked on the phone, you'd start off sounding thrilled to hear my voice, then you'd gradually tighten up. By the end, I felt as if I were concluding a business call. 'Thanks so much for calling.'" She imitated my sign-off perfectly.

I flopped onto the couch. Click. Highlights from Monica Seles' victory at the Virginia Slims. My eyes were riveted to the screen.

"Robin." Her voice was like honey. I almost turned around. "Robin," she repeated, her tone insistent yet unbearably gentle. "I know how hard it is to trust someone. Believe me."

She squeezed in next to me. My breath grew shorter. Images from my past were pressing in. I closed my eyes, but they were still there.

Soft fingers stroked the side of my face, circled my ear. "My father died when I was just eight years old. He was a truck driver. Big strapping man who looked like John Wayne. Boy, did he love country music. His favorite was 'Six Days on the Road,' by Dave Dudley." The affection in her voice was acute. Something in me begged to be let loose. I drowned it out by turning the volume up on the television. "He was the gentlest man I've ever known. When my parakeet died, he buried it under the dogwood outside my bedroom window. The day before the accident, we —"

She fell silent, and the noise in my head intensified. I saw my father's face at the funeral home where my sister's body lay prior to the service. His eyes steel-gray, his skin blotchy and scarred, his lips so tight they turned the color of raw chicken. He pushed my mother to one side then hauled me into the room by my wrist, my feet dragging on the floor, my cries bouncing off the walls like rubber bullets. He slammed open the coffin lid. "Look at her," he growled. "Look at your sister. What you have done." He hoisted me up by my collar, the top button of my starched white Peter Pan shirt pressing hard against my Adam's apple, choking me, stifling my sobs. Finally, the button popped and landed on Carol's horrifying wax-like figure. He tossed me then, like a bag of garbage.

"You, you ..." he stuttered in rage. With more emotion than I had ever seen him express before, he tore off his jacket and rolled up his sleeves. I cowered below the coffin, waiting for him to strike me. When the blow came, I barely winced. I remember thinking, I deserve this.

"You are no better than the Nazis that killed my family. Do you hear this?" Each word punctuated by the back of his hand crashing across my cheek. "No better than a Nazi." He spat something at me in

Yiddish, the first and only time he ever used the language in front of me. And the last words he ever spoke to me.

Du bist der malekhamoves. The harsh, guttural sounds haunted me for years, till I finally asked a friend to translate what I remembered. She had stared at me uneasily.

"You are the Angel of Death."

Now, my hands trembling, the memory strangling me, I turned to K.T.

She was lost in her own history. I watched conflicting emotions flicker across her face. Finally she said, "We fought that day. A stupid fight. I wanted him to work in the mines like the other fathers in the area, so he'd be home more often. He told me he didn't want to end up like my mother's father, a bitter, hacking old man at the age of forty-four. Then he drove off." Her eyes filled and I envied the easiness of her tears. "He was killed in a three-vehicle crash in Tennessee the very next day."

I had shifted toward her and now she cradled me in her arms. I shut off the television and tucked myself closer.

"No one told me he died. My mother said, 'Daddy's gone there.'" K.T. pointed upwards. "I thought I had been so bad he had run away from us. Then one day, I was playing with a wooden plane he had built for me..." She paused and looked at me closely. "I still have it. It was in the dining room the night I lured you to that dinner party."

I nodded, recalling the evening too vividly. It was also the night I found out someone else in my life had died.

"Well, I was outside playing with it and I saw a real plane roar overhead. That's when it hit me. My daddy was up *there*, flying around, waiting for me to apologize. For years, anytime I heard a plane, I'd run out and scream, 'I'm sorry, Daddy. You can come home now.'" Her look darkened. "My life became hell once he died, in more ways than I'd like to recollect."

I could feel her drifting away from me, and terror gripped me. Not now, I thought frantically. Not when I'm falling.

I kissed her mouth, hard and demanding. Then I let our eyes meet. Read what I can't bring myself to say, I begged her silently. She lifted a hand to my cheek and nodded almost imperceptibly, as if she could hear my thoughts. I moved her hand so that her palm rested on my lips. Her cool, long fingers smelled of exotic spices. I tasted each one. Then all at once, a cry broke from me and, clinging to her like dew to a petal, I disclosed my own painful memory.

Afterwards, we held each other, crying and drawing warm, moist lips over all the unhealed wounds.

My insomnia kicked in that night. After two hours of trying to adjust to K.T.'s still-new contour, I snuck out of bed. The soothing scent of burning wood traveled up to the second-floor landing where I stood. I'd rented this place on a dozen occasions, the first time just two months after Carly and Amy moved into Telham. The owners, two elderly women who refer to each as other as "close companions," had built the cabin in 1984 as a retreat from New York City's madness. Now that they'd retired, they spent most of the year in Arizona. They'd approached me about buying the place, but I'm not ready for a steady diet of country solitude. At least, not yet.

The second floor had three bedrooms, each just large enough to contain a double bed, oak quilt rack and dresser, a wicker rocking chair, and two nightstands. The master bedroom also held an antique pine dry sink with a copper basin. The bedrooms, like the whole house, were cozy and efficient. Downstairs was airier, mostly because of the beamed cathedral ceilings. Besides the living room, dining room and oversized country kitchen, the first floor boasted a large den and a screened-in porch that ran the length of the cabin.

I headed into the den. The room was littered with the laptop computer, portable printer, modem, and manuals I had dragged along with me. Just in case. The latest issue of *P.I. Magazine* peeked out of my attaché. I started to browse through it, then stopped abruptly. How *had* Noreen died? And why the hell did she have to die on my so-called vacation?

Du bist der malekhamoves.

Maybe my father was right.

With a shudder, I flopped into the desk chair and ran over the events of the past two days. Why was Helen so sure someone had killed Noreen? While I didn't trust Sheriff's Crowell's investigative skills, his assessment of Noreen's death as being alcohol-related seemed far more feasible than murder. Except that I hadn't found any empty bottles in the house. And Noreen had been stone sober when we talked.

I scrambled into the living room, then dug my note pad out from my jacket pocket. With a yellow highlighter, I circled Helen's name and the word "blackout." I didn't like the thought of a murderer roaming around a community in which two of my closest friends lived. Especially if the murderer was someone I knew.

By seven o'clock Monday morning, I had started an official case file on Noreen's case, complete with a list of everyone who had attended Robert and Allan's party. Lucky for me, my buddy Carly was always the first one to arrive and the last to leave any party she attended. I called her house and caught her just as she was leaving for work. She cursed me twice in English and at least seven times in Italian. Nevertheless, she spent the next twenty minutes recalling the sequence in which guests had arrived and departed.

The sun was just beginning to burn away the morning fog, but my adrenaline was already pumping. If I had stopped long enough to analyze my sudden obsession with Noreen's death I might have realized just how eager I was for a distraction from the pressures of my own life. At the time, though, I felt pretty damn heroic.

Ten minutes after eight, I was out of the house, leaving K.T. asleep. Assuming, at least temporarily, that Sheriff Crowell was right about the estimated time of death and that Carly's memory was accurate, I was able to whittle down the names of people I wanted to question. Top on the list were the people who owned the adjoining property on Forest.

Camilla and Fred DeLuca had moved into the pea-green ranch-style just ten months ago after converting an abandoned railroad station house in Mountainhome into a garden shop. Fred also sold fresh vegetables and herbs to members of the community. Amy had started using him as a supplier for her herbalist business last June. I remembered meeting and liking him, but enjoying his wife about as much as a New York subway in August. At night. I rang their doorbell and waited.

Camilla greeted me in a outfit that was the sartorial equivalent of uncooked Spam. A pink and green florid muumuu strained around her hard, pregnant belly. Her feet were clad in gray thermal socks that had bunched around her ankles. Curlers dangled haphazardly from her straw-colored mane. She wore a ribbon of hair bleach under her nose and stared at me with dull, startled eyes. Somehow managing not to leap backwards, I introduced myself. It took her a second to remember that we had met each other by the artichoke dip on Saturday night, then she was all smiles. "C'mon in," she said enthusiastically. "Fred's fixing the back door screen."

I followed her in and wrinkled my nose. I may have two cats of my own back in Brooklyn, but I firmly believe the furry darlings should be seen and not smelled. One of the distinct pluses of a vacation here in Telham was the absence of my sweet darlings' fur showers and ammonia-scented litter pans. The DeLuca house emitted the acrid odor of uncleaned litter leavened with the slightly sour

41

aroma of cheap cat food. Camilla sat at the knotty pine kitchen table mixing up another batch of hair bleach for God-knows-what body part.

"By the way," I remarked with studied casualness. "How well did you and your husband know Noreen Finnegan?"

She practically spat. "That's the bitch who's suing us . . ." She hesitated. "You aren't a lawyer, are you?"

"I'm a private detective. You may not have heard yet, but Noreen died yesterday. I was wondering if you knew anything about the circumstances."

Exhilaration flitted over her face. She hid it inexpertly. "Suppose I should say I'm sorry to hear the news. But I'd be lying. You know how much she was suing us for? Because of a little tap on her rear bumper? A quarter of a million dollars! Claims she hurt herself so bad she had to quit her business."

I remembered now. From what Noreen had described to me at the community's annual Halloween party, the accident had been no fender bender. The collision had sent her to the hospital for a week. Afterwards, her back pain was so intense she had to abandon her painting business.

Camilla's smile reminded me of the way my cat Geeja looks when she's stolen food from my plate without my knowing it. "Wait till Fred hears." She double-checked her watch, then shouted, "Fred!" A drop of bleach splashed off her upper lip and landed on the tabletop. I noticed a few pale stains dotting the pine and had no trouble guessing how they got there.

Somewhere in the back a door slammed, followed by steady footsteps. Finally, Fred entered the room, tugging his torn jeans up over his belly when he realized there was a guest. His dark brown hair was pulled back into a ponytail and he had an unlit cigarette tucked behind his right ear.

"Hi there," he said, extending a greasy palm. "Good to see you again." He glanced down at his blackened paw and smiled shyly. "Oops. I've been cleaning my bike. Sorry 'bout that."

I shrugged and reached for a napkin. "No problem, Fred."

Camilla excitedly muttered an explanation of who I was and why I was there, all the time scraping the bleach off her lip. I noticed Fred found the act about as appealing as I did. "Shoot, Camilla," he whined. Then he nodded me into the living room. The heads of deer and elk stared at me unrelentingly from two of four walls. I tore through a steamy greenhouse and exited onto the back deck.

"You do a lot of hunting?" I asked.

He cocked his head at me and said, "Don't tell me you're one of those animal rights fanatics. Well, just for your information, I never shoot anything I won't eat. And I hardly eat anything I didn't shoot. Or grow." He pointed proudly at the greenhouse. I gathered from his proud grin that he had used the line before. "I got a freezer downstairs with enough venison to last two winters. I betcha you taste a little bit of my stew and you'll be hankering for the hunt yourself."

"I don't think so, Fred. I never could understand how anyone could kill a defenseless —"

"Now, why do people always say that? I'm not minding your business, so why should you mind mine?" Fred shook his head. "Honey, let me tell you something, I got no interest in what other people do

43

in their own homes or on their own time. I used to live in Bensonhurst. My next door neighbors could open their window shades and watch me take a whiz. I was a mailman back then, and I'd spend all day trekking from one house to another, people stopping me and asking me to check their mail. Then they'd start whining at me. Where was their tax refund? Why didn't so-and-so's mother send a birthday card? Where was their J.C. Penney catalogs?"

He removed the cigarette from behind his ear and placed it between his lips, still unlit. "Trying to quit," he explained, chewing on the filter. "Anyways, I had people up to here." He poked his forehead. "We moved to the country so's we can have some quiet, alone time. And if some of that time I spend hunting, I don't see that it's causing anyone much harm." He bent over his mountain bike, spun the front wheel, and said, "Perfect," then he looked up at me. "So tell me, how'd Noreen die? My guess is she just drank herself to death." The gleam in his eyes undermined the tone of solemnity he was obviously striving for.

I evaded his question. Fred didn't seem to mind. He tut-tutted in the appropriate fashion, but he looked like he wanted to kick his heels together and hoot. "Real shame."

"Guess it's good news for the two of you."

He stood up, obviously surprised. "Camilla told you about the lawsuit?" I nodded. "Damn that woman." Squeezing the front brake as if it were someone's throat, he said, "Well, sure, it's good news. Just the legal costs alone could put me out of business. That's what she wanted to do. You know, that eye for an eye bullshit. My business for hers. Hell, Camilla just got startled by some deer on the road. She hardly touched Noreen's car. The suit was pure spite. But that doesn't mean I'm glad she's dead."

I wasn't convinced. I etched Fred's name down on my mental list of suspects and, with an exaggerated sarcasm he couldn't miss, asked, "So you don't have any idea who might have wanted to kill Noreen?"

Scratching his nose with the back of his hand, he said, "Who says she was killed? That's not what I'm hearing."

I raised my eyebrows. Obviously, Fred had heard about Noreen's death before I had ever opened my mouth. Wondering why he had pretended ignorance, I asked, "When did you hear the news?"

Averting his eyes with a grin I would have found ingratiating under other circumstances, he said, "Man, I can't lie for shit. Look, I remembered you telling me you're some kind of private dick. It don't take a genius to figure out you're here fishing for suspects."

"Who told you about Noreen?"

"Doug Marks, the coroner. You know he lives just around the corner from here. Ran into him at the gas station last night."

I nodded. Marks was the next person I planned to question.

Fred reiterated the coroner's abbreviated version of Noreen's death, which was less than I already knew. I turned to go, then had another thought. "By the way, did you happen to notice whether Noreen was drinking at the party?"

Fred scratched the skin under his ear and gazed

at me quizzically. "Nah. She was too busy stirring up trouble." After a moment of hesitation, he said, "But maybe I missed something. Hold on and I'll ask Mil."

I followed him into the greenhouse, then stopped. Outside you could taste the aluminum edge of winter in the air but in here, it was the heart of summer. I was surrounded by brilliant foliage, the aroma of roses, lilac, and dill. Sneezing with delight, I bypassed the roses and inspected the herb and vegetable garden. I surreptitiously tore off a mint leaf and nibbled it, then strolled over to a bed of flowers set off by aged railroad ties. Clusters of magnificent indigo-hooded flowers clung to tall stalks bearing lobed, rich green leaves. As I bent closer, I heard a sound behind me.

Fred had returned, a mop slung over his shoulder in a manner that reminded me of Elmer Fudd out to hunt some "wabbits." I pointed to the flowers and asked him to identify them.

He seemed uneasy. "Delphinium ... or maybe Monkshood. You'd have to ask Mil. That's her bailiwick. By the by, she says Noreen always seemed drunk. Even when she was sober. All I know is the woman was a damned witch. If someone had to go, personally I'm glad it was her."

My next stop was Douglas Marks' house on Blue Ridge. Still puzzling about Fred, I rang the buzzer.

"Door's open," Douglas shouted from the distance.

I stepped inside and almost collided with the stuffed, eight-foot grizzly in the entrance. Brooklyn was looking more attractive to me every minute.

"I'm in the office."

I followed his voice, weaving through a room littered with antiques and framed photographs of every size and shape. I paused to admire a spinning wheel whose wood finish had been worn away by time and the delicate touch of someone's hands.

"That's one of my favorites," Douglas said from the doorway at the other end of the room. He was at least six-two, with the dimples of a cherub and the easy grin of a con man. His coarse, brown hair was pushed back from his forehead in thick waves. As I stared at him, I vaguely remembered being told that Douglas had had a brief stint as a doctor on some daytime soap opera. No wonder. He had the face of a man who could operate with one hand, while stroking a nurse's back with the other.

I picked up an ancient mustard-yellow frame bearing a silvery daguerreotype of Confederate soldiers gathered around a grave site. "Family heirloom?" I asked.

"Hobby. I love historical photographs. It excites me to think that I own an image of someone who no longer exists on this planet." He gestured into his office. "Please, come in and have a seat."

I complied, curious that he had still not asked for my name. I started to explain who I was, but he waved his hand and said, "I know. You're my temporary neighbor. Close friend of Amy and Carly. You forget. This is a small, tight-knit community. If you sneeze, I'll know all about it." He lowered himself onto the scarred oak piano bench positioned in front of an equally scarred rolltop desk.

My skin felt itchy from his earnest scrutiny. I wanted to get back out into the late-fall sun. I squirmed in my seat and said, "You probably know that Noreen Finnegan was an acquaintance of mine."

He nodded meaningfully and steepled his hands under his chin. "A tragedy. One of the most dreaded aspects of my job is encountering untimely deaths. The elderly almost always look at peace, somehow at home, in their caskets. But the young... their skin looks more plastic."

Sweat broke out on my forehead. I couldn't afford to think of my sister. I shifted my attention to his desktop. A thick book on death-rate statistics in the United States since 1875 rested on a pile of legal pads inscribed with a precise, sharply edged print. Next to that was a model mahogany casket with silk lining. I scanned the spines of books lodged in a cubbyhole off to the right of the desk. His interests ranged from botany to basket-weaving to ballistics. Truly a man of the nineties.

I tuned back in to Doug's monologue. He was explaining how he served as both the township's funeral director and its coroner. "I must confess one of the drawbacks of the job is that I sometimes walk into a party and have difficulty viewing the participants as anything but walking inventory." His affect was so studied, I again recalled the rumors about his fleeting career as an actor.

I cut him short. "I forget now... just what soap opera *were* you on?"

The question startled him. "Come again?"

"I've heard that you used to be an actor."

He laughed, a little too loud. "A high school performance as Othello. Certainly you're not interested in my teenage aspirations." He patted my knee patronizingly, then said, "Let's get back to the real issue. I suppose you're curious about the cause of death. Noreen was clearly intoxicated. Her clothes reeked. She apparently cracked her skull upon passing out. A serious injury, certainly, but hardly the cause of death. My ruling is congestive heart failure stemming from alcoholic cardiomyopathy. The bottom line — cardiac arrest."

"Did you check the alcohol level in her blood?"

"Not necessary in this case. You could smell the booze all over her body. We knew she had spent the previous night at a party, and I am personally familiar with her history of alcoholism. The woman was extraordinarily volatile."

"So you just guessed at the cause of death?" I said accusingly.

He gritted his teeth. "You may be surprised to know that even a hick town like this one can have trained professionals. For your information, my ruling was confirmed by a colleague. Maybe you know Dean Flynn?"

One of the first homeowners in Telham, Dean lived two houses up from Noreen. The two of us had played water volleyball a few times in the community pool. He reminded me of one of my best friends from high school. "Isn't Dean a gynecologist?" I asked incredulously.

"He's a highly esteemed *physician*. We work at the same hospital."

"And neither of you think an autopsy is in order?"

He looked annoyed. "No. I've seen many cases like this. There was no sign of burglary or rape or even assault. Matter of fact, there was absolutely no indication of criminal activity in the home at all. Unless, of course, you deem alcohol abuse to be criminal. Under such circumstances, I had no legal obligation to perform an autopsy — unless the family insisted. And in this case, I was expressly directed to *not* perform an autopsy."

"By a family member?"

"Why, no. Finnegan was an orphan, raised in foster homes. There were no living relatives identified in her records. The individual acting as next of kin is ... hold on." He tossed his legs over the bench and shifted some papers around till he found what he was looking for. "A Ms. Emanuela Diaz, resident of Manhattan. We called her first thing this morning. She said, and I quote, 'No autopsy. You touch her with a scalpel without my express permission and I'll sue your ass off.' Police Chief Crowell and I decided there was no cause to upset her."

No cause at all.

Chapter 4

K.T. was in her element. I never imagined that a woman could look so incredibly sexy in an apron, flour smeared on her cheeks, her hands kneading dough for buttermilk biscuits. She brushed a strand of hair away from her forehead with the back of her hand and smiled at me enticingly. "I missed you in bed this morning," she said.

I lifted her hand and sucked the batter from her fingers. "Mmmm. Delicious."

"Where'd you go?"

I summarized my morning interrogations. "I

stopped by Dean Flynn's place, but he was already out. I left a note for him to call me."

I wrapped my arms around K.T.'s waist as she continued to massage the dough. We were standing so close, her body's motion became my own. Unexpectedly we began rocking together, her rounded ass tight against my hips. She murmured my name. Her tone was articulate. I could hear the desire. And something more. She wanted to possess me. And, God help me, I wanted suddenly to be possessed. The realization thrilled and terrified me.

"You're cooking," I responded inanely. I wanted to make love to her right there, on the kitchen counter. I also wanted to run outside into the bracing cold air.

"You bet I am," she said lustily, turning around in my arms and planting her full lips on mine. Her tongue, smooth and insistent, explored my mouth, licked the inside of my lips, curled around my tongue. The contact ripped through me, triggering a flash flood that drowned my senses.

I swept the dough aside, flour wafting into the air like spray from a curling wave. I lifted K.T. onto the counter, my pulse rushing. Our mouths had not parted.

I moved my head back, but the link between our bodies didn't break. Firmly, I braced my hands against her cheeks and pushed her away, then I stared into her eyes. I wanted to know her, to memorize her face so that I could visualize her features even in the dark, so that I could remember what she looked like even . . .

When she's gone, I thought, startling myself.

The words ricocheted inside my head.

When she's gone.

The assumption rested under my heart like a burr. K.T. would leave me. Like my sister Carol. Like my father. Like Mary. And Cathy.

Nothing lasts, I've complained to my therapist. Especially not love. Or the people you love. And each time someone leaves, a part of you is cut away until, like a tree struck repeatedly with an ax's edge, you can no longer stand.

I did not want to fall, but I could feel K.T. slicing into me, deeper than I had allowed anyone in my past to go.

Her eyes were boring into mine, their tenderness peeling away the layers of defenses, leaving me raw and exposed. Her kisses, light now, like the flutter of eyelashes against a pillow, sailed over my cheeks. "You're safe here," she murmured, again reading my heart with uncanny accuracy.

I closed my eyes. The death rattle in Carol's throat filled my ears. Once more, I tasted her warm blood as it spurted over my face and lips, smelled the acrid smoke from the gun as it filled the darkness of the closet, felt the cold metal in my small palm, the stillness of my own heart. Don't leave me, Carol. Don't.

I buried my head under K.T.'s chin. In the past six months, my memories had become sharper, more vivid. Sometimes, like now, I feared they would break me, shatter me like a rock hurled through a pane of glass. I started sucking K.T.'s neck, seeking to lose myself as I had so many times before, in passion, in fantasy, but the images pursued me.

My father ripping open the closet door, horror and fear distorting his stubbornly inexpressive face.

His thick, calloused hand grabbing the .22 caliber gun from me. The blue-tinged barrel pointing at my temple, still stinking of gun smoke, and then the distinct click, metal on metal. Afterwards he howled, the piercing cry of an animal whose body lay mangled in a hunter's steel trap.

The volatile memory, unexpectedly unearthed, detonated inside me.

He had pulled the trigger.

K.T.'s arms tightened around me as I shuddered. Softly, she sang into my ear, "Let me be your shelter."

My hands, cold and trembling, lifted her shirt and ran along the cool indentation of her back. I hungered for her in a way that felt unfamiliar. Our mouths met again, and this time our exploration was more urgent, more insistent.

I pulled off her apron, tugged open her powder blue shirt, and lifted her bra above her breasts. Her nipples were swollen before my lips even grazed them. Now I took one between my wet lips and sucked with steadily increasing pressure. Her moans filled the air the way sound swells under water. She was my only world. My center.

She moved a hand to her breast and wordlessly offered me more of herself. I took her, my palms pressed against her back, her body arching into me. I floated back and forth between her breasts. Then K.T. began talking to me in a hoarse sing-song, repeating my name, describing her sensations, urging me to please her, take her. With each beat of her sweet, ardent litany, my excitement surged, the sensation between my legs spinning into a painful whirlpool of need.

I unzipped her jeans, slipped them down over her butt, raised her, and swept them down her long legs. We were both groaning openly now, stripped of pretense, stripped of decorum, elevated to an intimacy at once vulgar and exquisite.

Biting at her thighs, I traveled up toward the source of her intoxicating scent, then I parted her and entered her first with my tongue, then my fingers. Her hands pulled my head to her as she bloomed in my mouth. I struggled to slow my pace, to savor her taste, the hot pulse of her body around my finger, the glorious rhythm of her hips as they rocked against me. I eased my other hand under her ass and K.T. beseeched me to take her. As I entered her, her moan collapsed to a mewling long past the realm of speech. Gradually I quickened the flicker of my tongue, the depth of my suck, the gentle pump of my hands, till her thighs clenched around my ears, her fingers curled in my hair and her cry reverberated through the room like the final thunderclap in the last storm of a torrid summer.

We were curled up on the throw rug in front of the stove, the odor of burned biscuits bringing us slowly back to earth. K.T. reached up and turned off the oven, then returned to my arms laughing. Flour and raisins coated our damp bodies. Sometime during our lovemaking, we had overturned a five-pound bag of flour and a bowl of raisins. I ate one off her shoulder and smiled contentedly.

"You actually look happy," K.T. said as she stood up and offered me a hand for support.

As soon as she separated from me, as soon as her words penetrated, my mood shifted. Guilt crawled over me, stinging my flesh like a swarm of red ants. Then horror.

My father had tried to kill me.

I ignored her hand and stood up.

"Whew, wrong words," K.T. remarked as I grabbed my corduroy pants from the countertop and smacked them clean of flour.

"Sorry, it's just the case."

The excuse sounded rehearsed, even to my own ears. I had used them before to distance myself from Cathy Chapman, a woman I met in San Francisco while I was investigating the death of my ex-lover Mary. Before I stopped writing romance novels and joined the Serra Investigative Agency, the catch phrase was, "I'm working." Or thinking about working. Or coming down from work. But there was always a place to which I could retreat at will. A travel article. A silly novel about hot hetero sex that had no connection to my emotional life. And now "the case."

Still, I knew that some part of me had stopped running.

I tied my sneakers and looked up at K.T. She had dressed and was now scraping burnt biscuits off the cooking sheet. Her face looked strained, confused. I crossed to her. Surprising myself I said, "I'm scared. I can't risk another loss."

She stared at me for a second, then nodded. I

waited for her to touch me, to fold me into her arms protectively, but she did nothing. Her stillness made me anxious.

"Do you understand?" I asked her, a slow burn beginning along my scalp.

Again she nodded, then turned away and began cleaning the burners on the stove top. Quietly, so quietly I barely made out the words, she said, "At some point you have to let go of the past."

I sensed she was talking more to herself than to me, but that didn't stop me from saying, "Don't tell me what the hell I'm supposed to do." How can I let go of my past, I thought angrily. It's all I have. The only barrier between me and . . .

Between me and what?

K.T. touched my arm and said, "Stop pushing me away, Robin."

Terror gripped me. Then indignation. "I'm not pushing you," I snapped, swinging my arm free. "For chrissakes, do you see how we make love? How can you say that to me?" The words pouring out of my mouth had nothing to do with what I was feeling. I wanted to scream out, "Hold me. Tell me you won't ever leave me, no matter what."

I picked up a sponge to violently scrub down the counter. "Look, I'm opening up to you and you respond with some cheap psychobabble you probably picked up in the supermarket back home in West Virginny, but I got something to tell you, honey. It doesn't fly here. Not in New York, and not with me."

K.T. was observing me with narrowed eyes. I had a feeling she was seeing me far too clearly, and I wanted desperately to render her blind.

"What you got, babe, comes cheap. Believe me." I winced at my own words. What the hell was I doing?

K.T. fingered the earring in her left lobe, then shook her head and walked out of the room. I had won.

I stood over the sink, watching the soap bubbles crackle into nothingness, and listened to K.T. stomping up and down the stairs. Then the front door slammed and I doubled over. By the time I straightened up and forced myself to follow her, the rental car was gone.

My therapist's answering machine beeped in my ear. I didn't need a recorded voice. I didn't need voices. Just silence. Antiseptic, deafening silence. I hung up sharply and went out for a run, pounding the road till my teeth hurt and the noise in my head turned white and sweet.

I spent the rest of the morning burying myself in housecleaning details and phone calls. The first call went to my housemate, Dinah, back in Brooklyn. She and her lover Beth were trying to adopt a child. Listening to the two of them chatter nervously about the social worker's impending home visit just made me antsier.

I cut the conversation short and made a quick call to Amy. She ran her business out of her home, so I assumed she'd be in. I gave her an update, then halted when I heard a voice in the background. "Who's there?" I asked, knowing Carly wouldn't be home from the school where she teaches for at least another hour.

"Helen. I'm treating her nerves with a new herbal remedy I've just developed. From the tension in your voice, you could probably use some yourself."

My teeth ground together. Something about their relationship worried me. I made a weak joke and hung up with a little shiver.

After a moment, I decided to contact Tony Serra, my partner in the detective agency. I informed him of my unexpected involvement in a murder investigation, then waited for him to numb me with a barrage of comfortingly useless Christian adages. Instead he casually updated me on his active cases.

Strangely, he saved the most important news for last. After months of negotiation, we had finally landed a big-ticket job with CompTek, a rapidly expanding mail-order company specializing in personal computers. The thirty-two-year-old owner was a tad paranoid, and a billionaire twice over. He had just moved the firm to Jersey City and wanted to install a state-of-the-art security system. My brother, a one-time burglar who now owns the largest locksmith shop in Staten Island, would handle the equipment selection and installation at a steep discount, while Tony and I developed all other security procedures. The five-year contract would push SIA far into the black, practically guaranteeing the agency's survival.

Tony evaded my questions about hiring additional staff and subcontracting with computer specialists, then drifted off into an explanation of how a peculiar chemical released from turkey meat causes drowsiness. A shiver of anxiety ran through me. Shit. Just what I needed. He sounded listless and unfocused. I waited till he paused, then asked him to transfer me to Jill Zimmerman, our office and research manager.

"Miss us already?" she quipped.

"Is Tony within earshot?" I asked impatiently.

"No. Why?" I could tell from her voice that she already knew the answer.

"He doesn't sound good. The old Tony would have been prancing around the office about closing the CompTek deal. He would've inundated me with quotes about how hard work pays off. Instead, I didn't hear a single disciple mentioned in almost forty-five minutes of conversation. And he kept digressing." I waited for Jill to respond to my implicit question. When she didn't, I hurried on. "Has he been to the doctor again?"

She sighed. "Who knows? When I ask, he jumps down my throat."

Tony has AIDS. He contracted the virus in 1985 when he made the mistake of entering a Brooklyn bodega at the wrong time. He had gone in to buy a pack of Marlboros and interrupted a robbery. As a decorated New York detective, his instincts were sure and fast. But not fast enough. Before he could draw his own gun, a .25 caliber bullet ripped through his shoulder. The bullet shattered his clavicle. The subsequent operation and transfusion left him HIV-positive.

After Tony confided in his partner, the news ripped through the NYPD like wildfire. Soon after, his partner was transferred to another precinct and

Tony was strongly "advised" to take an early retirement. He opened the agency almost immediately. Its success was the medicine that had kept him energized for almost seven years.

Two months ago Tony had another bout with pneumonia. In the past, he had bounced back with surprising resilience. But this time, recovery had been slow and painful. In recent weeks, his weight had begun dropping at an alarming rate. What concerned me most was his attitude. He had become apathetic and occasionally forgetful. I knew Jill and I were thinking the same thing.

She broke the silence first. "I hope it's not the beginning of AIDS dementia."

A horrifying chart detailing the various possible progressions of AIDS was hidden under the blotter on Tony's desk. Jill and I had discovered it one day when we were searching for a lost file. While Tony tenaciously avoided all discussion of the disease with anyone but his doctors, he had been carefully and grimly underscoring each and every symptom he manifested in yellow highlight. The chart was his road map to death. AIDS dementia, or HIV encephalopathy, was near the end of the line. But forgetfulness and distractedness did not necessarily herald AIDS dementia.

"Call his doctor and make sure he knows about Tony's behavior," I said.

"Robin, we promised to respect —"

"He's my partner, Jill. I need to know what's happening. Tell Tony if you have to, but make sure that his doctor gets the information. As a matter of fact, make sure you tell Tony I ordered you to call

Dr. Kleinau. It'll piss him off. Knowing Tony, he'll live another ten years just to get even with me. And tell him I called him an asshole, too."

Jill laughed. "A balding asshole. He'll be frothing at the mouth."

I felt my fears ease a little. Tony was a fighter. We just had to remind him about what he was fighting for. "One last thing. Make sure he realizes that the case I'm on right now is pro bono."

"You've got a strange way of demonstrating friendship."

"Glad you noticed. By the way, I could use a little help on this investigation. It's not really official, but still I'd like you to check Noreen Finnegan's financial transactions. Credit card usage, bank withdrawals, the basics. Let me know if there's been any unusual activity in the past few months. She also had a suit pending against Fred and Camilla DeLuca." I gave her their address and the name of their business. "Round up as much data as you can." It was routine work, but Jill agreed readily. We had computerized our offices only a few months ago, and she had already become adept at ransacking computer files.

Just before I hung up, I remembered something else. I explained that Noreen had apparently planned to hire me to search for siblings from whom she had been separated following her parents' death. "Can you check and tell me if Pennsylvania has a state reunion registry?"

I heard the thump of books, then Jill came back on. "They have one, but it's for birth parents only. Are you sure she was born in Pennsylvania?"

Reluctantly, I said no, then paused. "But I know how I can probably find out."

After banking the fire, I headed outside. For a few minutes I just stood on the front deck and listened. Tree branches swished in the chill breeze. I looked up through the twin white pines planted to the left of the house and watched birds flying south in ragged Vs. The sky was a rich late-autumn blue, dotted with brilliant cumulus clouds. A perfect day for rifling through files. I started up my car and began backing out of the driveway. A second later a dark blue Taurus whipped by the house. I recognized the driver instantly. I slammed on the brakes and cursed. Then I followed the car over to Valley Road.

Chapter 5

Manny Diaz was unlocking the front door as I
pulled up. She glanced over her shoulder at me,
then hesitantly turned around and waited for me to
climb up the driveway. Twice, her gaze darted to my
left. I checked behind me, but no one was visible.
Still, a shiver of apprehension ran up my spine as I
halted next to her.

Her eyes were bloodshot and the lids heavy. I
suspected that she had neither stopped crying nor
eaten since hearing the news. I took in her sallow

skin, the paleness of her lips, the droop of her shoulders, and shuddered. I recognized the blank stare of mourning that had not yet matured into conscious anguish. But there was something else — a distinct edginess that pierced her expression of grief like a knife point under silk.

My first impulse was to fire off a round of questions, but I shifted gears reluctantly. Tony had taught me that a truly good detective had to size up people rapidly, and instinctively track the right path around his or her defenses. My guts told me Manny was a raccoon trapped in a hot attic, and I had better move slow and smart.

"Let me go inside first . . ." I said, gently taking hold of one elbow and leading her into the alcove. As we crossed the threshold into the house, she slumped against me. A whimper rolled through her and I squeezed her shoulder. She whispered something in Spanish as I eased her into a leather armchair. The house still smelled of alcohol, but the odor was fainter now. The silence, on the other hand, had grown palpable, rubbing against me like burlap against raw skin.

Manny shuddered again and moaned, "I cannot believe this is happening . . ." Her bottom lip was cracked and bleeding. My mouth went dry just from looking at her.

I turned away and asked, "Can I get you something to drink?"

"Please," she said, but her hand was grasping mine tightly.

I knelt beside her. "Breathe deep. That's it. Close your eyes." She followed my instructions, but still I could sense her struggling for solace. She had to find that safe place in her head, a cool tunnel with no outlet, where thought and pain no longer had fuel to burn. I knew the place well — well enough to know that no one else could provide the directions.

I withdrew my hand and fled into the kitchen. The air was cold and acrid. I opened the freezer, found some coffee beans, and ground them with a vengeance. The aroma made the room feel somehow safer.

As I poured water into the coffee pot, Manny slipped behind me. "Do they suspect me?"

The question startled me. And made me instantly distrustful.

I faced her. Wearing a loose-fitting navy dress with a cinch waist, Manny was an attractive, heavyset woman, with the type of body Rubens loved to paint. But it was her eyes that made her truly extraordinary. Olive green and hungry, they probed my expression.

"Manny, what really happened last night?"

She shook her head and turned away. "The coffee smells good."

I repeated my question, cringing at the edge that had sneaked into my voice. She stood at the sink, her feet planted at the border of the stain that marked Noreen's fall. The only sound in the room was the percolating coffee pot.

"Noreen was my lover." She uttered the words as if they were a plea. She wanted comfort and I wanted answers. I stared at her back and waited. Finally she turned around. "I am not a murderer." Anger had replaced the grief, and I realized too late that I had stepped into a sinkhole.

"Why would anyone suspect you?" I asked, trying in vain for a neutral tone.

Her response was a sneer. "Thank you for the coffee, Robin. I think I will be better off alone for now."

She had dismissed me, but I wasn't ready to leave yet. I poured two cups of coffee and handed her one. My wrist almost gave way before she finally took the mug. I followed her into the living room and sat down opposite her. She leaned back in the sofa and glared at me as if we were enemies now and neither of us was about to make peace. "Can you think of anyone who'd have a reason —"

"To kill her," she interrupted with a burst of anger. "Almost anyone she ever met."

Despite myself, I felt accusation creep into my eyes. Manny picked up on it instantly.

"You think I killed Reenie." It was a statement.

I tried to backtrack. "Why do you even assume she was killed? Everyone I've talked to assumes it was an accident." Everyone but Manny and Helen, I noted with a chill.

Her eyes flickered with fear. Or perhaps recognition. Whatever it was, it convinced me that Manny knew more than she was saying. She wet her index figure with the pink tip of her tongue, then rubbed a spot on her black pump. "When I left here last night, she was alive."

"What time was that?"

"Midnight."

I made a mental note of the time. "Was she drunk?"

She gulped the coffee, then winced as if the liquid were too hot. I knew better. She was stalling for time. Lucky for me, Manny was a lousy liar. "Whiskey," she said at last. Her voice was wavering again.

"I didn't notice whiskey at the party," I said doubtfully. Actually, I hadn't looked further than the food.

"She wasn't drinking there," she said, her eyes darting everywhere but never resting on me. "It must have started afterward. When she got home."

"Curious. There aren't any bottles in the house. I know. I looked."

Her head snapped up. The trapped-raccoon look had returned. "Who the hell do you think you are? This is my house —"

My internal alarm went off. "Tell me, Manny, who inherits?"

She stood up. "That's enough, Robin." Her indignation was a thin mask. I had touched a nerve, and no one was more surprised than me.

"You inherit the house, don't you?"

The open door and Manny's fiery gaze told me everything I needed to know.

Or almost everything. I spilled my coffee on my lap. Honestly leaping up from the pain, I knocked over the lamp next to the armchair. Manny instinctively retreated into the kitchen for some paper towels, giving me time to scramble upstairs to Noreen's bedroom. I retrieved the metal file that I had wisely forgotten to lock and started shoving papers under the belt of my jeans.

From downstairs I could hear Manny cursing my name.

"I'm in the bathroom," I shouted to head her off. We met at the top of the stairs. Feeling devilish, I kissed her hot cheek before exiting the house, the stolen goods slipping halfway down my thigh before I reached the car.

I unloaded the crumpled papers from my pants and sat down in front of the smoldering fire. Sure enough, there was a birth certificate mixed in with the papers.

Noreen Sue Finnegan was born at 8:34 p.m. on August 3, 1952, to Adelaide and John Finnegan. Place of birth: Wayne County, Gladstone, Michigan. As I read her father's occupation, my lips puckered with surprise. Apparently, John Finnegan had been a police officer. A row of dashes filled the occupation box under her mother's name.

I marveled yet again at the wealth of information this one document yielded. I learned the name of the doctor who performed the delivery, the location of the hospital where Noreen was born, the family's home address, the number of children Adelaide had given birth to previously (one), and that Adelaide Finnegan had been tested for syphilis during the pregnancy. I had no idea what I was going to do with this information yet, but that didn't detract from my pleasure at having obtained it.

I called Jill back and asked her to check if Michigan had a state reunion registry.

After a moment she said, "You got lucky this time, Rob," and read off the number for the state adoption department in Lansing. I jotted it down and started concocting my latest fiction.

The woman who answered was practically in

tears by the time I finished explaining how I had two months to live and desperately needed to locate my siblings before I passed away.

"I'd love to help you, honey, but I'm going to need a written request and a copy of your birth certificate."

I've done adoption searches in the past. Few processes are more infuriating. Storming through the paper blockade was often a herculean task — one I didn't have time for in this case. I reminded her that Thanksgiving was just days away, and then I went for the jugular. "Please. I have so little to be thankful for . . ." My voice trailed off mournfully. Let her fill in the blanks. Experience has taught me that few people can resist playing the hero.

I silently began counting to ten. I didn't make it past five.

"Hold on. Let me see what I can do."

Ten minutes later I was ready to hang up. My friend in Michigan returned just in time. "So sorry. We're short-staffed this week." I could hear file drawers squeaking in the background, then the line grew unnaturally quiet. Speaking with trained delicacy, she said, "Sweetie, you must have forgotten. You already registered with us." Another uncomfortable beat of silence passed. "None of your siblings have contacted us."

The problem with lying so convincingly is that sometimes you fool yourself. Inexplicably, my eyes filled. My voice cracked as I said, "So no one in my family is looking for me," almost forgetting that Noreen was the orphan and not me.

"At least not yet. But don't give up. They may not know the registry exists." She started rattling off a plethora of standard adoption-search techniques. I knew them well — well enough to know how rarely they work.

I hung up, strangely depressed. With that one phone call, I suddenly felt a kinship with Noreen I had never experienced while she was alive. Whether it helped the investigation or not, I was now determined to find the siblings she had so desperately sought.

The good news was that I already had more information than I commonly had when searching for an adoptee's birth parents. I picked up the phone and dialed the National Locator Cross-Street Directory Service. By the time I hung up, my ear was bruised and the screen of my laptop computer filled.

John Finnegan's name disappeared from the directory in 1964 — which meant he had either moved or died. The service confirmed the date of death. October 15, 1964. I had to resist shouting "Bingo!" into the phone. I next obtained the names, addresses, and phone numbers of nine families living near the Finnegans at the time of their death. Only one of them was still at the same address. I tried that number three times before. I got frustrated and forwarded the information to Jill, who made a disparaging comment about my pro bono generosity. I didn't care. Noreen's one-hundred-dollar deposit was still sitting on the dresser upstairs. I wasn't about to let her down.

I could smell mothballs, and then fire. All at

once, the closet was blazing and I was trapped in the corner. Handcuffs bound me to the wall and my mouth was filling with blood so fast I couldn't scream. Then someone was slapping me, the palm slicing across my face like a metal bar. The gun barrel entered my mouth. The metal was scalding, tasting like charcoal. Clicking. Clicking.

My father's face flared with revulsion as he pulled the trigger.

I jumped up, my heart racing and the entire length of my body damp with sweat. A new nightmare. A new reason to avoid sleep. I threw the blankets aside and stumbled for the light. A glance at my watch told me I had slept less than three hours. Four o'clock in the morning and my adrenaline was running haywire. I dropped to the floor and did fifteen pushups. When that didn't work, I raided the kitchen and began assaulting the demons with Yoo-Hoos and Lucky Charms. I had resorted to picking the marshmallow rainbow bits out of the box of Lucky Charms, when I realized what I needed.

K.T.

More than anything else, I wanted to curl up in her smooth arms and listen to her heartbeat. I didn't care what time it was. I dialed the number of her Manhattan apartment and waited, each ring making my throat tighter. I was out on a limb whose strength could not be known. All at once, I began trembling uncontrollably. My fingers felt like ice and my cheeks burned.

"Hello."

At first I didn't recognize her voice, thick as it

was with sleep and surprise. I hesitated. What if it was someone else?

"Robin?" She sounded suddenly awake. "Is that you?"

Sobs blindsided me. Every muscle, every organ, tripped into spasm, tugging at my words. I balled my fist and rhythmically pounded the kitchen counter. The pain wouldn't stop.

"Robin," she repeated. The sound of my name, stated so gently, struck me like a battering ram. I folded, dropping to the cold, tiled floor that still smelled faintly of flour and lovemaking.

"I need you, K.T. Please." I hung up, more terrified than I had ever been in my life. And never more alone.

I was still huddled against the pantry door when K.T. arrived at the cabin, nearly two hours later. She came in with the sunlight.

The warmth hardened me.

I stood up and blew my nose with a paper towel. The roughness felt right. "Sorry about last night," I said. "I had this stupid nightmare . . ."

"Stop." K.T. ran a finger along the base of my neck, following my hairline. Goose bumps rose at her touch. I reached around her, pulling her toward me, anxious to lose myself in her mouth.

She pulled back tenderly and shook her head. "That would be too easy."

I hate intelligent women.

She wanted truth? Fine. "Yesterday I remembered that my father tried to kill me. After I murdered my sister. True poetic justice, don't you think?" I was defiant, angry, and in control.

Break out the champagne. The real Robin Miller was back.

But then I looked into K.T.'s eyes, the color of blue spruce in early morning light. She saw through me and disregarded the bravado I had adopted so long ago that even I can barely distinguish when it's real and when it's not. K.T. saw me as I was. Frightened and needy and aching for something in which I no longer believed. And she didn't avert her eyes.

In an instant, I transformed from oak to willow, my spirit bowing, accepting the hard wind blowing out of my past rather than bracing against it.

Suddenly, under K.T.'s silent gaze, I realized I would not break. I lifted her hand and kissed each knuckle. "God, I missed you." And with those simple words, I crossed from nightmare to dream.

Sleep doesn't come easy to me. I've had bouts of insomnia that lasted weeks, till I finally collapsed into near-coma states at friends' homes or in restaurant booths. Once, I slept for three hours on a subway car and awoke to find both my briefcase and my shoes gone. With K.T. holding me to her breast, her steady heartbeat drumming in my ear, I fell asleep in minutes. When I woke up, I was curled around her like a vine around a branch.

K.T. tapped my nose with a square fingertip. "Dagnabbit, woman, you are one stubborn son-of-a-bitch. I knew you needed to sleep. When I was growing up in Wizard Clip —"

I burst out laughing. "I went to sleep with an

angel and woke up with Daisy Mae, direct from Dogpatch."

Concern flitted over her features, then she grinned. "Sometimes, chile, I is afeered that you is one brick shy of a full load."

"Did you really grow up in a place called Wizard Clip?"

"Wizard Clip, West Virginia. Population... fifty-seven. Only twelve of them weren't relatives. Nearest real town was Stinking Gut. That's where the mine was located." The tease had left her voice. I had the distinct impression that K.T. was contending with one of her own demons.

"Did most of them work at the mine?"

She sat up in bed, steepled her hands over her nose, then rubbed the corners of her eyes wearily and said, "All of them did — except the women, children, and my father." Her smile was bitter. "He was the radical, the 'hillwilliam,'" she added, then noticed my puzzlement. "Folks called anyone with aspirations a 'hillwilliam' or sometimes just a 'biggety ole hillbilly.' In other words, my father was a snob." She said the words proudly. "I didn't appreciate it then, but he was killing himself to get us out of that town. Away from that damn mine and the narrow-minded drones that worked there, day in, day out, carrying the coal home on their clothes, in their lungs, on their filthy lips."

This was a side of K.T. I hadn't seen before. When she spoke of the mine, her face distorted with rage. And something else. Shame or distaste. Perhaps both.

"What happened after your father died?"

She pursed her mouth and said in a tight voice,

"Oh, life got real interesting then, believe me." She gazed over my head toward the nightstand. "It's lunchtime. Why don't I head out to the store and stock up the house. Tonight, I'll make you a Southern dinner like you ain't never seen."

She had ended the history lesson a little too abruptly. K.T. was hiding something, but I couldn't begin to guess what it might be.

I watched her slink out of bed and stretch luxuriously in the insistent sunlight. She was as sleek as an Abyssinian cat, with a body so tight my eyes could trace her muscles from across the room as surely as with my palm. Long and compact rather than slim, her body excited me in a new way. I was surprised to realize that I was slightly breathless and already aching for her touch.

I scampered across the bed and tackled her from the side, pinning her wrists to the floor with a mischievous laugh. "Now, you are mine," I said in a mock German accent. "You vill not argue."

Her eyes widened and her lips trembled. But the look wasn't excitement. I rolled off hurriedly, slamming my hip onto the pine planks. As she sat up and crossed her hands over her chest, her shoulders shuddered as if a brisk wind had passed through the room. I wrapped my legs and arms around her from behind and rocked her gently. She responded with what at first sounded like a sob, but rapidly became a self-conscious giggle.

"You startled me. I didn't realize you were such an insatiable beast," she said lightly. I wasn't buying the tone, but I wasn't about to push her.

I nuzzled her neck and whispered, "You promised

me a Southern dinner. You better deliver the goods tonight."

Just then, the phone rang. I disentangled myself and hopped over to the bed.

"Robin Miller?" The male voice was tentative and familiar.

"Speaking."

"How's your volleyball serve doing these days?"

He had to be Dean Flynn, my water-volleyball buddy who lived near Noreen. "Dean?"

"Dr. Dean to you," he said playfully. "I understand that you wanted to talk to me. I'm free now, if you have the time."

I glanced over to K.T., who was strapping a bra around breasts the color of marzipan. I sighed and said, "Give me five minutes."

Chapter 6

The Flynn house was remarkable, even in a community known for its haute rustic architecture. A modern, cedar-shingled colonial with a wraparound porch and forest-green shutters, the house was surrounded by young birch trees and thick rhododendron shrubs. The sun-dappled driveway was strewn with red ocher stones that rattled under my sneakers. I did a little tap dance and then headed toward the front steps. Dean was sitting on a glider watching me with amusement.

"Oops."

He smiled and stood up to greet me. "Don't worry. I don't trust adults. I'm a kid myself. Despite what my birth certificate says."

His palm was rough with some kind of scar tissue and his arms beefy, unlike the rest of him. He had more angles than a quartz crystal. As in the past, I felt momentarily disoriented by his pale blue eyes, a stark contrast to his too-tan skin.

"Great color," I said spontaneously.

His grin was self-deprecating, his teeth dazzling. "Salon bought. So's the hair color. That's it. The rest of me is real. Scout's honor," he said, flashing me the appropriate hand signal. "Want to go inside? I'm afraid you can already feel the bite of winter coming."

I was curious to see the house's interior, but Dean looked toasty in a wool fisherman's sweater and maroon corduroys. And a mug of spiced cider was steaming next to the glider.

"Tell you what — if you can share some of that cider with me, I'd be happy to talk right here."

He clapped his hands enthusiastically, looking remarkably like a teenager. "Great. I'll be right back. Have a seat."

The glider was constructed of unstained pressurized wood and had to be at least a decade old. My thighs rested comfortably in grooves worn down by years of use. I began rocking back and forth, the afternoon sun baking my forehead and cheeks.

"Now, there's a woman at peace." His voice startled me. So did his words. Strangely, I did feel relaxed. I accepted the mug of cider with a small nod. The liquid was perfectly spiced, and I told him so.

"The mulled cider's a specialty of Maggie's. You've never met her, have you?" he asked, his tone darkening. "Unfortunately, she's not here to accept your praise." All at once, his face crowded with lines, aging before me like the portrait of Dorian Gray.

Hesitantly I asked, "Where is she?"

"Wish I knew." He shook his head and made a halfhearted attempt at a grin. "But that's not why you're here. I saw Dougie last night. He told me about your concerns. So how can I help?"

The steam from the cider was beading on my upper lip and nostrils. It felt wonderful. "First of all, please tell me you haven't bought into Crowell's lame investigation."

"The man's an incompetent," he said sympathetically. "No doubt about that. But I'm going to have to disappoint you about the cause of death. I concur absolutely with Doug. Noreen was a drunk. All indicators point in one direction. She overindulged, passed out and cracked her skull."

I frowned. Didn't anyone but me wonder why an active drunk had failed to have a single bottle of booze in her home? "I still don't understand why an autopsy wasn't performed."

Dean pursed his lips, barely hiding a trace of annoyance. "We didn't need an autopsy to identify the cause of death. I happened to catch Doug at the hospital when he was examining the body. We both knew about Noreen's alcoholism. You couldn't live in Telham and not know. Doug had a hunch and he contacted the physician Noreen used in Philly, before she moved up here. He had noted an early stage of alcoholic cardiomyopathy, with increased wall thickness but normal diastolic internal diameter."

I liked Dean, but I wasn't crazy about doctors and right now he was more doctor than human. "Can you explain that in lay terms?" I asked impatiently. The cider was gone and the conversation was chilling me.

He smiled indulgently and checked my mug. "Sure, but first let me refill that for you." The man was a mind reader.

"Thanks. Mind if I follow you in?"

After a second of hesitation, he said, "No. But remember, Maggie's not around and, frankly, I'm not a great housekeeper."

He led me into a foyer filled with potted trees and hanging plants. A European-style kitchen was at the far end. High-tech kitchen accoutrements included a microwave that had more dials and buttons than a cockpit. The room was pristine white, with flashes of hunter green and peach. Dean's housekeeping apologies were unnecessary. The place was immaculate.

"Sorry about the cold medical terminology. It's an occupational hazard," he explained as he ladled cider from a Crock Pot. There was enough cider for a family of eight.

"Dean, I don't think I've ever asked you — do you have kids?"

He winced sharply, sloshing cider over the side of the mug and onto my hands. "Christ. Sorry about that." He turned on the cold-water faucet and held my hand under the spray. The pain hadn't hit yet, but I knew it would. "This will help take the sting out," he said soothingly.

Standing this close, I could smell his cologne, an odor not unlike fresh-turned soil. Heat radiated from his skin. We were the same height, and right now we were practically cheek to cheek. My instincts went up. Sexual pheromones were in the air, and they sure as hell weren't mine.

"You have incredible green eyes. They're almost jade." His lips were so close, I could feel his breath on my face. With my free hand I turned off the faucet.

"Thanks, Dean. For the water and the compliment."

He leaned back. "That sounded like a come-on, didn't it? Sorry for the eighteenth time. I'm really a jerk. C'mon into the living room. I promise I'll be halfway decent."

A shiver of anxiety came and went. I followed his lead into an expansive living room with a Palladian window facing the road and a massive casement window on the other side overlooking the Acee River. The teak furniture was Scandinavian modern, and showroom perfect, down to the undefiled medical journals, electronics periodicals and gardening magazines fanned out on the low coffee table. I crossed to the stone fireplace that extended at least sixteen feet upwards, ending just before the peak of the cathedral ceiling.

The ceiling fan was one of those newfangled ones that not only blew and sucked air, but did so at ten different speeds, with lights that flashed on when they sensed movement and dimmed when the room was still. A few feet to the left of the fireplace was an eight-foot-long entertainment unit that housed a flat-screen television, hi-fi stereo, laserdisk, CD carousel, and videotape editing console. Someone in the house was obviously an electronics freak.

Standing before the low-burning fire, I held my undamaged hand toward the flames, then after a moment turned and asked, "Where is Maggie?" If she really was the housekeeper, she couldn't have been gone very long. Even the slate mantel was free of dust.

He dropped into a tan leather coach, crossed his legs and stared at me. I had the sense that he was sizing me up, calculating his next words. "You have a knack for identifying sore spots."

"I guess it's my turn to apologize."

"Not at all. You're a detective. I imagine you're very good at what you do. As a professional, I can respect that."

Okay, enough with the cat-and-mouse game. I sat across from him. "What's up, Dean?" My tone was unmistakable. Time for business.

He adjusted his posture and I knew my message had penetrated. "My wife disappeared Sunday morning. I talked to Crowell about it, but he said there was nothing he could do until she had been gone at least forty-eight hours. Well, she's been gone two days, and now he's telling me 'there ain't much to do but wait.' I don't want to wait. I want my wife back." He sighed, then smiled sheepishly. "As you may have guessed, I'm not my best when she's not around."

I was barely listening. The coincidence was unnerving. Why hadn't anyone noticed?

Without thinking, I blurted, "Has Crowell even bothered to search the grounds?" As soon as the words were out of my mouth, I regretted them.

Dean recovered quickly. "No. He didn't think it was necessary." He stood up and paced over to the casement window, hands in his pockets. "Maybe I should give you some background. Maggie and I have been going through some . . . rough times. We've wanted a child for so long." He turned and faced me with red eyes and pale lips. "Ironic, huh, for a specialist in OB-GYN. I've delivered hundreds of children, for fathers far less qualified than me, but —"

He cut himself off, as if startled by his words. Scratching behind his ear, he continued in a quiet voice, "Maggie's had two miscarriages. The last one happened just three weeks ago. We were devastated. You don't know . . . well, maybe I shouldn't say that . . . Do you have children?"

For some reason, the question unnerved me. I shook my head and felt myself tightening up. I've never been at ease around children, maybe because I was cheated of my own childhood. Their innocence, their sheer delight in discovering life, always startled me. My hands began tingling and I rubbed them vigorously over my knees.

"Maggie's been so depressed. I've tried to comfort her, arranged for a colleague to counsel her, but she was inconsolable. But I guess I didn't fully understand what was happening with her. Saturday night I had a delivery at the hospital. Afterwards, I crashed in the physician's lounge. When I came home Sunday morning, the first thing I noticed was that her car was gone. I thought she was just out running errands. But then I checked the closets. Her suitcases were gone. And so were mine. No note, no explanation."

Dean squatted in front of the flagstone hearth and stoked the fire with a brass poker. The embers burst into flames. "I don't know what to do. For a man of action, that may be the hardest part," he said, sounding exasperated. He tossed another log onto the fire.

"Has she ever done this before?" I asked. Despite his explanation, the timing of Maggie's disappearance disturbed me.

"Never. She wouldn't even go to the local supermarket without leaving me a note." Wearing blackened fire gloves, he expertly rearranged the logs till the flames were licking the outside of the stones. A rush of heat swept toward me.

"Does she have any special friends, relatives, who she confides in regularly?"

He tossed the gloves on top of the wood ring and looked at me with concern. "Sure. Noreen Finnegan. The two of them were as thick as thieves."

My first reaction was anger. "Damn it, Dean. Don't you think that's mighty coincidental?"

The poor man looked startled at my outburst. I counted to five, then started over. "Does Crowell know about their relationship?"

His jaw muscles rippled. "Friendship. *Not* relationship." He stamped over to where I was sitting and eyed me with irritation. "I didn't say they were involved. My wife and I are in love."

Fine. I nodded meekly. Anything you say, Dean.

"And, no," he continued. "I didn't tell Crowell that my wife's new best friend happens to be the meanest dyke in eastern Pennsylvania. The man's a phenomenal bigot with the reasoning capacity of a Neanderthal. With that kind of information, I'd get a shit-eating grin and a pat on the back. I can hear him now. 'Well, buddy boy, I guess Maggie's found herself greener pastures to chew.' No. I didn't tell him."

He had worked himself into a rage that seemed to drain from him as rapidly as it had erupted. Now, he sat down next to me and shook his head. "Again, I apologize. I'm just on edge. What makes it worse is that Thanksgiving is just a few days away. My wife's gone and I can't do anything. I'm on call this whole week. I have seven patients on the edge of labor, and the grand pleasure of informing another woman that she has cervical cancer." His thick fingers rubbed his temples with unbridled anxiety. "Man. I'm going nuts."

Suddenly, he spun towards me. "Can I hire you? I mean, you do that sort of thing, don't you? Missing persons? Money's no object."

He rambled on while my internal alarm buzzed wildly. My instincts told me that Maggie's disappearance and Noreen's death were connected in some way. Taking Dean's case would provide me with an official reason — and finances — for pursuing the investigation. With a silent groan, I realized I probably would have to contact the National Locator Service again. My ear was still bruised from yesterday's phone call.

I explained my fees and shook hands with him. "I'll get started right away. But I'll need help from you. Pictures of Maggie. Access to her records, driver's license number, Social Security number, credit card numbers, any information you have."

Dean was nodding eagerly. Too eagerly. I don't like overly optimistic clients. The higher their hopes soared, the harder they crashed. Gesturing for emphasis, I said, "You have to understand, Dean, I can't make promises. I may not find her, and if I do, you may not like what I find."

"Fine, I understand. Just do your best."

I wasn't sure he did understand, but I continued anyway. "When did Noreen and Maggie first become friendly?"

He looked away. "Late spring, I guess, before Noreen and Helen bought the house. The two of them had been checking the community out for a few months. As you know, there aren't many places like Telham." He hesitated. "We're pretty liberal. Anyway, Maggie met up with them one day at the clubhouse while they were checking out the listings. She told them a neighbor of ours might be interested in selling his house. Two weeks later, they went to contract. Noreen and Maggie hit it off right away, God knows why."

"Any idea about what they had in common?"

A finger traced the scar on his right palm. Lost in memory, he hadn't heard my question. I repeated it and watched him flush. "Oh yeah. Drinking. Maggie has a little problem with alcohol. The one thing I can say about Noreen is that she helped Maggie recognize her disease. The two of them started AA together."

My interest piqued, I asked, "Do you know where the meetings were held?"

He pointed a finger and said, "Hold on a minute."

As soon as he exited I jumped up, a burning sensation running along the back of my right thigh — a worrisome signal that my sciatica was about to pay me a visit. I cursed under my breath, then shifted into high-snoop mode. An array of photographs was artfully displayed in a hutch situated in the hallway leading back to the kitchen. I hobbled over, the pain dissipating slowly.

The centerpiece was an elaborate wedding picture. Shot in a full-bloom rose garden, the picture showed a much younger and less polished Dean, his hair mousy brown instead of its current warm chestnut. He was at least fifty pounds heavier. The most remarkable features were his proud smile and piercing blue eyes. Seeing Dean now, and then viewing the photograph, was like seeing the lump of granite from which a fine sculpture had been carved.

Next to him was an average-looking woman whose heart-shaped face bowed toward the camera shyly. Her hair was coal black and gathered into a French knot braided with yellow baby roses. I leaned forward, struck by the look in her eyes. They had the beseeching gaze of a puppy caged in a pound. She was young. Younger than Dean by a fair number of years.

"She's beautiful, isn't she?" Dean stood at the end of the hall with an armload of papers. "I hate to admit it, but she's the spitting image of my mother. You know the song, 'I want a gal just like the gal that married dear old dad.' Guess that could be my theme song. But, then, you probably feel the same way."

The thought of settling down with anyone who bore so much as a vague resemblance to either of my parents was downright repugnant, yet I somehow managed to smile politely. I took a quick glance at the rest of the pictures, most of which seemed like childhood photographs. Of the many baby pictures, only a few were of Maggie or Dean.

"Whose kids?" I asked, following him into the kitchen.

He smiled broadly. "Mine." Then he shrugged. "Kind of. They're children I delivered." His face darkened. Another nerve hit. I was batting them home today.

Dean slipped the papers into a plastic bag from McDaniels, the local grocery store. "I pulled together a few things for you to review, plus this," he said, handing me a plain address book. "It's Maggie's old one. Noreen gave her a new one for her last birthday. On the back page she's listed all the local AA meetings."

Most of the meetings were at the Unitarian church on Route 390. The hours surprised me. The first one started at six in the morning, and the last ended at midnight. I flipped through the pages, noticing an unusual number of first-name-only entries. Under the L, I found "Lisa" written in block letters, the name starred and accompanied by three different numbers. I had a hunch that "Lisa" was Maggie's sponsor. I dropped the book into the bag. "Thanks."

Dean grabbed my hand. "One last thing," he said, his voice edgy with emotion. "After this last miscarriage, we discovered pregnancy's out for us. She can't carry." His eyes filled. "We decided to adopt. One of my patients is fourteen years old and due any day now. Just yesterday she decided to put the child up for adoption. But I know she won't turn the baby over to me if Maggie's not here. I'm not even sure I'd want the baby without my wife by my side. Please find her. I need her."

He was squeezing my hand so hard it almost hurt.

"I'll do my best. That's all I can promise."

There were times when I hated my job.

The sun was resting on the treetops by the time I returned to the cabin. K.T. was still gone, but I felt my heart do a little kick at the thought of her return. Then I remembered how tortured Dean had looked. Love was a dangerous emotion. A tremor passed through me.

Sitting in the den downstairs, I leafed through the papers and pulled Maggie's credit card and Social Security numbers. Back in Brooklyn, Jill Zimmerman would need them to start a skip trace. I plugged in my modem and laptop, ran off a standard contract, typed in my notes, and transmitted the whole file to her. Some holiday, I thought. My therapist would be so proud.

While I was on-line, I decided to sort through my notes on Noreen. As much as I hated to admit it, I was still kicking at the starting gate. Her death could really be accidental, for all I knew. I scrolled through the file and halted at the word *cardiomyopathy*. The term had never been fully explained. Flynn's line was busy, so I resorted to my own personal expert.

Beth Morris and Dinah Zahavi, my housemates back in Park Slope, not only serve as step-parents to my cats Geeja and Mallomar, but also as my personal nurse and therapist. Beth is so thin, a stiff wind could easily transform her into a kite. She has spiky blonde hair, an even disposition, and a fondness for corny show tunes. She is also a highly qualified nurse. I know her schedule as well as my own. At three o'clock on Tuesday, she was probably in her office at the Methodist Clinic. I dialed the number from memory.

"Dahling, it's me. How do the two of you survive without me there?"

She laughed good-naturedly. "Funny, but our food lasts a little longer, the block's a little quieter, and we all feel a little safer. But it is more interesting when you're around. So are you in trouble yet?"

Beth knew me too well.

I yawned for effect. "Just the usual. A little murder, a little romance, a missing wife or two."

"Well, be patient. Things will heat up any day now." She broke off as the hospital paging system kicked on. "I had a feeling you weren't just feeling homesick."

"I need a little medical debriefing." I summarized what I knew about Noreen's death.

"Interesting," she said, her tone reflexively dropping into a more professional cadence. "Typically, cardiomyopathy's a chronic disorder of the heart muscles. Usually involves hypertrophy and obstructive damage."

Now she sounded like Flynn. I responded sarcastically, "Want to try English on me?"

"That is English. But I'll simplify. Cardiomyopathy's a progressive weakness and enlargement of the heart."

"And it's related to alcohol abuse?"

"It can be. Hold on, I want to look something up." She put down the phone, flooding my ear with urgent buzzes and beeps. I started feeling ill, as I usually do thinking about hospitals.

"Okay, I'm back. Let's see . . . almost one-third of all cases of congestive cardiomyopathy are related to alcoholism. But the condition can also be caused by rheumatic fever, a vitamin B deficiency, viruses, autoimmune diseases, toxic agents—"

I interrupted. "Toxic, as in poison?"

"Sure. But I wouldn't jump to any conclusions," she cautioned me. "How advanced was her condition?"

Without an autopsy report or a full medical history, I was working blind. "I have no idea."

"Do you know her age?"

"Thirty-nine."

"What about her health condition over the past year? Had she experienced fatigue, chest pains, palpitations? Loss of sex drive? Anything like that?"

I answered in the negative.

"Without all the facts, I really can't help you much. Think of it as just another type of investigation, Rob. A good physician has to trace disease as surely as you trace clues in a criminal investigation."

The comparison didn't exactly have me jumping for joy. Beth had no idea how much of my job was sheer guesswork. Or maybe she did. The possibility further unnerved me. "That's fine," I muttered, feeling anything but fine. "But given what you *do* know, would you draw the same conclusion as Marks and Flynn?"

She paused. "I get the sense you want me to say no. I can't. If this woman really had a history of alcoholic cardiomyopathy *and* she continued drinking, sudden cardiac arrest is not unexpected. I doubt any physician would react differently than they did. To tell you the truth, given the circumstances, I'd have to say an autopsy *wasn't* warranted."

"Thanks anyway." I scratched at an unruly cuticle, wondering if I was inventing a mystery where there wasn't any, and shifted gears resignedly. "By the way, how did the social worker's visit go?" Her hesitation made me uneasy. I rushed to fill the silence. "I'm sure you wowed her."

"Oh, we wowed her all right." The bitter edge was atypical of Beth. "Dinah and I made a few tactical errors. We thought honesty was the best policy. What morons we were."

She was fighting back tears. Unexpectedly, so was I. I hadn't realized till now how much I wanted the adoption to go through for them. "What happened?"

"The bitch strolled into the house and in less than five seconds zeroed in on our portrait gallery." She was referring to the framed photographs lining the hallway on the parlor floor. Images popped into my head. Dinah and Beth dressed in silver-blue dresses, exchanging vows in Prospect Park's picnic house. A group of us attempting to mount a giraffe raft at Herring Cove Beach in Provincetown. The three of us standing entwined in front of the Washington Monument during the morning rally of the 1987 Gay and Lesbian March on Washington. Off to our right, if you looked real close, you could see two shaved-head lesbians signing each other's boobs.

I closed my eyes tight. "Shit."

"The ironic thing was, we talked about taking down the photographs. But we decided that it was unscrupulous. And God knows, we *have* to have our scruples."

I hated hearing the stony self-ridicule. The few arguments I've had with Beth and Dinah have been over principles. My work often necessitates a little ethics-bending, and the two of them have judiciously tracked every reported indiscretion. The strange thing was, I realized with a start, their criticism helped me keep peace with myself.

Bolting for the high ground, I blurted, "Don't talk like that. You did the right thing —"

"The *right* thing," she said, cutting my lecture short. "Robin, she didn't even pretend to take us seriously. She told us right off, 'You ladies are not qualified for adoption.' "

I stood up and winced. A line of fire was running along my thigh and into my spine. I headed into the bathroom for an aspirin and said, "We'll get a lawyer —"

"Wait. You haven't heard the best part yet. Dinah went on a rampage, citing cases and spewing legal terms like Perry Mason. The woman just sat there nodding impassively. When Dinah was done, she smiled and said she was sure we could adopt an AIDS baby or, and I quote, 'another undesirable.'

But the 'normal' babies were reserved for 'normal' couples." She was crying now. "You know how I feel. It's not that I don't care about those other children..."

She didn't have to explain to me. Beth used to work in pediatrics. After six years of pediatric intensive care, she had been on the verge of a nervous breakdown, the strain contributing to the dissolution of a three-year-old relationship. Soon after, she moved into a studio apartment with a view of a brick wall, totaled her car, and started dosing up on valium. Trapped in a downward spiral, she was lucky or healthy enough to enroll in a special workshop for health professionals that Dinah was leading at the clinic. The subject was coping with death.

Dinah recognized the seriousness of Beth's depression and urged her to get into therapy. Six months later, Beth transferred to triage and moved in with Dinah. I was adamantly against the arrangement, warning Dinah that she was on the verge of becoming another "U-Haul lesbian." The past five years of domestic bliss have happily proven me dead wrong.

I took a deep breath and asked, "So what happens now?"

Her laugh was abrupt. "Who knows?" In the distance a deep voice bellowed her name. She grunted into the phone. "Duty calls." She hung up before I could say another word.

I was still staring at the phone when K.T. came back to the cabin. The sound of my name springing from that honied tongue made me scoot out of the den like a child running for an ice cream truck. Her hair, the color of Sedona mountains at dusk, was windblown, the curls clinging to her neck and forehead like ivy. The weathered denim shirt she wore drove me crazy. Somehow, perhaps from her lugging the groceries from the car, the shirt had lost a middle button. Her cleavage was a magnificent tease, a delicate curve plunging into a tantalizing shadow.

She lowered the bags onto the kitchen table as if in slow motion. Through the gap I saw a portion of her foam-green bra, a hard pink nipple pressing against the lace. I started to pulse and twitch. But it was the eyes that did me in, the leaf-green glow, the intent gaze. The communication between us was silent and indisputable.

I don't remember crossing the room, just the way our mouths met and danced together, a ballet of tongues and lips, slow and yet rousing. My fingers lifted her shirt, traced the deep indentation that culminated in the small of her back. I was shivering. Lips to ears, small cooing sounds, the sweetest music. I grasped her hand and started to lead her upstairs. She protested briefly, pointing to the groceries, whining about pork chops and fried green tomatoes.

I reached around her, lifted the phone off the receiver and flipped the power off. "I have my own tomato to fry," I said with a racy twitch of my eyebrows. She chuckled, but her hips gyrated against me with purpose. An eyebrow winked back at me and then we kissed again, this time longer, the urgency building. Our bodies began rubbing together in a now-familiar rhythm. A river over rocks. My juices rushed.

I walked us out into the hall and started up the stairs backwards, our lips locked, knees banging together. I tripped over the last two steps, landing hard on my butt. A sharp pain shot down my leg, but I was too busy to pay it much attention. K.T. fell on me, giggling. The weight of her body lit me like a match to kerosene. I rolled her over and covered her laughing lips with my hungry mouth. She responded instantly, one arm wrapping around my neck, pulling me closer. Her legs trapped my thigh against her groin, begging me to pump. Using the top of the step to brace myself, I pressed myself into her, feeling her hip bone against my own groin, the friction almost too much too soon.

I lifted myself on one elbow, opened her shirt, and struggled awkwardly, anxious to undo her bra. Impatiently, she pulled it up over her breasts. Groaning, I took a nipple into my mouth, sucking harder than I had before, knowing instinctively that we both needed this contact, this intense taking. With the other hand, I stroked her, from her belly to her other breast. Finding the bud hard and waiting, I kneaded it with my fingers then, greedy, sought it with my mouth. I oscillated between her breasts like a pendulum, while my thigh kept time between her legs, pumping steadily.

All at once, words filled the air like the scent of our aching bodies. She urged me to suck harder and I responded gratefully, my own body tightening and straining toward her in answer to her groans and heated directions. Without realizing it, I had gone over the edge, rubbing my still-clothed body over her full thigh till I came in a shuddering explosion. I stripped K.T.'s jeans and underwear, the waves of

97

my orgasm pitching me forward with fierce need. What I wanted was K.T.'s shiver against me. I backed down the stairs and knelt before her, opening her with cold, trembling fingers.

"You're so beautiful," I said, the words surprising me, but not as much as the tears and choked-back sob.

K.T.'s hand found the top of my head, her fingers catching in my hair like fire. Her touch seared me. "Oh, take me, baby. I want you inside. I want you." Her voice was hoarse with need. I pressed my mouth against her, slowly entering her with my fingers, sucking her fervidly. I loved hearing her voice as I explored her, carried her from crest to crest. She began saying my name over and over, and I punctuated her cry with my tongue. Painfully, purposefully, I tried to slow myself down, to intensify her sensations, but her thighs tightened and she bolted toward me.

"No, no. Don't stop. Now. Please."

She blossomed on my mouth, twitching against my tongue like the wings of a butterfly.

"Oh, God, Robin, I love you."

Suddenly stone cold and mute, I rested my head against her as she throbbed.

Neither of us acknowledged my stillness. We retreated to the bedroom, where K.T. promptly made love to me, as if to cover her declaration with the blanket of passion. I couldn't come. We fell asleep in each other's arms, in a room so hushed the silence shrieked like wind through a ruin.

When I awoke, K.T. was gone and the air smelled like hot apples. I was at once relieved and famished. I dressed quickly, feeling strangely shy, and started downstairs. The first step ignited a nerve in my right leg. The second sent an electric shock up my spine. I cursed my way into the living room. No question about it, I moaned to myself. The sciatica was back.

I stopped in the bathroom for two Motrin, then headed into the kitchen. K.T. was cooking with a vengeance. Every cupboard was open, pots simmered on the stove or soaked in the sink, and the microwave was counting down like a mad scientist.

"Whew. Did you leave anything untouched?"

"Uh-huh," she said, barely noting my comment as she beat a bowl of creamy orange batter.

I crossed to the pine table and fleeced a slice of apple, then opened the fridge and downed a Yoo-Hoo. We all choose our own medicine.

"You'll ruin your appetite," K.T. said in an offhanded way that reminded me of someone's relative. She was right, but it wasn't the Yoo-Hoo that was killing my hunger.

"What smells so delicious?"

She finally made eye contact, then immediately looked away. In that one glance she conveyed so much emotion — pride, fear, affection, confusion — that I wondered how she was able to stand.

"Hope your cholesterol is good." She tried to adopt a lighthearted tone.

Maybe if we both pretended . . .

"If it is, I have a feeling it won't be after this meal."

"Good guess. I'm making fried green tomatoes

99

which, despite rumors to the contrary, were made famous by my mother and not by Fannie Flagg. That appetizer of haute grease will be followed by pan-fried pork chops with apple jelly, spiced mustard greens, and my own specialty, sweet potato hush puppies."

"What, no dessert?"

She laughed. The effect was like rubbing Noxzema on a sunburn. "No self-respecting Southern woman would commit such a travesty. I made a cherry cobbler. And if you think finding all these ingredients in this neck of the woods was easy —" She planted one hand on her hip and with the other pointed at me playfully. I kissed the tip of her index finger and winked.

"Why, ma'am, I am honored to be your guest tonight."

"You should be," she said with mock sternness.

I smiled. We were back on solid ground.

While K.T. was finishing dinner preparations, I holed up in the den to review my notes. When she finally called me to dinner with a light kiss on my neck, I was fully immersed in the case. I wolfed down the fried green tomatoes, which were served with some sort of goat cheese and spicy sauce, and made a lame attempt at conversation. K.T. caught on quick. She spooned the apple jelly onto the pork chops and said, "Okay, detective, why don't you spill the beans?"

She didn't have to ask twice.

What troubled me most was the contradictory information I had gathered about Noreen's alcohol consumption on the night she died. Helen had insisted that Noreen was already bombed when they were fighting at Robert and Allan's place. Yet when we had talked on the deck, I could have sworn she was dry as overdone turkey. That was around ten o'clock. Then there was Manny's testimony. According to her, Noreen didn't start drinking until after she *left* the party. By midnight, she was supposedly stinking of booze. But if she started drinking *after* the party, why weren't there empty bottles in the house?

"Maybe she stopped off at a pub, or a friend's house," K.T. offered.

The nearest bar was a good half-hour away and populated by rednecks who'd be more likely to smash a bottle over a bulldyke's head than share a counter with one. I should know. An urgent call from nature once forced me and my friend Leslie into the bar. Three men with pool sticks started approaching us before we made it to the bathroom. We'd ended up peeing in the bushes.

The second option wasn't much better. All of Noreen's friends were at the party. Then it struck me.

Maggie.

Had Noreen stopped at Maggie's? Both women had drinking problems and from what Dean told me, Maggie had good reason to be teetering in her resolve.

"I have another theory," K.T. mused. "What if the two of them were more than friends? Maybe Dean came home and caught them in some compromising position. He could have followed Noreen home —"

"And did what? Pour alcohol down her throat till

her heart gave out? Maybe this job's made me overly suspicious," I said, spearing another slice of pork. "Maybe her death is just an unfortunate tragedy."

K.T. tilted her head and stared at me with doubt. "You don't believe that."

She was right.

The night before she died, an unusually lucid Noreen had expressed an interest in hiring me. I had assumed that Helen was right and all Noreen wanted from me was assistance in searching for her siblings. But there was another possibility — that Noreen had been in some kind of trouble and needed my help. Rational or not, I felt obligated to fulfill that impromptu commitment. Besides, the inconsistencies taunted me. So did Maggie's disappearance.

My former lover Mary once said that one of the stupidest things in the world anyone could do was piss off a Scorpio like me. She was right on. My venom was surging. And I was aching to sting.

We made love again after dinner, this time playfully, both of us so full from dinner that energetic lovemaking was out of the question. Instead we giggled and groaned our way into sleep. My insomnia in abeyance, I awoke shortly before dawn, rested and incredibly grateful for the weight of K.T.'s leg over mine. I kissed her moist arm and eased out from under her.

During the night, the fire had died. Even so, the house was chillier than it had been the previous week. One look outside told me why. A light snow was falling. Bending over, I could feel the pain in my lower back flare up. The cost for energetic lovemaking, I thought. I arranged logs on the grating and watched the flames pop over the bark, blue smoke rushing up the flue. I wanted desperately to feel content, but my mind was already racing.

With every minute, the trail leading to the truth was getting muddier. Instinctively, I knew I had to move fast. But what the hell could I accomplish at five in the morning? The answer dawned on me, bright as a Kansas morning. I showered, directing the head so that hot water pounded the base of my spine and upper thighs. I dressed, scribbled a note to K.T., and grabbed my notebook.

My running sneakers crunched through the thin layer of frost lining the driveway. The nip in the air warned of a long, hard winter. I envisioned the soot-blackened ice that marks winter in Manhattan and sighed. As I started the car, I imagined buying the cabin as a retreat for K.T. and me. The thought made my teeth chatter and I slid the temperature control lever to high.

Keep your feet on the ground, I warned myself — wings clipped, talons dug in. The car revved and I dialed an oldie channel. Frank Sinatra was belting out "I Got You Under My Skin." I sang along with something akin to hilarity bubbling in my chest.

Maybe it's just gas, I mused, my fingers crossed on the wheel.

Chapter 7

The Unitarian church was hewn from native stone. In the gray-pink light, the snow glistened softly on the steeple. There were eight cars in the lot. I pulled in next to the last one and parked, the slam of the door sounding like an explosion in the snowy hush. I gathered my flannel jacket around me and climbed the stairs. The carved-brass doors grated to a close behind me as my heartbeat raced. I stood stock-still till my eyes adjusted to the dimness, a faint smell of incense tickling my nostrils. In the distance was the drone of voices. I followed the sound.

The meeting was already underway. Eight pairs of eyes, at once suspicious and curious, turned toward me. I muttered an apology and headed for a metal chair positioned near the coffee urn. Before I could get there, a slender older woman with frosted hair and cheap lipstick took hold of my hand. "Sit in the circle, dear." She slid a chair next to her and patted my shoulder. I smiled weakly and obeyed.

Now that I was here, I felt like a mean-spirited jerk. The man across from me, clad in a plaid hunting shirt and heavy boots, looked like an aging lumberjack. He was sniffling into a woman's handkerchief. "Man, I was close. This close. But I knew if I did it, if I touched that bottle, it was over for me and Cynthia. And no one's ever stuck by me like that woman has."

I looked away. The group consisted of five men and three women. If Maggie's sponsor, Lisa, was here, it shouldn't be hard to find out.

The lumberjack was bawling now. "How can she even face me in the morning after what I done? Shit. I can't sleep no more, thinking of how I run that little kid down..." The woman next to him grasped his hand.

As he spoke, my eyes filled and my stomach churned. This was not a good idea, I admonished myself.

"I thought that poor baby was a deer. Got out of my Bronco cursing the beast for bolting in front of me. When I saw what I hit... Lord, I ain't never going to have another minute of rest."

"You will, Bill. Someday, somehow, you'll have to find a way of living with the truth without a bottle in your hand." The woman holding his hand had the smallest voice I had ever heard. But her words were spoken with indisputable conviction. "We all have to make peace with ourselves, with our pasts. I know you don't believe in God anymore, Bill, but there are other higher powers you can hold onto. Cynthia's love, for instance."

It was as if she were talking to me. When she and Bill hugged, my body shook involuntarily. The elderly woman to my right wrapped an arm around my shoulders. I wanted to bolt. Instead I cried along with the others, all of us lost in our own lives. Finally, the official part of the meeting ended and we all stood up, held hands, and recited the serenity prayer.

I was anything but serene. As soon as the circle broke up, I dashed for the door.

"Was it that hard for you?"

I turned and looked into the gentlest blue eyes I had ever seen. She was the woman who had comforted Bill. With a sinking instinct, I knew this was Lisa. I nodded dumbly, my emotions tangling me in thoughts totally unrelated to Noreen or Maggie.

She grasped my upper arm with surprising firmness and said, "Why don't we talk outside? Groups can be awfully intimidating for first-timers." A discreet gesture informed the others that she would return soon. Still holding my arm, she steered me to the center of the church. She was at least six inches shorter than I am and so slight she seemed free from the weight of gravity. Next to her I felt ungainly. We settled on a side pew, the cold, hard seat pressing into the back of my thighs. I could feel the sciatica taking its revenge.

"This is better, isn't it?" she asked kindly.

My eyes darted around the room. This modest chapel with faded stained-glass windows and a scent that commingled incense, mold and human flesh, made my heart clench. Looking at the woman next to me, I realized it wasn't just the church. "Is your name Lisa?"

Her eyes widened. No mistrust, just interest. "Yes." I had intended to wheedle my way into her confidence. Instead I plunged into the truth. When I finished detailing my suspicions about Noreen's death and Maggie's disappearance, she looked tired.

Without a word of reproach, she stood up and grimly pursed her lips. "I know few believe in our vow of confidentiality, but I take it very seriously. You're asking me to violate a trust people have placed in me, and I simply won't do that." She started to walk away.

"What's more important, your confidentiality or someone's life?" My voice boomed.

Lisa turned slowly. Her gaze was so direct, it burned. "When I saw you crying during Bill's story, I sensed you were in trouble yourself. Your pain seemed so real, so close." It was as if she were subjecting me to a Vulcan probe. I took a step back. "Perhaps it is," she said, with a sympathetic tilt of her head. "Noreen's death is very sad for me. She reminded me so much of myself."

I couldn't imagine two women less alike. My confidence wavered.

"I was so proud of her. She had turned her face

to the light and was determined to keep it there. My greatest disappointment was that she didn't reach out to me before going over the edge."

Frustration shook me to the core. "Even if you believe it's too late to help Noreen, what about Maggie? Aren't you even worried about her?"

Her face clouded and she continued, more to herself than to me, "I have to remember that I can rescue no one but myself. Ultimately, we all have to choose. It's hard to put aside responsibility and take up acceptance, but I know of no other way to make it through the day."

Her language was stilted, but I sensed it was more from emotional strain than from artifice. This woman was in a battle for her life. I suddenly felt ashamed. Resigned, I exited the church, the blast of cold air a welcome slap of reality. I was halfway to the car when I heard feet pounding toward me. I spun around, immediately on guard.

It was Bill. He glanced over his shoulder furtively. I strode ahead, opened the passenger door and gestured to him, then got into the car.

Bill's volunteer fireman cap pressed against the roof of my Subaru. I stared at him and waited for him to speak. He scratched the side of his nose nervously, his shoulders hunched forward. A faintly sour smell emanated from him. It was well below freezing and the man was sweating bullets. "I heard you talking to Lisa," he said guiltily. "About Noreen."

He fell silent again, licking his cracked bottom lip with a white tongue. At a loss, I popped open the glove compartment and offered him a Life Saver. He grabbed for the roll, jamming his elbow into the dashboard. It seemed like his bulk was expanding before my eyes. Any second, my car would explode.

"I got a daughter, you know." The non sequitur was uttered with incredible tenderness. With a tentative glance toward me, he faltered, "She's, uh, you know —"

I finished the sentence for him. "A lesbian."

His head wrenched in my direction. "Yeah," he said, looking startled at my apparent clairvoyance. "Like Nor. Only not as, uh, manly. She's twenty-four now. A few years ago, when she told me and my wife about her, you know, her ways, we was floored. She's a pretty girl. No reason she couldn't hook some decent feller. We tried to get her help, but she took off to Philly and wouldn't have none of our interfering. We didn't talk till this past summer." Beads of sweat were pooling on his forehead, running along his sideburns, and through his rough beard. His broad hand swept over his face self-consciously.

"After the accident, she come home to see me in jail. What a moron I was, acting like she was no good while all the time I'm the one sitting in that cold cell — a boy's life gone 'cause of me. Soon after I started these meetings, and me and Nor hit it off right away. I could see she wasn't so bad as she liked people to think. She got me talking to Jane again ... Lots of people tried to get through to me, but Nor was the only one that could. You don't let a family slip through your fingers." He wiggled his sausage-thick fingers toward me for emphasis. "She said, 'Love makes a family. Love's got to hold it together.'"

His eyes turned glassy. "I'll never forget that. What I'm getting at is this. I called Nor the night she died. I was in a bad way . . . she carried me over the hump. I read the paper, all that talk about her being drunk. That simply ain't true. I talked to her at two in the morning and she was as straight as you are right now." He rushed ahead awkwardly. "I mean sober. It ain't right everyone saying she went off the wagon. I don't know how she died, but I know she wasn't drinking when she did."

I drove directly to Helen's house, the windows wide open to clear out the car. And my head. It was just before eight when I parked outside her garage. If Helen had anything to do with Noreen's death, one possible motive was sitting in front of me. Instead of the 1,800 square-foot contemporary on Valley Road that she had purchased with her own funds, Helen was living in the smallest two-bedroom ranch in Telham.

The snow was heavier now and the wind no longer gentle. I scurried up the stairs. The doorbell screamed through the ranch with a too-high pitch. On the second peal, Helen opened the door wearing a white terry-cloth robe loosely tied around her waist. I knew instantly that she was naked under the gathered fabric and felt an unexpected surge of hormones. She blinked at me, still groggy from sleep. Or perhaps something more. As she stepped aside to let me in, I noticed the darkness under her eyes, the way she shuffled into the living room. The air in the house was stale from smoke. And alcohol.

She fell into a tailored, gray tweed couch and plopped her feet onto a matching ottoman. When she crossed her legs, the robe fell half open, revealing a pale, smooth thigh. I averted my eyes with some difficulty.

The house felt uninhabited, the walls bare of artwork and the furniture so new you could smell the plastic in which it had been wrapped. The only exception was the computer desk near the window. Reams of printout paper filled the corner, and the desktop was littered with floppy disks and technical manuals — graphic reminders that Helen earned her living as a programmer. With an uncomfortable flutter, I realized that both she and Amy worked out of their homes. When I looked back at her, I noticed that her features had turned wry.

"Not exactly material for *House and Garden*," she said. "But then again, who cares these days?"

I automatically glanced back to her thighs, which were parted slightly. "Have you been drinking?" I was too irritated, and turned on, for small talk.

"Someone's feeling feisty. Come, sit next to me," she said, patting the couch. Since there was nowhere else to sit except the desk chair, I complied. "To answer your question, not since yesterday afternoon. Which is pretty good for me."

To my chagrin, she didn't smell stale like the rest of the house. A muskiness rose off her skin. I realized she smelled like a woman who had just made love. With a lazy amusement, she watched me grow flustered. I felt trapped. My guts told me someone was in that back room, but there was no way I was going to find out. The power play between us was in high gear. And she clearly had the upper hand.

She reached out, caressed the side of my neck the way you'd pet a cat, and mewled, "So what can I do for you, detective?"

I was twitching down below and pissed at myself for allowing my hormones free rein. "You lied to me, Helen." I practically spat the words in her face. "Noreen wasn't drunk when you two fought at the party, and you know it."

She looked perplexed for an instant, but her hand never stopped moving. God help me, I couldn't pull myself away from that even stroke. "I never said Noreen was drunk," she said with conviction.

If I didn't know better, I would have believed her. "Helen, don't play with me."

A flicker of delight entered her eyes, and it dawned on me that my past infatuation with her had not gone entirely unnoticed.

"You sure about that?" She leaned forward, her robe draping so that her creamy, full breasts were just a glance away. With a flick of my hand, that robe would be open and her body laid bare. She scissored her legs, shifting closer to me. Her unmistakable scent was making me dizzy. With incredible difficulty, I stood up. I wanted to run outside and hump a snow bank.

I gulped and said, "Why'd you lie?"

She gazed at me through half-lowered lids and shrugged, "Honestly, I don't remember saying she was drunk. But if I did, you have to understand that I was pissed off and scared silly. Besides, whenever Noreen went into one of her rages, I just assumed she was drinking. Maybe that's all I meant."

She stood up and crossed to me. I wanted to send her into the bedroom for more of whatever she had been receiving. Anything to escape the web she was weaving around my clay feet. A slender finger teased the top button of my shirt. There was no doubt about her intentions now. She was seducing me. Successfully, I might add. I held her hand still, ignoring the sparks between us.

"Helen," I said, then repeated her name as if that would protect me from succumbing. "Helen, we need to talk. I need to know more about Noreen."

My hips were a second away from pumping against her. K.T. had unleashed a monster. I envisioned K.T. the way she had looked this morning, the sheets tangled around her moist calves. I swallowed hard and asked, "Do you know that Manny inherits the house?"

Unexpectedly, the magnetism between us lost its charge. Maybe it was the impact that the memory of K.T. had on me, or maybe Helen picked up on the determination in my voice. All I knew was that she tightened the robe's belt and sat down again.

With a sigh, I pulled over the desk chair and sat opposite her.

She ran a hand through her dark, tangled hair, pausing to sniff her fingers surreptitiously in a final tease. "I just found out yesterday. Ironic, isn't it? Manny did two lousy months, and she gets *my* house." I didn't have to be an expert in body language to read how the words stung. She was hugging herself like someone who had been kicked in the stomach.

"When I signed the house over to Noreen, we had an understanding. She'd keep my name in the will. I guess that's another reason I was so scared when I found her body. If anyone questioned her death, I had to be the number one suspect. As it turns out, no one seems to give a shit."

Except me, I thought.

"Wasn't that unusual, your asking to stay in the will?"

She exclaimed, "It was my fucking house. Noreen may have been the one to decide where we moved and what we bought, but it was my money that paid for the place. All because that stupid detective's cousin said Telham was a good place for dykes. None of it ever made sense to me." Her face was beet red. "I gave up a good job in Philly to move here. Noreen was running her own house-painting business, we could have gone anywhere. I wanted to move to San Francisco, but Noreen got it in her head that she had to be here. In Canadensis. In goddamn Telham Village. Who the hell knows why? But I went along with her. And you know what? I ended up loving that damn house. When the house was quiet, you could hear the Acee River rushing over the rocks. It was magical." I could almost hear her counting to ten before she spoke again. "Maybe you didn't know this, but Noreen was physically abusive to me."

My eyes must have narrowed in doubt because the next thing I knew Helen had dropped the top of her robe so that her shoulders were bare. The sight elicited no delicious twitch from down below. A puckered scar ran along her left collarbone.

"About a year ago, before we moved here, she flung me through our living room window. If you're interested, I can also show where the iron landed on my hip. Or maybe you're not into burns." She was taunting me now, her eyes sparking with past nightmares.

I was barely breathing. "God, I'm sorry, Helen. I didn't know." The robe was back in place, but the images she planted rooted instantly in my mind.

"Right," she said. "No one did. Except me."

"Why didn't you leave?" I sounded like an audience member on *Oprah*. I wanted to shove a sock in my mouth. Helen looked like she'd be happy to help me.

"I did." Her chin was lifted defiantly. "Maybe it took seven years, but I *did* leave. At the time, the house felt like a small price to pay."

There was a part of me that wanted to back off and leave her alone, but the need to know the truth was far stronger. "What happened when you broke it off?"

She laughed unpleasantly. "Not much. My timing was ideal. About a month before we closed on the house, Helen found out she had a mild heart condition. The doctor said if she kept on drinking the way she had in the past, she was bound to have a heart attack. She finally got herself into AA. I had already been there for years." Wiping her eyes wearily, she said, "Guess I'll be starting up again," and exhaled like someone tossing an anchor over the starboard side. "When we broke up in August, Noreen was saner than at any other time in our relationship. I think the appropriate term is 'window of opportunity.' I saw it and I leapt for it." With a sneer, she added, "She was pretty civil. I'm sure the house helped."

"Did she stay sober?"

"You'd have to ask Manny that, now, wouldn't you?"

The woman was an aerosol can under pressure, and she was working hard not to explode. I didn't want to be around when she did.

After the interview with Helen, all I could think about was curling up with K.T. near the stone fireplace. It struck me that for the first time in years it was my work I wanted to escape from and not my life. I pulled up to the cabin and frowned. K.T.'s car was gone. I scampered to the door, afraid of the emptiness and yet hopeful she'd somehow still be there. I could feel her absence as soon as I opened the door. The fireplace was littered with ash and the only sound came from branches scratching against the roof. The rush of snow outside only added to the sense of stillness.

I shuffled into the kitchen, a strange queasiness sweeping up from my stomach. I stopped short in the doorway. A note fluttered under a basket of golden corn muffins. Without touching them, I knew they'd be warm to the touch and I almost cried.

Dear Robin —

I waited as long as I could. When you weren't back by eight, I assumed you were still out doing the Columbo thing. My restaurant manager called. The sous chef was in an accident this morning. Nothing serious, but there's no way he can come in today. I arranged for a backup tomorrow — Thanksgiving Day, for heaven's sake — but I had to drive down and help out this afternoon. Hope you understand. I'm still planning on joining you at Carly and Amy's house tomorrow, if you still want me there. I'm anxious (nervous) to meet your friends. Do you really think we're ready to go public? I think of you and things happen to my body that would make Madonna blush. Well, maybe not Madonna.

I miss you already. I pray that you feel the same way.

Kentucky

I fingered the signature, wondering why she had signed her full name rather than the more familiar K.T. Lifting the note, I sniffed it for a trace of her scent. All I smelled was damp paper. And the corn muffins. I happily downed two.

Whatever's happening here, I thought, felt damn wonderful. Singing the Frank Sinatra tune I had listened to earlier in the day, I headed back outside. I wanted to share my excitement. I'm ashamed to say I skipped outside. Yes. Skipped. Damn the sciatica. Besides, Amy would be only too happy to whip me up some potion to deaden the pain. Like a five-year-old, I opened my mouth to the sky and drank in the slow drifting snow. Then I started the car and drove up the hill to Amy's.

It wasn't until I knocked on the front door that I realized there was no car in the driveway. I puzzled

117

briefly, then remembered that tomorrow was Thanksgiving; Amy was probably shopping. I smiled broadly. Unquestionably, a feast was in the works. I headed back to the car, then paused. Amy wouldn't be gone long, I mused, and I was in urgent need of her ministration. I tried the door and was surprised to find it locked. I fingered the usual hiding space — a perpetually broken hurricane lamp tacked to the right of the front door — and found the key and let myself in.

Carly and Amy had decorated their house with items bought at local auctions, the eclectic mix including an aluminum-edged formica kitchen table from the fifties, bearing a unique centerpiece constructed of antique Coke bottles. In the living room was a painter's bench, a butt-worn tapestry-covered Queen Anne chair, an array of milk cans painted with country scenes, and a bamboo rocker etched with peace signs by a former hippy since turned stockbroker. I loved the place. Warm and inviting, their home had been the site of countless anniversary, birthday, and holiday celebrations. Right now, I was desperate for the coziness.

I was kneeling in front of their compact disk collection in the den when I heard a sound coming from the kitchen. I straightened up, the fire in the back of my thigh raging. Damn. Then it happened again.

A cat. Nothing odd about that. Except for the fact that they don't own one. I followed the sound through the kitchen and into the windowless annex that served as Amy's homeopathic "lab." I switched on the light and discovered a beat-up tabby chasing her tail. Despite — or maybe because of — the half-chewed ear, the waif was adorable. I bent down and scratched under her neck, suddenly missing my own two girls back in Brooklyn. I'd have to call them tonight, I chided myself.

An empty food bowl placed under the butcher block counter was the cause of her distress, I deduced with remarkable quickness. The fact that the cat practically socked the bowl between my legs was my first clue. Five cans of Alpo sat on the counter, next to a note from Melissa Moses, Amy's eccentric next-door neighbor.

I know you're both pretty allergic to Hassle, but she got pretty badly whipped in a cat fight last week. I hated to leave her alone till Monday. Since you weren't home when I came by, I put her in here until you can familiarize her with the rest of the house. Hope I'm not pushing our "good neighbor" policy too far.

Knowing how Amy felt about her lab, I had a feeling Melissa might have just run out of favors. I couldn't remember the last time anyone besides Carly had been allowed in here. Amy was very particular about keeping the space "neutral." I never knew what she meant by that, but I had learned not to question her work. I had benefited too often from her skills to remain a skeptic.

She had reorganized the office, lining up jars of herbal extracts along one wall, next to plastic bags of dried roots and flowers. On the shelf below were the accoutrements of a mad scientist: beakers, scales, a Bunsen burner, gourds, mortar and pestle, eye

119

droppers, and small glass vials filled with what looked like miniature cotton balls. Hassle rammed into my ankle, a not-too-subtle reminder of why I was in here. I grabbed a can of chicken and cheese and retreated to the kitchen, opened the can, then remembered the bowl was still in the lab. Hassle, smart beast that she was, had not moved from the bowl.

As I knelt down to pick it up, I noticed a row of prepared solutions strategically lined up in a rack suspended from the left side of the counter. A small vial with the handwritten words, *Sciatica elixir, potency one, NSF-1121*, caught my eye. My head jerked up, smacking straight into the edge of the counter. The *Alpo* can dropped from my hand and rolled onto its side. I was too distracted to worry about the mess. At least not right away. The bottle was almost identical to the ones Amy's prescribed for me in the past. Fate sometimes works in our favor.

I unscrewed the dropper top and started to drizzle the prescribed ten drops onto my tongue when I heard the door slam. I jerked like a guilty child, cringing as the bottle crashed right beside the cat food. Shit. Amy would kill me. At least the bottle had broken cleanly, into just two pieces. I put the dropper down on the counter carefully, shoved Hassle away with my foot, scooped up as much of the mess as I could with cupped hands, then rushed into the kitchen. Amy caught me with my hands in the garbage can. She stared at me and then at the open lab door. To say she looked displeased would be a drastic understatement.

She practically slammed her pocketbook onto the kitchen counter. "What the hell is going on?"

"Ame, I can explain —"

Her nose flared. "What's that smell?" She stared at my chicken-and-cheese coated hands and groaned. I was in deep doo-doo now. "That's cat food. Shit, Robin, what the hell are you up to?"

Amy didn't use words like *shit*.

She looked around the kitchen floor and then focused like a marksman on the yawning entrance to the lab. "Fuck! Not the lab!"

Just then, a howl snapped through the air, then ceased almost instantly. I darted through the door. Hassle was breathing rapidly, her chest heaving in severe spasms. I held her against me and dissolved into tears when her heart kicked against my fingertips.

"Call a vet!" I hollered at Amy through my sobs. *Don't die, don't die, don't die.* I was kissing her head, rubbing her jerking stomach. She began vomiting violently. I didn't care.

"Get it out, Hassle," I urged her. Please, God, I prayed, don't let me be responsible for another creature's death.

By the time I finished my prayer, Hassle was limp in my arms.

Chapter 8

I was shivering, despite two down comforters and the hot teacup riveted between my palms. Amy and Carly were whispering heatedly in the bedroom off the living room, where I had been sitting numbly for the past two hours. With each passing minute, the cold had penetrated deeper. I was afraid that if I moved, my limbs would crack off like icicles.

Amy's indignation had apparently evaporated soon after I passed out in the lab. When I came to, she was red-faced and hovering over me with panicked eyes. She pleaded with me to speak to her, but I was strangely mute. I felt emotionally anesthetized, but there was something else too. My tongue was paralyzed.

The door beside the couch opened with a whine. Carly shot an angry look over her shoulder, then came and sat beside me. "Please, Robbie, talk to me."

At first, I didn't want to utter a sound. Now I felt as if I couldn't. My tongue was swollen and my throat so tight, breathing took intense concentration.

"We contacted Dean. He's on the way. You hear me, honey?" She stroked the back of my hand. Her touch felt like a coal-hot razor scraping my skin. The trembling worsened. Carly was crying softly. I knew because I could hear the sudden intake of breath. But I wouldn't look at her. I knew if I did she would be a yellow blur. I squeezed my eyes tight as Carly cradled me in her arms and began rocking me. The motion hurt, but I couldn't tell her that. I couldn't tell her that I had killed Hassle as surely as I had killed my sister Carol, that the cat's death rattle was horribly like a human's, that death seemed so close to me I could almost shake its hand.

There was a distant car-door slam. Carly disengaged from me slowly, as if she were afraid that I'd fall apart without her arms around me. For an instant, I feared I might. I looked up and saw Dean gesturing angrily at the lab door. Amy had crossed to him and now the two of them were standing toe to toe, shouting words that I somehow couldn't decipher. Carly stood by quietly, but I could tell by the color of her cheeks that she was reaching her limit. Finally, she swelled up to her full five-three and slapped first Dean, then Amy with the back of her hand.

I was surprised to hear myself chuckle. All of a sudden I was strangely giddy. And sobbing uncontrollably.

Carly was next to me before I knew it. "Rob, what's happening?"

"I'm so cold." My words were thick, the aural equivalent of curdled milk, but somehow Carly understood. Two minutes later she was wrapping a sleeping bag around my shoulders.

Dean approached with his little black bag and I wanted to kiss his knuckles. "You're not looking so good, kid," he said, sounding like Marcus Welby. I went limp in his care. He took my blood pressure, examined my eyes, nose, ears, listened to my heartbeat for what seemed like hours, and palpated more parts of my body than K.T. had. All the time, he kept muttering inane words of comfort that I drank in like brandy.

He opened my mouth and pulled my tongue out with a piece of gauze. My eyes almost crossed from staring at the way he bit his lower lip with his front teeth. I felt like giggling, but threw up instead.

Amy and Carly rushed to clean me up. After each heave, they washed my face with a warm rag. I wanted to die. When the spasms stopped, Dean leaned toward me with a heavy sigh that smelled of the spiced cider we had shared yesterday. "The worst is over, Robin. You're going to be fine."

Maybe physically. But I could already feel this

new nightmare taking root in a corner of my brain like a weed.

He prepared a hypodermic, cuffed my arm, and injected something into my vein. To Amy he said, "I want to bring a sample of that potion in for an examination, if you don't mind."

"I'm telling you, Dean, she's taken this exact formula before and it's never had this effect. She probably took too large a dose —"

"Not even one full drop," I said, jumping in. Something was buzzing in my ear. With a start I realized it was the rush of my blood. "Ame, it was barely a single drop." I wanted her to explain this away.

Fear crowded into her eyes. "That's impossible, Rob."

Dean broke in. "What's in the stuff, for chrissake?"

Amy was still staring at me as she answered him. She ran through the list of ingredients the way K.T. would on her cooking show. Dean pounced on her before she finished. "Aconite?" he shouted in disbelief.

At the word, Amy closed her eyes and trembled. "We've talked about this before, Dean. There's so little of it in there —"

I looked past her to where Carly stood, soundlessly opening and clenching her fists. I was having difficulty following the conversation. My heart was pounding and I wanted to bury myself deeper into the blankets.

His tone modulated now, Dean asked, "How many grains?"

She said the number as if she could hardly

believe her own words, then collapsed into the rocker. It creaked dangerously under her weight. Her skin was so pale, you could almost trace the veins running along her cheekbones.

Dean coughed. I had the sense he was trying to keep his composure. "Well, Amy, I've told you how dangerous I think it is to be fooling with such poisons, natural or not. Maybe you miscalculated. In any case, we have to bring in a sample and try to get an accurate breakdown —"

Amy stopped him with a wave of her hand. "Do what you have to, Dean."

Carly said, "I'd feel better if you stay here with Robin. I'll drive the sample in myself. Just tell me who and where."

"Well," he hesitated, then turned to me. I could tell from the shake of his head that I looked like hell. "You're right. I better stay close." He wrote something down on a prescription pad and handed it to Carly. "While you're out, have this filled. I'm sure she's out of any serious danger by now, though God knows why you didn't bring her directly to the hospital . . ." He stopped himself. "Sorry. You two must be upset enough."

I heard Amy sniff and I looked over. She slumped in the rocker, shook her head in disbelief and said, "There goes my career," with a sadness that chilled me.

As I looked at the woman who had been one of my closest friends for nearly twelve years, I recalled the label on the bottle I'd broken and felt sick to my soul. The label had read *Sciatica elixir, potency one,*

NSF-1121. Suddenly, the significance of the last few digits became clear: Noreen Sue Finnegan, November 21.

With a horrible certainty, I knew Amy's medicine had killed Noreen.

Amy set me up in the front guest room. Neither of us exchanged a word. Desperate for sleep, I covered my head with the blankets. It wouldn't come.

One drop of that herbal concoction had kicked through my body like a Kung Fu master. Ten drops would have killed me almost as quickly as a gunshot to the head. And with a lot less mess.

I reran the last few days. Perhaps Amy had simply, and tragically, made a fatal mistake in mixing the medicine. I threw the blanket aside and paused. Amy and Dean were talking quietly in the other room. Occasionally I heard a sob. I cracked the door. Holding my breath, I could just make out the words.

"Amy, I'm not questioning your qualifications. Or even the value of homeopathy or herbal remedies. Just because I'm in traditional medicine doesn't mean I'm automatically against alternative treatments."

"It usually does. Come on, Dean, you think I'm a quack. You and Douglas have made that clear on numerous occasions."

"Well," Dean said, "I have to admit the theory

that you can somehow increase the efficacy of an agent by diluting it till the point that it's almost one hundred percent water —"

"We've gone through this before," Amy interrupted impatiently.

"Right. Fine. So let's get to the point. Why the hell did you use Monkshood? You have to know aconite is one of the deadliest poisons around."

"And an ingredient that's been used by herbalists around the world for centuries. Ask Fred or Camilla, if you don't believe me."

"Explain that to the authorities. If this gets out, you'll be lucky if all that happens is the dissolution of your practice."

The springs of the couch squeaked. "Damn it. I did nothing wrong, Dean. I'm telling you there wasn't enough aconite in that potion to kill anyone. Including Hassle."

Footsteps stormed toward my direction. I shut the door and waited. A minute later I heard first the coat closet and then the front door slam. I walked to the window and watched Amy pull away from the house. The road was matted with snow. I prayed that she would drive slowly.

I was standing there when Dean tapped twice and came into the room. He looked surprised to see me standing. "I thought you'd be asleep."

I turned back to the window and said, "Is that why you knocked?"

At first he didn't answer. Then he said, "I need your professional advice."

I blew onto the window till it fogged and began scribbling images. "Go ahead," I said without feeling. I knew what was coming.

"That potion could have killed you."

"Uh-huh." I stared at my handiwork. I had drawn a cat. My forehead dropped to the frosted window.

He hesitated. "Maggie told me a few months ago that Noreen had back problems. I recommended a doctor, but she said Amy was treating her." I heard him click the bedside lamp on, then off. "You don't happen to know if she was being treated for sciatica, do you?" The question was phrased so innocently, it was hard to keep from sobbing out loud. What could I do?

I grilled myself as Dean waited. If I told him about finding the sciatica preparation in Noreen's medicine cabinet, Amy would automatically be implicated in Noreen's death. How could I do that to her? And what if it was just an accident? I knew better than anyone the torture of being responsible for another person's death. She would carry that around for the rest of her life.

But I also felt a reluctant obligation to Noreen. Without full disclosure, I could in effect be an accessory to a wrongful death.

A hand closed around my shoulder. "Sorry. This has to be harder on you than on me."

With a gulp, I whispered, "Can you order an autopsy?"

His grasp tightened. "Do you think that's necessary? You know what —"

"We have to know what killed Noreen."

I waited until he left the room, then I sat down on the bed and held my head. In the distance, I heard him hitting the buttons on the phone with undue force. Twice I almost cried out for him to stop. Then it was too late. I heard him explain to Douglas Marks, the coroner and funeral director, that circumstances had changed. Information had come to light that would seem to indicate that an autopsy was in order.

Then something went wrong. His tone changed. He said, "I see," about five times before hanging up. By the time I entered the kitchen, he was staring at the receiver. When he looked up at me, I could tell he was struggling for composure.

"Noreen's body was cremated this morning."

It took ten minutes, but I finally convinced Dean that I was well enough to return to my cabin. He agreed only after making me promise to rest in bed for the rest of the day. I had no intention of keeping that promise.

Outside, sitting in his car, he rolled down his window and asked how my search for Maggie was progressing. I felt guilty telling him I had barely started. For an instant, he looked as if he were about to explode in rage. I was getting ready to defend myself — I'd had the case for one damn day! We stared at each other for a second, communicating without language, then he nodded glumly and pulled away in his Audi. I climbed into my car and rumbled onto the road. My tail swerved on the packed snow, but I straightened quickly and headed downhill. By noon, I was home.

I felt as if there were ice in my veins, so the first thing I did was change into thermals, thick corduroys, turtleneck, and a quilted flannel shirt.

Then I popped a container of *faux* chicken soup into the microwave, watched the counter tick off time as it nuked the chemical-rich brew, then reluctantly dialed K.T. at the restaurant.

The soup tasted like freshly mown grass leavened with roach spray. But it burned on the way down and right then that's all that mattered. Beads of sweat formed on my upper lip as I waited for someone to pick up. The receiver finally lifted on the other end, then crashed into something hard. In the background, K.T.'s soft drawl tangled around a few choice curse words. Inexplicably, my eyes began to burn. I swallowed hard and said, "You sound busy." Cool, very cool.

"Robin?" she asked, her excitement clear and unaffected. "It's so good to hear your voice. You wouldn't believe the zoo I'm managing. I've been away from here so long, the chef thinks he owns the damn place. Can you believe he altered my Thanksgiving Day menu without consulting me? If Jonathan hadn't been in that fender bender —" She broke off suddenly and shouted something that sounded like "ginger, not curry, you possum-headed idiot." Her voice carried over the sound of clanging pots, hissing grills, and heated multilingual arguments. I could picture her standing amid the frenzied prep staff, bellowing orders with all the grace of a tugboat captain, her hair damp with steam and perspiration, her green eyes flashing ire. Without question, she would look gorgeous.

I smiled grimly. Somehow, K.T. had already come to mean too much to me.

"K.T.?" I tried to attract her attention. She answered the third time.

"Sorry, Rob. We'll have to make this short. But tonight," she said, lowering her tone seductively, "tonight, you will have my undivided attention . . . and all the time you can stand."

"That's why I'm calling, K.T. We have to call this off."

All I heard on the other end was what sounded like a Cuisinart on full power.

Suddenly she blurted, "Damn, Selmo, the pan's on fire!" Then to me, "This is the wrong time for this conversation. We'll talk tonight." Her intonation was pure business.

"No, K.T. I don't want you here. This is going too fast for me. I need—"

A twisted sound, like a sob hacked off just before the intake of a breath, exploded in my ear. "If you dare say either 'space' or 'time' to me, I will come up there and strangle you with the damn phone cord. You've had more space and time than God."

She was right, of course. But when did that ever matter?

"There's just too much going on. I can't explain." I stopped myself abruptly. My breathing was changing and I knew I was close to breaking. "I'm sorry about the last-minute notice and all, but—"

"Shit. You are the damnedest creature. Look, I'll stay away, just give me Carly's number."

It was an order. "Why the hell do you need her number?" I answered, puzzled and irritated by her demand. Why couldn't she disappear quietly? So many others had.

"She invited me to dinner tomorrow. That was

pretty gracious. I want to at least apologize for not showing up."

I had never heard her tone so sharp. "I'll explain," I said.

"The hell you will. Give me the number, Rob."

A second away from hysteria, I blurted the phone number and hung up. Just in time. The phone wasn't back in the cradle before I started bawling. I wanted her so much, I felt sick to my stomach.

I grabbed the phone again and crashed it against the wall. I was out of control and furious at myself for letting K.T. in.

I replaced the phone, jerking back as it rang under my hand. Maybe it's K.T., I prayed spontaneously. Maybe she sees through all this crap. I lifted the receiver, fear and hope braided together like a two-wick candle, both emotions in full flame.

"You should have an answering machine up there, oh captain mine." It was Jill Zimmerman, my office and research manager.

My sigh was heavy.

"Trouble in paradise?" she quipped in response. When I didn't answer, she continued in a serious tone. "You blew it again, didn't you?"

I wasn't in the mood for a lecture, especially from a newlywed who still acted as if she were on her honeymoon. I slurped down the rest of the soup and said, "Save it for someone who cares." Sometimes, the brilliance of my repartee is blinding.

"Rob, you've been dreaming about this woman for months. What happened?"

I gave her a rundown of the day's events.

"Got it." I could almost picture her nodding smugly. "You came down with the heebie-jeebies. That 'Robbie, the Death Master' thing you go through. Honey, it's time to shelve that phobia. You are a fine —"

"You have anything to report on Maggie Flynn, or have you been taking psych courses while Tony and I fork over your weekly paycheck?"

It was a slap in her face, and I knew it. Jill deserved to be a full partner in the business, but Tony didn't trust her skills yet. Underscoring her employee status was a cheap shot, but as my therapist once explained with annoying accuracy, self-sufficiency was one of my oldest defenses. And one of the surest ways for me to get there was by being a downright bitch. Cats know the strategy well. When someone realizes you have teeth, claws, and a mean hiss, they think twice before approaching you again.

The tactic worked as well now as it had in the past. "No, ma'am, that's why I'm calling," Jill snapped back.

Tapping into a computer network that regularly made mincemeat of the individual's right to privacy, she had run a trace using all the identifiers I had provided — Social Security, bank account, and credit card numbers. "No large cash withdrawals and no credit card purchases. I checked with the airlines, Amtrak, local bus lines, and came up empty. So how do I proceed from here?"

"Have you tried to locate her car?"

She harumphed indignantly into my ear. "I tried to contact your cop friend Zack McGinn. But he's in the Bahamas. My own search turned up nil."

I picked up a pen from the kitchen table and started doodling on a napkin. "Have you run down the identifiers for Noreen Finnegan yet?"

"No. And I didn't start on the DeLucas either. I've been focusing strictly on locating Maggie. It was a judgment call, Rob. From what you told me, she has to be the prime suspect." She was sounding defensive now. "And before you ask, no, I haven't begun calling up those nine numbers you gave me. I'm assuming that the murder investigation takes precedence over the adoption search. Besides your odd vacation diversions, I'm bogged down with background work for four of Tony's cases. You know, the jobs that actually bring in money — the money that, as you so graciously reminded me, pays my salary."

The barb hit its mark. I knew she was right. From an economic perspective, my investigations were low priority. Unfortunately for Jill, the fact only heightened my irritation. "Fine. Silly me. For a moment, I thought a murder investigation was more pressing than combating business fraud. Look, Jill, just do what you can on your end. Whatever computer work you can't manage, pass on to the Roach." Michael Flanagan — a.k.a. the Roach — is an old friend of mine who crawls around computer networks and data banks with the arrogance of that infamous insect. "I'm sure Michael will be able to plug me into some solid leads in less than an hour."

With that parting shot, I hung up. Five minutes later, I tried to call her back to apologize. The line was busy.

Annoyed with myself for letting my frustrations splatter over Jill, I headed gingerly into the den with a second cup of soup. My laptop was still set up from yesterday. I sat down and attempted to sort through recent events. I retrieved my notes on Noreen's murder and adjusted the tilt of the screen.

The basics of any investigation are means, motive, and opportunity. The test results weren't in yet, but there was now a strong possibility for the means. Someone had tampered with the sciatica treatment prepared for Noreen. I tried to remember the word Dean had used.

Aconite.

I called up my on-line dictionary and typed in the word. The drive rumbled as the definition popped on screen.

> aconite *(kuh-Nit)*
> *noun*
> 1. *The monkshood.*
> 2. *A medicinal preparation made from the roots of monkshood.*
> [< *Greek akoniton.*]

The word *monkshood* tripped a switch in my memory. Fred DeLuca's greenhouse. Suddenly I remembered the gorgeous blue-hooded flowers that he had seemed so reluctant to identify. Just an hour earlier, Amy had defiantly informed Dean that Fred would confirm the fact that aconite was a traditional element in herbal remedies.

I would have snapped my fingers if they hadn't been frozen on the keyboard. Fred was Amy's supplier.

Impulsively, I dialed his home number. When no one answered, I called information and obtained the number of their garden center. An obviously harried Camilla answered. "Green Promises. What can I do for you?"

She sounded anything but helpful, but I wasn't about to let that stop me. "It's Robin Miller. Can I speak to Fred?"

"Robin who? Oh. You. Sorry but Fred's occupied right now. You don't know how crazy people get around the holidays. I just saw two women practically wrestle each other to the ground over some squat blue pine —"

Impatient with small talk, I aimed and fired. "I'm calling for Amy. She needs to stock up on some herbs."

"Damn her. We just delivered a shipment to her last week. What is she doing? Medicating all of Japan? Tell her it'll have to wait. We're shorthanded enough without taking on more work. That damn doctor's wife just took off and left us —"

Zing. The nerve endings in my brain were sizzling. I didn't bother listening to the rest of her tirade. "Are you talking about Maggie Flynn?"

"You got it. I know the woman's been depressed about her miscarriage . . . and seeing me pregnant probably just made it worse. But still, she didn't have to pick Thanksgiving week to tear off to God knows where. Days like this, I'd rather be back in New York waiting tables."

I couldn't have agreed with her more.

She promised to have Fred call me, then shouted a price to someone as she hung up. With Camilla's "Fourteen-fifty for the mini-wreath" still echoing in my ear, I typed in the new information and continued mulling over the case.

Noreen Finnegan died early Sunday morning, possibly as a result of consuming a tainted herbal remedy. If the sciatica treatment was in fact the cause of death, there were at least five people who could have known how to transform a medication into a murder weapon: Amy, Dean, and now Camilla, Fred, and Maggie. All of them could have easily gained access to Amy's lab, especially since she rarely locked her front door.

But who had a motive?

In my eyes, Amy seemed a distant possibility. The fact that she was my friend made me doubt my instincts for less than half a second. Friend or not, Amy simply had no reason to kill Noreen — or at least as far as I knew.

Dean had a motive only if the relationship between Noreen and Maggie was more than just a friendship. Although I didn't think that scenario was likely, I couldn't rule it out.

Fred and Camilla had a solid reason for wanting Noreen dead — the pending lawsuit. I had already asked Jill to run a full background check on the couple. With information on the business's financial status, I'd be able to better judge whether they were desperate enough to kill. Camilla was an obnoxious lout, with a style unique to native New Yorkers, and she grated on my nerves like a backfiring truck. But she was part of the landscape of my youth. In a strange way, I liked her.

After seeing Fred's decapitated-head gallery of death, I knew he was capable of killing. But when he said he only killed what he could eat, he sounded pretty damn credible.

Which brought me to Maggie.

As Jill had surmised, her disappearance made her the likeliest suspect — that role now compounded by the fact that she occasionally worked at the garden center. But what reason could she possibly have had for murdering Noreen?

I stared at the blinking cursor, stumped. Was it possible that a sexual advance from Noreen had sent Maggie over the edge? The idea was so farfetched, I almost chuckled. Lesbian sexual energy was a powerful force, but not that powerful. Then I caught myself. Remembering a few bizarre cases from my past, I warned myself: Don't rule anything out.

Finally, I had to consider Helen and Manny. Each had classic motives. Revenge and greed.

Aside from Maggie, Helen was my top choice, for obvious reasons. Who knew what had really occurred during her alleged alcoholic blackout? She had opportunity and she certainly had cause. Since she hadn't known that Noreen's will named Manny as sole benefactor, her motive could have been sheer avarice. But when I tried to imagine her plotting to kill Noreen just so she could repossess the house, my confidence dissolved. The scenario wasn't consistent with what I knew of her. A sultry, passionate woman, Helen was more likely to murder for revenge than money. For some reason, this line of conjecture didn't comfort me.

Manny inherited the house and whatever estate Noreen had left. She certainly could use the money. On more than one occasion, Manny had complained about the cost of supporting her mother and brother, and she hated the fact that she couldn't afford to

139

move them out of that Bronx tenement. I tapped the keyboard, then scrolled back through my notes. From what I had learned since questioning her, I was positive that she had lied to me about finding Noreen drunk when she arrived home at midnight. And Manny had as much access to Amy's lab as anyone in the community.

I scrolled again through my notes, hoping I had missed some obvious lead. There was nothing. The more I read them, the more confused I became. Why had Noreen's body been doused with booze, and who had ordered her cremation? How come there was such conflicting information about her level of intoxication? The authorities, including Douglas Marks, had been quick to gloss over her death. Was their haste due to more than just incompetence and prejudice? And why had Noreen been so interested in locating her siblings?

I put in a call to Douglas and got his machine. I left a message, and then considered picking up the adoption search again, but when the laptop screen melted into a gray haze in front of my eyes I gave in to exhaustion. I lumbered into the living room and dropped onto the couch. I had just nodded out when the phone rang.

"Honey, you are going to love me." The tone was so jubilant, I barely recognized Jill's voice. "The Roach just taught me some tricks that would make your toes curl. The man's a genius."

I tried to interrupt, but she gunned past me. "We did a trace using the information you gave me on Noreen Finnegan. Seems the lady's alive and well and charging up a storm in Atlanta, Georgia. Matter of fact, she's staying at one of your favorite locations — the Hotel Nikko in Buckhead."

There was exactly one seat left on a seven-ten flight leaving from Newark, New Jersey, that evening. On a clear day, driving a steady seventy, the trip to the airport would take an hour and a half. Today, in the midst of the early snowstorm, I'd need every minute of the three-and-a-half hours I had left.

After confirming that "Noreen" was still checked into the Hotel Nikko, I called Dean and received his go-ahead for a first-class ticket to Atlanta, then I dialed Carly's number. Helen answered.

"Amy came by my house," she said. The hasty explanation unnerved me. "She was too upset to drive home alone, so I came back with her. She's really devastated about what happened."

I didn't want to speak to her, and I wasn't up for Amy either. Curtly I said, "Put Carly on."

Her hesitation worried me. After a beat, she said, "She's not back yet."

I didn't know which troubled me more: the prospect of Carly being stuck on a snowbound back road or Helen being alone with Amy. "Where's Ame?"

"Lying down. We saw your car buzz by my place a few hours ago. She lost it then. Said she was afraid your friendship would never be the same."

I was worried about the same thing. But I wasn't about to convey that to Helen. Instead, I asked her to tell them that I had to take an unexpected

141

business trip to Atlanta, but I was still planning on joining them for dinner the next night. It was the last thing I wanted to do, but I couldn't stand the thought of further upsetting Carly. Or Amy.

I packed an overnight bag, then headed for the door. The phone rang. I hesitated, then ran back to the kitchen.

"Hi, it's Douglas." He started to talk about the weather in the laconic Pocono fashion I suddenly had no patience for.

"Look, I'm trying to catch a flight to Atlanta, so let's make this fast. I need to know who ordered Noreen's cremation."

"I'm sorry, Robin, but that's confidential."

"The hell it is. I'm investigating a death and you're withholding information."

He laughed. "So what? You have no authority here. But I'm feeling generous today on account of the holiday. So here's a little gift. A family member came forward and ordered the cremation. Now, as a special treat, if you tell me where you're staying, I'll even check with the party in question and see what I can do for you."

I hated coyness, especially when I was losing a power battle, but I needed answers. I gave him the information and hung up. The phone rang again instantly. Great. Now that I was running out of time, everyone wanted me. I picked up the receiver and said, "Yeah," with as much belligerence as I could muster.

"Whoa, what's wrong, you having a bad hair day?"

It was Fred DeLuca. I promised to call him from

Atlanta, then rushed out of the house. In the car, my stomach heaved. I was still far from one hundred percent, but I craved action more than I needed bed rest.

The motor turned over easily. Five minutes later, I was passing the domed gates that mark the entrance to Telham Village. I pedaled the gas and switched on the radio. The weather report was pretty grim. Four inches had fallen, and more was on the way. The road was slick, especially when it started running parallel to the Stone Hill river. I checked the car clock. Quarter after four. At the current speed, I'd probably miss my flight. There was one more flight, at eight-forty, but I knew from past experience that even a single hour could make the difference between a successful and a failed skip trace. And unless there was a last-minute cancellation, I'd be out of luck.

If Maggie was smart enough to use someone else's credit cards, she was smart enough to know how easily her movements could be traced. Obviously, this woman was desperate to disappear for a while. I just didn't know why.

I sliced into a bank of fog that completely obliterated the road. The car skidded into the left lane. In the rear view mirror, I could just make out the glow of headlights charging toward me. In a flash, I decided to make a sharp turn onto Snow Hill Road instead of edging back into the right lane. The short cut over the mountain was twistier, but free from fog. I picked up speed, whipping around the curves with a recklessness that made my blood rush. Finally, my limbs began to heat up. Branches from the pines lining the road slapped against the windshield, pounding the car roof with miniature avalanches. I felt like singing.

My foot twitched from the gas to the brake and back again. It was like music, the rhythm pounding in my veins. Good, I thought, as my flesh began to sweat, the thermals growing damp around my thighs, in the small of my back.

Under my skin, bullshit. I could expel the memory of K.T. as surely as I was discharging the poison from my blood.

I fishtailed around an S-curve, a satisfying crunch rattling the car. Must been a rear light, I mused indifferently. I glanced into my rear view mirror to see if my brake lights were working. Dim headlights were still behind me, matching me curve for curve. The adrenaline rush derailed. I hunched over the wheel and hit the accelerator. There was a series of tight curves ahead that were a challenge even on a clear day. I took them at top speed. The car behind me kept pace.

I checked again. No. It hadn't kept pace. The lights were gaining on me.

My confidence shaken, I scanned either side of the road with concern. I'd driven Snow Hill many times in the past. I was smack in the middle of a wooded stretch that ran for three miles, without so much as a mailbox to indicate signs of inhabitation.

Concentrate on the road, I warned myself. But I was edging around the curves with less sureness now, my wheels swerving in the thickening snow. Another glance in the mirror made me gulp hard. My pursuer was close enough for me to identify the make of the car. A Ford Bronco. A four-wheel drive van with chains on its tires. The vehicle was tearing up the road like a snowplow.

The driver was invisible behind the rapid swish of windshield wipers and the spit of snow from the van's wheels. But as I felt the jolt on my bumper, the intention was clear. The Bronco was trying to run me off the road.

I turned my eyes back a second too late. I bounced over a snow drift and landed hard on my front tires, the back tires skidding violently to the right. A second later, I felt another impact that rattled my jaw. I revved the engine and jerked forward. A speed sign warned me to slow down to twenty-five. I gritted my teeth and pressed the speedometer to forty. By now, my heart was beating so fast I was afraid I'd pass out. I took the next turn way too fast and lost my nerve, slamming hard on my brakes. The car spun one hundred and eighty degrees, sideswiped a young birch, then shot over the shoulder. With a jolt, I smacked into a snow-filled ditch, the shoulder harness whipping me back with a snap.

My head wrenched forward, glancing off the steering wheel. In shock, I stayed like that for a moment. Then I rapidly released my seat belt, fumbled for the lock, and fell into the snow. I didn't have to turn around to know the Bronco had stopped as well. The rushing silence was horrifyingly articulate. I plunged ahead into the woods, the snow blinding me. There was nowhere to run. Already, the snow was calf high. Despite my bravado, I knew I wasn't strong enough to outrun my pursuer. The chill had penetrated my bones again and I felt as if an ice pick were cracking through my scalp.

The ground sloped suddenly and my toe caught on an unseen root. Tumbling headfirst, I rolled forward in a whitewashed hush. When I landed, I spit blood onto my parka. Then I gave up. I turned around, ready to greet whoever had chased me here.

Surprisingly, I was alone.

My eyes darted in every direction. All I could see was the hard-driving snow. Even the road was invisible from here.

Even the road.

I spun around, panicked, each intake of breath a fiery assault. I forced myself to stop. The icy air sandpapered my cheeks. Sweat beads on my forehead began to freeze. Using the back of my wool gloves, I patted my face dry, then unfolded my turtleneck till it covered my mouth. I was still shaking, but my breath was less ragged.

Stay calm, I urged myself frantically.

Right. Three miles from anywhere in the middle of a snowstorm. Why worry? I was surrounded by evergreens and brown-edged rhododendron stretching in every direction, the only trace of color visible. Where the hell was the road? I was on the edge of state game land. If I headed in the wrong direction my chance of surviving would plummet from improbable to "don't count on it, kid."

All I had to do was follow my own footprints back up to the road. I studied the drifting banks of snow and felt my hopes shrivel. The snow and wind had already swept away my trail. I squinted into the wind. I knew I had fallen downhill, but there was no slope discernible. The snow had rendered my surroundings dimensionless. It was as if I were standing amid a cloud. A strange peacefulness descended on me. For an instant, the cold dissipated and I wanted nothing more than to lie down. Then a sound, a moving stillness in the muted rush of air, jerked me back to attention.

Snow masked the details, but I could just make out the swash of cocoa-colored fur as it bounded around a bramble a few yards away. It stopped short, sensing my presence. My first thought was, the bears had not yet begun hibernating. But then its head turned toward me. The buck's antlers were magnificent, the glint in his eyes at once defiant and indifferent. He bowed his head, once, then disappeared into the cover of snow.

The buck had unmistakably come downhill. I fixed my sight in that direction and started trudging through the drifts. Within seconds, I realized my eyes were useless against the snow. I had to rely on instinct. And I had to keep moving. Even as I paused I could feel my toes and fingertips losing sensation. I closed my eyes, bent my head into the wind, and concentrated on the crunch of snow under my feet, the steady pulse of the wind. I felt the ground pulling up and I knew I had found the slope.

When I opened my eyes, I was a few feet from my car. I dove inside, pumped up the heat, and dug my elbow into the horn.

Chapter 9

I opted for first class. It seemed that there had been several cancellations due to the snow. Dry socks and new sneakers on my feet, a cup of coffee between my palms, and lobster thermidor in my stomach, I was remarkably content.

A state trooper had responded to my horn's relentless blare. I lied pitifully about my dying grandfather back in Decatur, until tears formed in the young stud's eyes. He turned on his siren and in the spirit of the holiday whipped me over to the local airfield. American Express took care of the rest. I had missed my scheduled flight, but caught the eight-forty, which didn't take off till midnight. I didn't care. I was warm and full. Best of all, I was alive to take revenge on the bastard who had run me off the road.

Of course, there was the possibility that the driver was unrelated to either Noreen or Maggie. But I doubted it. The timing was too coincidental. For the hundredth time, I reviewed the list of people who knew I was on the way to Atlanta. Dean, of course. Then Helen and Amy. Shoot. I had opened my stupid mouth to Douglas Marks and Fred DeLuca. Who the hell *didn't* know I was leaving town?

I downed the last sip of coffee, flipped up the food tray, and dragged my overnight bag from under my seat. A flip of a switch and a perky beep told me that my Dell laptop had valiantly survived the accident. I wasn't sure my new Subaru had been so lucky.

I stared at the list of names, struggling to figure out who could have been so anxious to get rid of me that they had run me off the road and presumably left me for dead. The only logical explanation was that someone figured I knew too much. Then another thought hit me. Maybe it's Maggie who knows too much.

After fifteen minutes of staring at the screen, I rubbed my eyes, suddenly bone-tired. I glanced at my watch. Nearly one in the morning. The plane would be landing soon. I tilted back my seat and closed my eyes, the image of a blue-hooded flower flickering just at the edge of consciousness.

The doorman opened the taxi door with a condescending nod. I knew I looked like hell. The flight attendant had mentioned it to me sympathetically when I downed two brandies shortly after take-off.

The Hotel Nikko was a class operation. The place was Japanese-American modern chic, complete with a gurgling rock garden and black glass and marble check-in counter. I propped myself up on my elbows and waited for the cashier to hang up the phone. I was seconds from collapsing and this jerk with a hawk-nose was whining to his girlfriend about having to work a double shift on Thanksgiving eve. After a minute, I thumped the counter like a true New Yorker. He hung up with a grimace, then turned on the charm. I checked his name tag.

"Hi, Billy. I called earlier. I wanted to surprise my sister Noreen. Is the room next to hers still free?"

His eyebrows furled together. I had a feeling I wasn't going to appreciate his next words. "Sorry. She checked out a little while ago. Just after your mother showed up. I guess your family doesn't communicate too well." He was trying to be cute. I wanted to slap him. I just didn't have the energy.

"My mother?" Even to my ears, my voice was shrill.

"Yes, ma'am. I don't mind telling you, your family's been marching through this place like Sherman." I noticed he heightened his Southern accent for effect. I groaned silently.

"What did my *mother* look like?"

With a subtle flare of his nostrils, he described an elderly woman who could be anyone or no one. Matter of fact, it sounded as if whoever "mother" was had done an exceptional job of impersonating the kind of homeless person who propels others into mystical meditations on shoe leather.

"Great." I needed an aspirin badly. I rubbed my temple and asked, "Did they happen to say where they were headed?"

He shook his hawk nose at me, obviously bemused. "They didn't leave together. Your mother said she needed to make a phone call. I had to give her a quarter," he said meaningfully. "Two minutes later, your sister called down for her messages. I told her your mother was in the lobby and she hung up. Next thing I know, the old —" He caught himself and smiled. "Your mother caught a cab." He scratched his stubbly chin and laughed. "Man, you Northerners."

"When did Noreen leave?"

"I'm not sure. I was on my break."

I tried to match his laugh, but snorted instead. Nothing like a world-class goose chase to piss someone off. Without another word, I headed back toward the front door. It was already three-forty. The first flight to Newark left at 7:00 a.m. I intended to be the first one in the cabin. Assuming there were seats available.

"Hey, Ms. Finnegan!"

It took me a second to realize Billy was calling me. I barely had the energy to turn around.

"I almost forgot. I got another message for Noreen after she checked out. She told me she was waiting for an important message. Thought this might be it, so I took it down thinking she might still call in." He was waving a striped sheet of paper that I suddenly wanted very badly. I practically snapped Billy's wrist as I jerked it from his hand.

Message delivered for Noreen Finnegan at 12:40 am:

Your sister Ellen called. Said she's sorry you had to wait so long. She's home now. Come by as soon as you can. The apartment listed under Addison.

The Peachtree address couldn't be more than fifteen minutes away.

I don't remember tipping Billy. But I should have slipped him a ten.

The cab driver was a Haitian who, for some reason, wanted to know if New York City had as many gays as the papers said. I had never seen any official numbers so I wasn't too helpful. We had a brief but fascinating political discussion before he dropped me off at the Peach Haven development, on Peachtree Street near the corner of Peachtree Road. If the word *peach* is ever stricken from Atlanta addresses, half the city will be nameless. At four-ten in the morning, I found the thought hilarious.

The upscale development consisted of seven painfully modern buildings, none taller than four stories. I headed down a brick path lined by — what else? — peach trees and magnolias. Giddy with lack of sleep and the excitement of tracking down Noreen's sister, I could barely focus on the brass address plates. Finally, I hit on the right one. A quick scan of the windows told me which floor probably housed Ellen Finnegan. In an otherwise darkened building, seven windows on the third floor were blazing.

The intercom plate looked like oiled steel. I scanned the names, which read like the roster for the Mayflower. Jefferson. Madison. Aldicott. I pressed the button next to apartment 3F, T. Addison, and waited.

The reply was almost instant. Without asking my name, the party on the other end buzzed me in. In New York, I would have had to supply my driver's license and birth certificate.

The elevator doors slid open so fast I barely had time to check my image in the corner mirror. I charged out just before they snapped shut again and collided with a woman who looked nothing like Noreen. Blonde hair teased into a Dolly Parton coiffure, she was an aging debutante. Here it was, the dead of night, and the woman was wearing a pearl choker with matching earrings, a tidy shirt-collar dress with puffed sleeves trimmed with lace, and delicate leather pumps. The only thing not delicate about her were her boobs, which strained against the dress's cotton fabric like a cat trying to fight its way out of a plastic bag. I had a feeling they rarely won.

She looked at me quizzically and asked, "Noreen?"

That answered my first three questions. This was indeed Ellen. She had no idea what her sister looked like, and Maggie had failed to inform her of Noreen's demise. I almost giggled. This day was definitely one to remember.

I took her by the elbow and said, "We better go inside."

She nodded, apparently dumbstruck, and led me through the open door at the far end of the corridor. My stomach sank at the sight of her meticulously arranged home. Ellen was a woman who liked order. And I was about to shoot it to hell.

The Berber carpet was camel, the wallpaper had pale yellow stripes with hand-painted vines running along the border, and the casement windows were so clean the glass was invisible against the night sky. Opposite the couch was a mahogany wall unit in which books were arranged by size, and knick-knacks by composition — crystal figurines on shelf one, ceramics on shelf two, and pewter on shelf three.

Ellen lowered herself into a Bentwood rocker and said, "You don't look like me at all."

I exhaled abruptly and shook my head. "I'm not your sister."

Apprehension sprang into her eyes. "Then who —"

I spent twenty minutes trying to explain. When I was done, Ellen's composure had completely dissolved. She blew her nose noisily with a handkerchief she had retrieved from the bedroom, then crossed to the wet bar separating the living and dining rooms.

"This Maggie," she said with distaste as she poured herself a bourbon, "this Maggie may have killed Noreen?"

"Honestly, I have no idea. Do you mind explaining —"

"Again?" She grimaced as the liquor went down her throat. Obviously, Ellen was not a practiced drinker. I was relieved. "Why not?" she said, pointing the bottle at me as an offer. I waved my hand and waited for her to begin.

"My husband Tyler works for American Airlines. The company just transferred him to Dallas, so I've been down there the past two weeks examining properties." She licked a drop of liquor off her lips with such salaciousness that I wished I hadn't turned down the drink. "I just got home a few hours ago. You can probably tell from the mess."

I looked around. In the hallway was a single bag of tweeded Samsonite strapped to a luggage cart.

She threw another ice cube into the glass and continued, "The first message came in on Sunday. She said it was Noreen. How was I supposed to know it wasn't her? We had only talked once before."

Shifting uncomfortably in the straight-backed couch, I asked, "When was that?"

"Last April. A detective tracked me down. What was his name. Oh, yes. George Morris. Apparently, I was the first one he located."

"The first one?"

"There were six of us. Three girls and three boys. I'm the youngest." She swirled the glass with a teal stirrer shaped like a coyote that made me crave margaritas and chips, then she sat down next to me. "When our parents died, a cousin took me in. I was raised here in Atlanta."

"What happened to the others?"

She shrugged. "Who knows? Susan, the woman

who raised me, didn't think it was wise to stay in touch with the family. This may sound cruel, but I have to agree with her. I don't remember much of those early years, and I'd like to keep it that way." Her chin jutted toward me defiantly. "That's what I told Noreen when she called." Then, as if she suddenly remembered Noreen's fate, her eyes softened. "I know she was my sister, but she was a total stranger to me. You have to understand, I was just four when the house burned —"

"Your parents died in a fire?" Helen had told me it was a car accident.

As Ellen continued, I could feel sparks igniting in my head. "My parents and a sibling. I was never told which one. Frankly, I was too young to understand. And life with Susan and Gordon was so much better than anything I had known . . ." A surprisingly mannish hand fluttered to her cheek. "Listen to me. I must sound downright boorish to you." She looked genuinely horrified.

I said, "Not at all," and meant it. I wasn't sure anything could sound boorish to a New Yorker.

"Gawd, if Tyler could hear me now."

"Tyler?"

"My husband. He knows nothing about this. I hate being dishonest, but I'm not sure he'd understand. Tyler comes from a true American family, unlike mine. If there are skeletons in the Addison family closet, you can bet that they boarded up the door decades ago. Being a Northerner, you may not appreciate how . . . tiresome it can be maintaining an image, but down here it's a job a lot of us take real seriously. Susan taught me that early on."

Averting her eyes, she paused to smooth down an invisible strand of hair. "My father," she continued, with a peculiar downturn of her lips, "my father was an immigrant and a true son-of-a-bitch." The words ran together with vehemence.

"Pardon my French," she said, looking not the least bit apologetic. "When Noreen contacted me she fired up old memories I hadn't even known existed. Can't say I was real grateful to her." The bourbon was settling in, her words slurring ever so slightly. "Seems she was starting to have some unsettling nightmares, faint recollections from childhood that were truly plaguing her. My father was a violent man, you see. I have just one memory of him. My mother was an elegant woman who played violin like an angel. One night I was having trouble falling asleep and she came into my room to play me a lullaby. My father was, let's just say, displeased. He smashed the violin over my bedpost. So maybe you can understand why I wasn't exactly overjoyed when Noreen called me, trying to piece together the past. As far as I'm concerned, life began here in Atlanta, in a civilized home with civilized people."

"What about your other siblings?"

"Amazing, isn't it?" Ellen said with raised eyebrows. "But I can barely remember them. There was Melanie and, of course, Noreen. Then Frank, Daniel, and John Junior. We weren't a close family, at least not as far as I can recall. Though mother did have a peculiar fondness for Daniel."

157

"How did the fire start?"

"Don't know. Don't want to know." She stood up abruptly. "Why do you suppose this Maggie was calling me?" she said with renewed agitation.

I answered with a question of my own. "What exactly did she say?"

"That she was in trouble, she didn't know who else to turn to. After all, despite the distance and the years, we *were* sisters." I watched the words sink in, like an anchor diving into still water. "She was my sister, for heaven's sake," she said, as if the thought had just occurred to her.

Helpless, I watched her dissolve into tears. There was nothing I could say to comfort her. She turned her back to me and, sensing that she needed a moment alone, I retreated to the bathroom. I was washing my face when the phone rang. I waited for her to pick up, but the phone kept ringing. I grabbed a towel and heard the answering machine click on. "Ellen, it's Noreen." At the first words, I darted into the living room. The tremulous voice continued. "I'm catching a seven o'clock flight. If you get this phone call before then, please meet me outside the Roy Rogers in the American Airlines terminal."

Ellen was immobile, her hand extending toward the phone, but her feet wouldn't budge. I ran past her.

"It's urgent that I speak to you before I leave."

I grabbed the receiver and hollered her name, but there was no answer. Then I realized the phone was a damn cordless. By the time I pressed "talk," Maggie had hung up.

158

*　*　*　*　*

Ellen looked like a debutante, but she drove like a truck driver. It had taken me less than a minute to convince her that I had to stop Maggie from leaving. Murderer or witness, she was the linchpin in my investigation. I had tried to wrestle the car keys from Ellen, but she had insisted on driving the BMW herself.

Now, I braced myself against the dashboard as she cut through three lanes to take the airport exit. We whipped around the ramp on two wheels. I was trying to read the signs, but she was zipping past them. Ellen obviously knew exactly where she had to go.

We screeched to a halt outside the American Airlines terminal, the front wheel of the BMW bumping onto the curb. We jumped out simultaneously and shot through the automatic doors so fast they barely had time to hiccup between our entrances. I paused to get my bearings and shift the strap of my overnight bag, and Ellen barreled past me. I followed her lead, my breathing labored and my head pounding. The events of the last twenty-four hours had taken their toll on me. I could barely keep up.

At one point Ellen disappeared and I panicked. Then I saw her running up an escalator. The Roy Rogers sign loomed before me as I hopped up the moving stairs. At the top, I spun around in place. There were three phone banks, all of them empty. Ellen and I stared blankly at each other across the food hall.

At five-thirty in the morning, there were less than ten people milling in the terminal. Eight, if you discounted Ellen and me. None of them were female. Cursing in frustration, I circled the phones over and over. We waited till seven, when the first flights departed. Then Ellen drove home. I bought a return-trip ticket and dulled my senses with a Boston cream donut, scrambled eggs, hash browns, and three coffees. I was searching for a place that sold Yoo-Hoos when my name came over the loud speakers. I darted to the nearest airport phone.

"What the hell have you gotten me into?" It was Ellen. She didn't give me time to ask for an explanation. "Someone's ransacked my home. Ripped up my photo albums, upturned my bookcases, my desk. I've never seen anything like this in my life. What am I supposed to tell Tyler?" Her anger dissolved into hysteria. "I don't need this. I want my life back, goddamn you!"

My first thought was, not again. "Where are you now?" Fire broke out in my stomach. I had to make sure she was safe. "Ellen, do you hear me?"

After another moment, she answered uneasily. "In my living room."

I suddenly felt queasy. "Have you checked the rest of the apartment?"

Her hesitation was all I needed. "Go to a neighbor's now! Then call the police."

"But what —"

"Do it."

I grabbed the first taxi back to her apartment complex. The cab pulled in behind two patrol cars. I paid the driver to wait, then approached the vestibule with studied nonchalance. The young officer at the entrance had a soft chin and eyes too small for his head. I rummaged through the briefcase for a set of keys that wouldn't open a single door in town and headed inside.

"Name," Soft Chin asked, blocking the apartment listing from my view.

"Jane Aldicott. Apartment 3D. What's the trouble, officer?" I sounded like Scarlett.

Reviewing the directory to confirm the name and apartment number, which I had remembered from my earlier visit, he said, "Nothing to worry about, ma'am. We have it all under wraps." He opened the door and waved me in.

Fighting the impulse to charge upstairs, I waited for the elevator. When I exited on the third floor, Ellen was in the hallway, sobbing to a neighbor who reminded me of June Allison. They both turned at the sound of the elevator. Ellen's eyes caught mine and she widened them in warning. I took one step in her direction and she whirled around, grabbing her neighbor by the elbow. Her back sent me a too-clear message. She wanted me to disappear.

Reluctantly I obeyed.

Soft Chin was leaning into his patrol car and talking on his radio when I left the building. I hopped into the waiting cab before he noticed me. The whole way to the airport, I tried to make sense of what had just happened. The obvious answer was that someone had followed me to Atlanta. What I didn't understand was why they had ransacked Ellen's place.

I forked over the fare to the driver and reentered the terminal. Suddenly another thought occurred to me. What if Maggie's call had been a ruse to lure

Ellen out of her apartment? Then I remembered how frantic she had sounded on the phone. Besides, she had had plenty of time to break into the apartment while Ellen was in Dallas. No — whoever ransacked the place must have trailed me there from the Hotel Nikko. So why hadn't he or she followed us to the airport?

There were two possibilities. The first was that Ellen's apartment had always been the primary goal. After all, Maggie herself obviously had a pressing need to contact Ellen. The second possibility was that we *had* been followed, but when we were inside aimlessly circling the airport terminal, the perpetrator had returned to the apartment to search for some bit of information I didn't even know existed, or maybe a lead on where Maggie was headed.

I was just about to pass through the metal detector when it hit me. If someone had followed me here from the Poconos, he or she had to still be here. Or on the first leg of a flight home. With an unnatural calm, I headed back into the waiting area. I found an inconspicuous phone booth with a view of the taxi stand. People were arriving now in droves. I stared at the doors, trembling as I dialed information. I wrote down the numbers on my palm, the ink smearing in the sweat.

I plugged in my calling card number, my fingers turning cold. With each peal of the phone, my throat tightened. Don't let it be Dean, I found myself pleading silently. By the eighth ring, I was almost in tears. My index finger was reaching for the disconnect when his voice cracked over the wire.

Every muscle in my body went limp. "Dean?" I practically wailed.

"Robin? Where the hell are you? I was up all night waiting to hear from you." Despite the lousy connection, I could hear the edginess in his voice. I knew from experience what lack of sleep could do to a person so I trod lightly. I rapidly brought him up to date, leaving Ellen out of the picture temporarily. Disclosing the full story would have taken too much time, and I still had four other numbers to call. He was barely breathing by the time I was done.

"Do you have any clue about where she may have gone?" he asked quietly. I had the distinct impression he was seething just below the surface. I couldn't blame him. I hated to say no, but the fact was that Maggie had successfully evaded me. Temporarily. With what I now knew, finding her was just a matter of time. "She was using Noreen's credit cards," I explained, "but I doubt she'll continue doing that. Without cards or cash, she'll have to stop running soon. That's when we'll find her. Who knows? Maybe she'll even come home on her own."

He sighed. "Why is she doing this?" His voice cracked.

I didn't have the heart to tell him that one possible reason for Maggie's disappearance was that she had been responsible for Noreen's death. Dean was smart. Soon he would have to start facing facts. I didn't want to rush him. "Look, Dean, I have to go now. I'll call you as soon as I know anything else."

"I don't understand. This is crazy. Why the hell was she even down there?" He shouted questions at me I couldn't begin to answer. In the distance, the speakers crackled with the boarding announcement for my flight. It echoed in my ears.

"I really have to go now —"

"Fine, fine. Do what you have to. Can I do anything to help?"

"Just sit tight. I'll call back soon."

"Maybe I should run over to Carly and Amy's and let them know what's happening. I'm sure they're worried about you."

I told him I intended to call them myself. I didn't tell him why.

Carly answered on the second ring. She sounded too wide awake for my liking. "Is Amy there?" I asked, not bothering with pleasantries.

She was equally abrupt. "What are you doing down in Atlanta?"

"Didn't you get my message last night?"

"Oh yeah. I got it." She was incensed. I couldn't understand why.

"What's wrong?"

"Amy and I had a blowup last night when I got in. I walked into the house and found Helen rocking Amy in her arms. I lost it, Rob. That woman's been around here way too often lately." She started to cry.

It was almost more than I could stand. "Carl, let me speak to Ame."

"She's not here. When I started screaming, Helen told Amy she shouldn't put up with me. Can you believe it? Like I'm some kind of monster. They left right away. I stewed for an hour and then drove down to Helen's place. Her van was gone. And so was Amy. She finally called a little while ago just to tell me she was safe. That was it. She hung up on me before I could say a word."

I swallowed hard before asking the next question. "Carly, what kind of van does Helen drive?"

"A Ford Bronco."

I almost crushed the phone in my hand.

Chapter 10

The plane ride back to Newark was agonizing. Every air pocket jolted me into near cardiac arrest. I ate incessantly, begging the flight attendant for a second breakfast like a homeless person who hadn't eaten for days.

I didn't know what to make of all the information rumbling inside my head. After talking to Carly I had dialed, in rapid succession, the numbers of the other people who had known I was on my way to Atlanta. Neither Douglas Marks nor Fred DeLuca had been home. For good measure, I tried Manny Diaz. Another no answer. Cursing, I slammed the phone down. Where the hell was everybody? Then I remembered. It was Thanksgiving Day morning. Any one of my potential suspects could have just as easily been on vacation or visiting a beloved relative as they could have been ransacking an apartment in Atlanta. Unfortunately I couldn't advance my investigation a single inch.

I had one·hard fact, and it stuck in my throat like a dry chicken bone. Helen owned a Bronco. Could Helen have run me off the road, returned to Amy's house, then raced to the airport ahead of me? The timing was possible, but the scenario still struck me as unlikely. Why would Helen have wasted time by driving back up to Telham? The only possible answer was that Amy was more involved in this madness than I wanted to imagine.

I remembered the way Amy had consoled Helen the morning of the murder, how uncomfortable their closeness had made me feel. Had I picked up on some sexual energy between them? Could they be lovers? Then it hit me between the eyes. Amy could very well have been the woman lurking in Helen's bedroom yesterday morning, before I stumbled on the sciatica potion. The very thought made my stomach revolt.

I tried to recall whether she was carrying anything with her when she caught me in the kitchen. With a stabbing disappointment, I couldn't recall seeing a single bag of groceries. Where had Amy been at nine in the morning?

Even the sixth cup of coffee wasn't helping me sift through the muddle that used to be a rational mind. I needed sleep. I forced myself to close my eyes, but my body almost laughed. It was like asking a racehorse to nap after just running the Kentucky Derby. I was functioning on sheer adrenaline now. Decades of insomnia had taught me that it doesn't pay to fight physiology. If my body wanted me to stay up, that's exactly what I was going to do. And when it allowed me to collapse, I wouldn't resist.

I whipped out my laptop. The self-test lights winked at me while I struggled to think clearly. Start with the obvious questions, I admonished myself as my fingers tripped over the keyboard.

Why is Maggie running?

Maggie had disappeared the very morning Noreen had died. The timing had to be related. If she didn't kill Noreen herself, then I was sure she knew who did. I gestured the flight attendant over for another coffee refill. She looked at me with incredulity, but filled my plastic mug with a Miss American smile. I swallowed it with relish, my heart skipping a beat in response.

From what Jill had discovered in her computer search, I knew Maggie must have appropriated at least two of Noreen's major credit cards, as well as her ATM card and driver's license — which meant that Maggie probably had been in Noreen's house shortly after she died.

Whoever killed Noreen had been clever enough to arrange the murder so that he or she didn't have to be present when Noreen actually took the fatal dose of medicine. And if Maggie didn't have to actually *see* the murderer to know enough to panic and run, then she had to know with horrifying certainty who had an overriding reason for killing Noreen — and anyone else who knew as much as Maggie. And I, great detective that I am, had let her slip away. I groaned out loud. I had to find her. But I didn't know where to start. After all, I still wasn't sure why she had chosen Atlanta in the first place.

The laptop screen flashed off in warning. My batteries were low. I hit the space bar and was about to sign off when my eyes centered on Ellen Addison's name.

Maggie had sprinted to Noreen's *sister* — the sister few people even knew existed. My hands froze over the keyboard. I slapped the tray, sloshing coffee over my lap. Damn! I wasn't thinking clearly. There was one factor I hadn't even considered yet, though it was leaping off the screen.

Who the hell was the unknown family member who had ordered Noreen's cremation? Noreen had hired a detective last year to find the siblings she had lost following her parents' death. Ellen said she was the first one identified. But it sure as hell didn't mean she was the last. And if Ellen wasn't pleased to have her past rear its ugly head, I had a sinking feeling someone else had reason to be downright furious. I replayed the conversation with Ellen. Her father had been abusive. The family's life had been a turbulent one — enough so that a four-year-old child had blithely accepted strangers as her parents and never once looked back.

Was it possible that one of the Finnegan children had set the fire that killed both parents and one sibling? And what if in the process of struggling to reunite her lost family Noreen had unearthed an early, insufferable memory? Would that be reason enough for someone to kill Noreen? I was projecting my own life into this scenario, I recognized. But — if the truth would destroy a life painstakingly built on the ashes of a first murder, I had no doubt that the answer was yes.

The adoption search no longer seemed incidental.

If my hunch was correct, any one of the potential suspects in the case could have a plausible motive I hadn't yet uncovered — including Maggie, Fred, Camilla, Amy, and Douglas. Even Helen. The implications of the last name made me shiver. Surely that would have been too hideous a coincidence, for two women to become lovers without realizing their shared parentage? I thought of their sudden breakup last summer and shuddered.

No. It just wasn't possible.

I stared at the remaining names. Maggie was the only suspect who even vaguely favored Noreen, but then again I hadn't recognized a family resemblance in Ellen either.

With the insistence of a stubborn dog, the presumption that Noreen had found another sibling dug its heels into my thoughts. Suddenly even Noreen's insistence on moving to not just Canadensis, but into Telham Village in particular, seemed suspect. I had a strong hunch she had been interested in more than just the scenic views. In fact, hadn't Helen said that it was the detective's *cousin* who had recommended Telham? Perhaps Helen had lied to me once again. Or maybe she really didn't know the whole story. And then a scud missile exploded between my eyes.

The detective Noreen had hired died in August.

Had that been the murderer's first attempt to silence the past?

I was playing a mean game of chess with a cunning master. With that realization, my body finally capitulated and allowed me to collapse.

The cabin was Oz at the end of the brick road, Valhalla to a slain hero. Home. I unlocked the door with a sense of peace I rarely felt running up the steps of my Park Slope brownstone. Maybe I really would buy the place one day, I considered with surprise.

I had slept for less than an hour on the plane and awoke more exhausted than before. I had rented a car and driven back to the Poconos with both eyes half-closed. There was one thing I wanted now more than anything in the world, and that was at least five hours of uninterrupted sleep. But I couldn't waste the time.

Dropping my bags on the den floor, I pulled out the sheet of paper where I had written the phone numbers of the neighbors who lived near the Finnegans at the time of the fire. Eleanor Dunn was still listed at 723 Hennessey Lane. I dialed the number. It rang ten times before I hung up. Barely pausing to breathe, I stabbed Jill Zimmerman's home number onto the phone. "Is your CD-ROM system fixed yet?"

She didn't bother answering. I heard the phone drop onto a hard surface, then feet retreating. She muttered a hasty explanation I could barely hear. I didn't have a similar problem understanding the various profanities spewing from her husband's mouth. It was the first time I had ever heard John curse. A second later Jill picked up the extension. "It's up and running. What do you want?"

I was straining our friendship, but my back was against the wall. The case had pushed me there. "Plug in the PhoneDisc USA-Residential directory."

She hesitated. "You want the current phone numbers for the eight names you gave me the other day?"

"Right."

"Get a pen, boss lady." Without skipping a beat, she read off six numbers.

I was so startled by the immediacy of her response I had to ask her to repeat them. "How'd you do that so fast?" I asked. "Those discs contain over eighty million names."

"I conducted the search late yesterday. I already interviewed two of the parties. They didn't remember the Finnegans."

Properly chastened by her efficiency, I hastily apologized.

She chuckled and said, "Maybe there's hope for you yet. Want to hear the rest of my news?" After pointedly updating me on Tony's health, she explained that the probe into the finances of the DeLucas had revealed that the gardening business was barely running in the black, but that wasn't unusual for a new venture. Both Fred and Camilla had impeccable credit histories. The only detail of any interest was the fact that they had been late on their mortgage payments for the last two months. At the same time, there had been three substantial withdrawals from their joint account. The total amount withdrawn came to just under $10,000. The balance of the account was a little over $13,500.

"There's one last piece of information you'll find interesting. Your friend Fred was a bit of a juvenile delinquent. There are two counts of car theft on his record. He served one year when he was eighteen. No *known* criminal activity since then."

I jotted the information down and said, "Good work," the words sounding lame even to my own ears.

Her tone was curt as she said, "Glad you noticed."

Hating to further cut into her holiday, I nevertheless instructed her to check whether any suspect besides Helen owned a navy or black Ford Bronco. Then I asked her to look into the death of the detective Noreen had hired last spring. We ended the conversation with a hint of civility, but I knew I would have to work long and hard to compensate for the way I had treated her the last few days.

The guilt propelled me into the kitchen where the discovery of a six-pack of Yoo-Hoos chilling on the bottom shelf of the fridge rendered me instantly delirious. Downing two bottles in succession, I decided to give my partner Tony a call. Jill had said he was acting like his old Bible-quoting self yesterday, but I wanted to see for myself how he was faring. His machine abruptly reminded me that he was in Phoenix for the next week. The mechanized version of his basso profundo just made me feel worse. I had forgotten Tony was planning to spend the holiday with his sister.

Once again convinced that I was a no-good louse, I got back on the case. In less than one hour, I ran through the numbers Jill had given me. No one could tell me more about the Finnegan fire than I already knew, and two offered obviously distorted versions of the truth. One querulous woman related how the house had exploded, killing three families on the block. An elderly man first explained that the whole family had burned to death, and then corrected himself by saying the house had been struck by lightning, leaving all the occupants unscathed except the family dog — whose charred skeleton he had personally buried. I figured the guy was a retired editor for the *National Enquirer* and hung up before he started telling me about the Nantucket alien who had given birth to a talking chipmunk.

None of the neighbors knew what happened to any of the kids, other than the cute four-year-old who had been shipped to Atlanta.

At two of the homes, I received no answer at all. I wrote asterisks next to those names, then returned to the top of the list and tried Eleanor Dunn again. An elderly woman picked up almost immediately. Her voice had the squeak of an ungreased wheel. With gritted teeth, I plunged into my pretext. I explained that I was a private detective hired to locate the Finnegan children. One of them had died and in her will had named the other siblings as equal beneficiaries. To add weight to my story, I mentioned that we had already located Ellen Finnegan.

"Why, I'm sorry about Noreen but I'm real glad you called, dear. It's so sad the way she lost her family. As I said the last time, that incident was the worst tragedy I ever witnessed." Talking to me as if we were old friends, she obviously relished the chance to rehash the incident. "Those poor children had enough to deal with before the fire. I don't mind telling you there were times my heart would break at the sounds I heard coming from that place." She lowered her voice as if she were afraid someone might overhear her. "That John Finnegan was a vicious man. He once kicked my poor Sally in the head just 'cause she relieved herself on his lawn. She was only a silly pup, for heaven's sake. But the man was a police officer, so I just kept mum."

"Did the newspapers ever say what started the fire?"

"Well, dear, there was some nonsense about a pan catching fire in the kitchen, but none of us ever bought that."

I sat up in my chair and asked, "Why not?" If she started talking about lightning bolts, I promised myself I would retire instantly.

"Too much of a coincidence, if you ask me. John had run into trouble on the force. I only knew because I could hear the two of them fighting about it almost every night. He was drinking more and more. So was Adelaide. I could hear his ugliness all the way across the street. He was calling her a tramp and accusing her of plotting to steal the kids from him."

"Was she?"

She practically cackled. "Now how would I know that, honey? That other detective asked me the very same thing —"

The phone slipped in my hand. "What other detective?"

"Don't you know?" she asked, immediately distressed. "I just assumed you two worked together."

Eleanor was a gossip, but she wasn't a fool. She clammed up, clearly on guard now. I had to win back her confidence. "You mean my uncle? Jeez. I hate when he does this. I end up wasting time covering ground he's already left far behind."

"What's your uncle's name?" She had dropped the endearments.

The question was obviously a test I needed to pass in order to obtain more information. I coughed, stalling for time as I rifled through my files, trying to locate the detective's name Ellen Addison had casually mentioned during our discussion in Atlanta. The name had reminded me of a cat —

"Morris," I erupted. "George Morris. When did he call you?"

"Last spring, I reckon. He said that Noreen Finnegan was trying to reunite her brothers and sisters. I thought that was about the sweetest thing I ever heard. I told him about Ellen, you know, the one in Atlanta. But here's the strange thing. Just last week I was cleaning out the attic and I came across a letter one of the Finnegan kids sent my youngest son. Hold on, let me get it."

I was breathing so heavily I was dizzy by the time she picked up again. "The letter's real short, saying how unhappy they were about leaving their friends behind, how their new parents were almost as mean as their old, stuff like that."

"You keep saying 'they' —"

"Of course. The twins. Daniel and Melanie. They got placed together, I knew that much from the start. But I couldn't remember where. Then I found this here letter. The return address reminded me. They were adopted by a family in Wilkes Barre,

176

Pennsylvania. The Van Eycks. The father, I think his name was Andrew, was a minister of some sort. I don't recall hearing anything about the wife."

"What happened to the other siblings?"

She tut-tutted into the phone. "Well, poor Frankie died in the fire, along with his parents. He was the youngest boy. Five years old, and yet the man of the house. John favored him, so he had an easy time of it. The other boy, John Junior, was shipped off to some family in California. Now there was a child who would've made most parents real proud. A gentle boy with a mind as sharp as a whip. His father hated him ... I never could figure out why. Can't tell you how many times I'd see that man smacking the child alongside his head, calling him all sorts of names. Adelaide told me once, had to be no more than three weeks before the fire, John was fearful the boy was too soft. You know what I'm saying? He didn't want a son — especially one carrying his name — to end up ... queer."

I was jotting down notes so fast, my hand started to cramp. I stretched out my fingers and asked, "What do you think caused the fire?"

"Now, dear, you should really get your uncle to share information with you. This seems an awful waste of time."

For a second, I was afraid that she would refuse to tell me more. But Eleanor was on a roll.

"As my late husband Harold, may he in rest in peace, used to say, someone in that house just didn't want no more hurting. He thought Adelaide set the fire herself. I always guessed it was John Junior. Though it could've been Daniel — the boy was way too attached to his mother, if you ask me. In any

177

case, that was no kitchen fire. I've never seen anything go up so fast in my life. One second, the house was there, the next there was nothing but ash. The bodies were so badly burned, they had to identify them by their teeth. And let me tell you something else, I knew that family. They ate at six-thirty sharp. If Adelaide was a minute late, you could hear John tearing through the house. So you tell me how a grease fire started just after eight. No. Someone set that fire, that's a sure thing. Who knows? Maybe John's friends on the force covered up the truth. That's what most of us thought. You know, protect the reputation of the dead, save the kids more anguish. Anyway, the second time your uncle called, I told him if Noreen was interested in a reunion, she had better watch out which siblings she found."

Five minutes after we hung up, I was on the phone with an FTD florist. Eleanor Dunn would have a dozen yellow roses on her doorstep by Friday. She deserved better, but I didn't have time to send Hallmark.

With a solid lead at hand, I felt as if I had topped a mountain crest that revealed a new and unexpected vista. My body's response was to instantly crash. At last, I allowed myself to head upstairs for a nap. I popped some Advil, then crawled into bed fully clothed and curled around my pillows.

The box spring creaked beneath my weight. But I hadn't shifted. I awoke suddenly, skittered off the bed, then spun around in a crouch that would enable me to strike out with my palm or heel.

Dressed in a loose lilac satin nightshirt, K.T. was kneeling on the mattress, her face caught somewhere between a giggle and a howl. "Boy, you Brooklyn girls really are tough."

She looked radiant, her autumn-red hair freshly washed, her scrubbed skin the color of peach blossoms, and her eyes as green as pine leaves in a spring rain. For once, I didn't stop to think. I pounced on her. After I had refreshed my mouth with the sweet taste of her tongue, I raised myself up on my elbow and stared at her in disbelief. "When did you get here?"

"Here, in the cabin, or here, in Telham?"

She looked so delicious, lying just within reach of my lips, I had to lower myself to her earlobes. Nibbling lightly, I said, "Here, here."

She laughed. "Is that a cheer or an answer?"

Still chomping at her ear, I didn't bother to reply.

"I drove up around eleven this morning. Carly gave me the rundown," she continued in a tone that was distinctly censorious. I didn't care. At that moment, she could have spanked me. Matter of fact, I wished she would. "The two of us took a walk about three hours ago and saw the car. We came in together, but when we heard you snoring from way downstairs, Carly headed home. I've been here ever since."

I didn't want to think about Carly. Or Amy. I wanted to think about skin. I licked her shoulder, "And you haven't ravaged me yet?"

Squirming away from my mouth, she said,

"Robin, stop for a second." This time her tone commanded my attention. "I've been worried about you. Carly and I spent all morning trying to figure out what's going on."

Instantly defensive, I blurted, "I didn't realize you both were in the PI business."

"Not with the goddamn case. With you. Why you tried to chase me off that way. Don't you realize I'm crazy about you?"

I tried to ward it off, but it was too late. The gates slammed down. I sat up and crossed my arms across my chest. K.T. tucked a strand of hair behind one ear and waited. So did I. If she wanted to have this kind of conversation instead of making love, she could have it with herself. I didn't have the energy.

She looked at me and smiled. Smiled! I didn't know how to react. Those leaf-green eyes were defiantly amused. They seemed to say, "I knew that's how you'd react."

I was pissed off but unexpectedly struggling to not laugh. My mouth betrayed me. She wrapped me in her arms and said, "God, you're impossible."

Nestled in her damp curls, I felt giddy. "Chalk it up to lack of sleep."

"Honey, I saw your boarding pass stub on the floor downstairs. You must have arrived back here by one, at the latest. It's about five-ten now."

My eyes darted to the window. The blinds were nearly closed, but I could see that the sky had turned deep plum.

"Carly and I decided to postpone dinner till nine. By the way," she said, pulling me toward her, "Happy Thanksgiving, darling."

For the next two hours, she gave me plenty to be thankful for.

It wasn't until I was scrubbing myself in the shower that the case tackled me again with a full body blow. I shifted the curtain to one side and bellowed to K.T. the question that I had been reluctant to ask. "Has Carly heard from Amy yet?" I braced myself for the answer.

"What?" K.T. was still inside, straightening the bed. I rinsed off and repeated the question a full decibel louder. I was too busy chastising myself to hear K.T.'s reply. I shouted to her again and stepped out of the tub.

"You're deafer than an old hound dog with a branch stuck in its ear." K.T. had joined me in the bathroom. "I said she called around noon to say she was at Helen's. Apparently, they had themselves a night on the town last night. From what I heard, the fight with Carly was pretty messy. I guess after twelve years, your patience can wear out."

Toweling down I said, "Remember that twelve years from now," and almost slipped on the tile.

"What?" she asked anxiously.

My mind was already somewhere else. "So Amy's home now."

"Probably. She said she was still planning to make us all a Thanksgiving Day dinner. She just needed some more time alone."

"At Helen's?" I nearly shouted. I started wondering if I really knew Amy at all. Twelve years of friendship suddenly seemed horribly insufficient.

K.T. frowned. "Of course not. She meant at home. That's why Carly and I went for a walk."

"Did she explain what she and Helen did during this 'night on the town'?" I had my own theory and it wasn't a pretty one.

"Lord, you're angrier than Carly was. They saw a show, for heaven's sake. Helen was just trying to distract her, give her a break from all the craziness up here. Personally, I don't think it was such a bad idea. Even Carly understood after Amy explained everything."

But Carly didn't know everything I did.

And I didn't know half of what I needed to.

I dressed rapidly and asked K.T. to head up to Carly and Amy's place without me. She resisted at first, but one good look at me convinced her this wasn't an argument she could win. As soon as she left, I pounced on the telephone.

From the background noise, I knew Ellen Addison was in the midst of a holiday dinner. Given the circumstances, the celebration seemed about as appropriate as a bikini in a blizzard. As soon as she heard my voice, she put me on hold. A full minute passed before she picked up in another room. I briefly wondered how she had explained my call to her guests, then I started shooting questions. She told me the most important news first. Maggie had not tried to contact her again. Then she castigated me for plunging her into the midst of scandal. I allowed her to proceed at full steam, patiently listening to the lies she had provided to the police. When she was done, I told her about my conversation with Eleanor Dunn. If I expected gratitude, I was dead wrong.

"Don't you get it by now? I don't want to know. Period. Tyler and I have worked too hard to create the life we're living. I wouldn't let Noreen destroy our happiness while she was alive, and I sure as hell won't have her destroying me now that she's dead. I want no part of your investigation. Do you understand?"

My teeth were jammed together so tight I'm sure I cracked enamel. Struggling to keep my temper in check I said, "I have an obligation —"

"Let me tell you about obligation, missy." Her voice was a hard whisper in my ear. "The way I see things, you're responsible for what happened down here. If you keep hounding me, I swear I'll tell the police how you lured me out my apartment just so your partner could rob me."

Surprised, I asked, "You were robbed?"

"No. But the police think I lost nearly ten grand in jewelry. I considered that little white lie my protection. And payback for the grief Noreen has caused me." Suddenly her voice was muffled. I had the sense someone else was in the room. When she started speaking again, she sounded even more agitated. "I'm serious. If I want to, I could make more trouble for you than you have ever seen. So don't mess with me."

The bitch had me on the wires. "Don't you even care —"

Again, she cut me off. "What I care about is preserving my way of life. I am sorry about Noreen, but what's done is done. As far as I am concerned, this whole thing is a bad dream. And honey, I just woke up."

The dial tone was a relief.

I glanced at my watch. I was overdue for dinner at Carly and Amy's place. And I hadn't yet phoned

Dinah and Beth, never mind my sister and brother. I made the obligatory calls, grateful for once that my mother and I — like Ellen, I realized with a start — had stopped pretending a long time ago that blood is anywhere near as thick as water.

So much for Thanksgiving.

Next year, I planned to be in Bermuda.

Chapter 11

I headed outside, clad in smothering plastic boots and a seven-ton parka. Just then, a car stopped at the head of the driveway, the door opened and Manny Diaz got out. Leaning back on the car door, she said, "Heard you had a pretty rough time yesterday."

I shrugged, as if to say, "All in a day's work." I wasn't about to let Manny know how shitty I felt. "I'm on my way to Carly and Amy's."

With a dazzling smile, she offered me a lift. I hopped in. Douglas Marks's card was on her dashboard. I fingered it, then our eyes locked. My question was unspoken, but Manny heard it loud and clear. She left the car in park and shifted around in her seat to face me. "You heard about the cremation," she said.

"Who ordered it?"

She narrowed her eyes. "I've been asking the same question. Douglas is keeping mum. He handed me some hogwash about client confidentiality, like some spic from Harlem wouldn't know he was bullshitting. Since when do funeral directors have the right to invoke client privileges?"

"He's also the coroner."

"And I'm Noreen's next of kin! It was my decision that counted. Noreen is . . . was . . . terrified of fire. She wouldn't even let me use the fireplace in the house." She closed her eyes and inhaled deeply, her lips trembling. A single tear squeezed out from under one tightly pressed lid as she continued. "She was always putting on this macho crap, but when it came down to it Reenie was like an abused puppy. More than anything, she just wanted to be loved. She just didn't know how to go about getting it. I tried, Robin, I tried, but she couldn't let me in. And then, shit, Helen —"

Her eyes were wide open now. I took her hand. Even through my gloves, I could feel her chill. "Talk to me, Manny, please."

She withdrew her hand, spun forward and shifted into drive. I had learned from the last time I questioned Manny that I had to back off. I leaned against the headrest and bit my tongue. Literally. We had skidded. Manny slammed the gear into park, half cursing, half sobbing.

"I don't know what the hell to do."

When I remained silent, she turned the motor off and slid the seatbelt over her head. Her right arm slipped behind my neck. The next thing I knew she was practically sitting in my lap. For a second I thought she was going to kiss me, then I realized she was reaching for the glove compartment with her left hand. She pulled out an empty liquor bottle and unceremoniously dropped it onto my lap. I picked it up and stared at it, puzzled.

"I've been driving around with that thing in the car since Sunday, trying to figure out the right thing to do. Now you can worry about it."

As soon as I read the label, my head snapped toward her. "You found this near Noreen's body?"

"Better than that," she said, in a tone that convinced me she was finally telling me the truth. "I saw Helen pouring the booze over her."

I wanted to shake Manny. Instead I waited for her to explain. The next ten seconds lasted an hour.

Biting the tip of her thumb, she mumbled, "Hope this isn't a mistake," then said, "Helen and I left the party around the same time. Noreen had taken the car, so Helen had to walk. I picked her up."

I was glad the car was dark so she couldn't read the cynicism on my face. Remembering the conversation I had overheard between them, I doubted that their departure was coincidental.

"Helen was still pretty upset so I decided to go inside with her and stay a little while."

Uh-oh.

I must have made an involuntary sound because she hesitated, bit the inside of her cheek, then smiled nervously. "Right. My first mistake. Helen's a damn attractive woman. Not really my type, but still . . ." Her voice trailed off. Manny didn't have to tell me how seductive Helen could be. The memory of Helen clad in a loosely tied robe would probably taunt me for the rest of my days.

"There's a vulnerability to her. All I wanted to do was comfort her. She started hitting the bottle right after we came inside. I'm not a drinker, but I thought a glass or two would take the edge off. Noreen and I had been fighting for the last few days about her decision to sell the house. She wouldn't explain why, just kept saying she had her reasons. Then there were all these secret phone calls. I'd walk in a room and she'd clam up. I started thinking she was sleeping around behind my back, and I panicked."

Even in the dim light, I could see how hard Manny was clenching the steering wheel. "Reenie had her problems, but she was good to me."

I interrupted. "She never hit you?"

Manny shook her head. "She came close once. I saw her raise her hand and I flinched. My stepfather used to beat me pretty badly. If she had hit me then, I don't know what I would have done. But she didn't. Instead, she called someone in the program and stayed on the phone for hours. I'm not saying she was perfect, but she was trying hard. To be honest, I think her struggle was part of what enticed me in the first place. It's easy to grow up cool and controlled when you've been showered with all that good, clean, white middle-class privilege."

The words were clearly directed at me. I would have laughed if the words hadn't stung so much. "What happened between you and Helen?"

188

She cocked her head at me knowingly. "You gotta ask? The booze had me flying in minutes. And Helen, Helen was winging right next to me. One minute, she's crying in my arms. Next minute, she's ripping open my blouse and sucking at me so hard I almost exploded. I pushed her away — I don't go in for that crap. You know the joke about U-Haul lesbians? That's me, all the way. I sleep with a woman, the next morning I wake up in love, two days later I'm handing out the keys to my apartment. So, when Helen started touching me, I tried to stop her. She wouldn't take no for an answer, but she didn't force me either. Instead, she unzipped her jeans and started playing with herself, licking her lips, and moaning my name over and over. I was mesmerized. When she finally grabbed my hand and slipped it under her waistband, I was a goner."

Suddenly the car seemed unbearably hot. I cracked the window and breathed deep. Feeling like a peeper, I asked, "What happened next?" I'm embarrassed to say that I half-hoped she would tell me more about the sex.

"We went at each other like bitches in heat. That's the first time I did it with a lover's ex. It added to the excitement, like there were three of us rolling around on that floor. When it was over, I felt like hell. The booze had burned off, my mouth tasted like ashes. When I saw what time it was, I really freaked. I knew Noreen would be furious. I dressed and tried to run out, but Helen came after me for more. I told her it was a huge mistake, and crazy as it seemed to her I still loved Noreen and wanted to make it work. She opened the Dewar's," she said, nodding at the bottle in my lap, "before the door closed behind me."

I looked down at the bottle as if it had acquired a life of its own.

"When I got home, Noreen was pacing on the outside deck. As soon as I pulled into the driveway, she came storming at me. I spun out of her way and she fell on her back. I ran upstairs and locked myself in the bedroom. I was too guilty to face her just then, so instead I just curled up on the bed and listened while she rampaged through the house. Around two o'clock, the phone rang. I finally fell asleep. Then, about two hours later, I heard Noreen screaming again. I thought, not again. Usually, her rages lasted for an hour, tops. First she's calling my name, then it sounds like she's slammed open the kitchen window. I mean, the walls were shaking. So was I. I never heard her like that. Then she shouts Helen's name and something about being poisoned. That's when I got really scared, 'cause I thought somehow she'd found out about what happened. But all of a sudden, there's this horrible thud and a real eerie silence. I open the door and hear this squeaking sound."

I reached over and held her hand, though I knew she probably wouldn't feel my touch. Her eyes were wide open and fixed on memory.

"Helen is barely standing straight. She has the bottle in her hand and she's pouring it over Noreen, laughing. 'Have another one on me, Noreen, honey.' That's what she says. I must have made some sound, 'cause she stumbles around to face me. 'Cozy picture, isn't it?' she says, tossing the bottle at me. I catch it before it hits me. Then she says, 'And

Manny makes three,' giggling like just another ugly drunk. 'Nothing like a little incest to get the juices flowing, right, Manny?' "

She crashed down to the present, squeezing my hand so hard I was afraid my fingers would crack off. I was too numb to react. The word *incest* was rocking in my head.

Tears streaming down her face, Manny continued. "All I could think about was I slept with this bitch. I was so ashamed, I just stood there. She just laughed at me and shuffled out the back door. By the time I knelt down by Noreen, it was too late. Her eyes were glazed. There was no pulse."

With my free hand I stroked the side of her head, wondering how she had kept all of this to herself for so long.

She turned to me, as if she suddenly realized where she was. "Robin, I'm a Latina lesbian in a white, redneck town where the word *colored* still means something you do with crayons. My fingerprints were all over that bottle, I'd just cheated on Noreen, and from what I knew, the woman I'd had sex with was probably the one who had killed my lover. Add to that the fact that Noreen had altered her will to make me sole benefactor. Christ. You don't have to be a rocket scientist to know whose ass was going to be dragged off to jail."

With a tremor, I realized she was right. If she had told Sheriff Crowell the story I just heard, he would have locked her up and prided himself on having earned his wages with such brilliant investigative skills.

"I couldn't let that happen to me. Or my family. You may not know this, but I've been managing an antique store in Cresco. The money's pretty good. For the first time in my life, I have a chance to take care of my mother and brother the way I want to. If I get tangled up in this murder investigation, everything I've worked for is blown. So I decided to save my own ass. I took the bottle with me and hightailed it to my mother's place. Got to tell you, it was scary to find myself seeking haven in the same rat-infested dump I've spent my life running from."

Now that the whole story was out, Manny's face had lost some of its tightness. I rubbed the back of my neck and grudgingly asked, "What do you want me to do with the information you just gave me?"

She emitted a caustic laugh. "Damned if I know, Robin." She started the car. "But if there's any way you can keep me out of this, I would really appreciate it."

Once again, I felt boxed into a corner. "Have you talked to Helen since —"

"Once. Late on Sunday. I wanted to give her a chance to explain. She said she couldn't remember anything about Saturday night. And she meant *anything*. As far as she could recall, I had stopped in for a quick drink and left. So if you want to confirm my story, you're going to be pretty dissatisfied."

Manny was even sharper than I had realized.

She pulled into Carly and Amy's driveway. "Guess this is where you get out. I was invited too, but I had plans with my family this afternoon. Anyway, I would have declined as soon as I heard the full guest list."

My hand froze on the door handle. "Helen was invited?"

She smiled at me with a shrewdness I had learned to respect. "Happy Thanksgiving, detective."

I pledged to kick the next person who said those words to me.

As it turned out, I couldn't keep my pledge. Carly opened the door with such exaggerated good will that my anger dissipated instantly. The youngest child in a family of eight, Carly was a fanatic about keeping holidays. She wanted them noisy, crowded, and overfed. The combination had worked for me in the past. Tonight, I felt sick at the prospect.

Amy's kiss on my cheek was constrained, her lips as dry and stiff as commercial carpet. Our eyes never met. Carly shot me a glance that said, "Get over it." I smiled as if I couldn't read the implicit warning.

K.T. was in the kitchen, basting the turkey with something that smelled like buttered wine. I bent over to kiss her and wasn't sure if the blast of heat emanated from the oven or from our lips. In a sly whisper, she said, "Later."

I straightened up and felt a hand firmly grasp me by the waist.

"Hi, sweetheart." It was Helen.

She pulled my head down toward her and kissed me full on the mouth, without the slightest hesitation. My face flushed. The kiss was voluptuous, a sliver of tongue darting into my mouth, the pressure of her palm increasing ever so slightly. Aroused and embarrassed, I backed into the stove.

"Whoa, Robin," K.T. said, laughing good-

naturedly. "You're dangerous in the kitchen. Get out
of here this minute." She ripped off some paper
towels and sopped up the sauce my jolt had spilled
onto the stovetop. With a playful slap on my rear,
she pointed me into the living room.

Helen was on my heels. I wondered if anyone
would notice if I bolted out of the house.

"You seem a little edgy," she said with a
meaningful curl of her lower lip. "Maybe you haven't
been getting enough lately." She had lowered her
voice. Why was she suddenly so hot for me?

I leaned forward and said, "Maybe you've been
getting too much. And from too many people."

Her left eye twitched. I was about to probe
another nerve when the phone rang and Carly called
my name. "It's Dean," she said, with eyebrows that
angled up like a puppy dog's. We had been friends
so long our best communication was nonverbal. Right
then she was asking me not to make trouble. I
nodded and took the phone.

"I've been sitting here on my hands, waiting for
you to call me," Dean blurted. "I wasn't even sure
you were back yet. It's Thanksgiving, for chrissakes.
Didn't you even think I might want to hear an
update?"

I told him to hold on, then changed to the phone
in the guest bedroom. He wasn't happy to hear my
news.

"So you know absolutely nothing new. How the
hell am I supposed to accept that?" he shouted. "I
just paid good dollars to send you traipsing down to
Atlanta and you didn't learn anything?"

I didn't think he'd be pleased to know that all

his dollars had accomplished was to bring me one step closer to finding Noreen's siblings, so I kept mum while he shot questions I had no way of answering. When he quieted down I said, "First thing tomorrow, I'll start making calls. We'll find her, Dean, I promise."

I heard him exhale. "Caroline's just a day or two away from going into labor. She won't make a commitment until she meets my wife. And if it's not us, that baby's just going to end up tangled in the system."

For a second I was completely baffled. Then I remembered. Maggie and Dean wanted to adopt. And Dean had a fourteen-year-old patient who planned to give up her child. "I'm sorry, Dean. There's nothing I can do."

"Well . . ." There was an uncomfortable hesitation and I cringed. I silently begged him to not ask me for the favor. Given the circumstances, I could hardly refuse.

"It's not ethical, but if you could come to the hospital and meet her. She has an eight o'clock appointment tomorrow —"

"You want me to pose as your wife?" I blurted.

"Forget it. I just wanted . . . I mean, if Maggie knew . . . Damn. Why the hell doesn't she come home? We could have so much —"

He didn't finish the sentence. He didn't have to. The guilt trip worked magic on me. Now, not only was I responsible for his wife's safety but also for the future of an as-yet-unborn child. Kicking myself even as the words were stumbling out of my mouth, I said, "I'll go with you if it'll buy you time."

He sighed again. "Forget it. The idea stinks. Besides, why would I want a child without Maggie around."

"It's worth a try, Dean. Who knows? Maybe I'll locate Maggie by tomorrow and we can explain the whole situation to the birth mother." I couldn't believe what I was saying.

According to my therapist, my work is probably some stupid attempt at correcting the wrongs of my past. When she first said that to me, I told her she was so far out of the ballpark she could be sipping tea in China. But the truth was that she had slid into home base. I knew what I was about to do was wrong, but believed it was for all the right reasons. Or so I tried to convince both Dean and myself. "We'll leave the exact nature of our relationship nonspecific. After all, I don't have to actually say I'm Maggie, do I?" It was a stupid compromise, but Dean leaped on it.

"Tomorrow at eight then," he said excitedly. "My office is on the third floor." He hung up, a man with a mission. I felt like a rabbit in a bear trap.

A floorboard squeaked behind me. Without turning, I knew who had just entered the room.

"What was that crack in the living room supposed to mean?"

I spun around and watched Helen close the door behind her. The trap just got tighter. I said, "Look, we'll discuss this later," and headed for the door.

She leaned against it and crossed her arms over her chest. "We have time now."

"Fine. In that case, let's start with Saturday night."

"First tell me why you made that remark in the living room just now."

"I heard about your adventure with Manny."

With fire in her eyes she stomped over to me until we were practically nose to nose. I caught a whiff of alcohol that had been poorly disguised by a mint lozenge. In a tight hush, she said, "That's Manny's story. Frankly, I don't remember much beyond my third drink."

"But she *did* leave with you?"

She nodded. "I didn't think her short visit was worth mentioning the other day. Guess I was mistaken."

Her tone had turned conciliatory, which made me more wary. If this were a game of Hot Potato, I was definitely nearing cold-spud territory. The look in her eyes slowly changed from confrontation to come-on. "Were you jealous when she told you we had sex, or did it just turn you on?"

She was too close to the truth for my comfort. "I have a question for you. Why have you suddenly started pursuing me?"

"Is that what I'm doing?" she asked, raising her knee and bumping it lightly between my thighs. My body responded instantly. It wasn't the first time my hormones had exhibited a will of their own, and I was sure it wouldn't be the last. What saved me was the knowledge that K.T. was just beyond that closed door.

"Why are you doing this?" I asked with a gulp, my mind already racing ahead to what I intended to do with K.T. once we got back to the cabin.

"Amy told me you had the hots for me. If I had

known earlier..." That clever knee had found a tender spot. She jiggled it like an expert. Ouch.

I stepped back with difficulty and said, "When did she make this announcement?"

"About a week ago. I thought she was teasing me since I've had a crush on you almost since the day we first met. In August. You were wearing a metallic blue swimsuit. I could barely stand to watch you rub lotion over those deliciously long legs. But when you rescued me at the party, I just knew it was true." She had pursued me, step for step, until I was backed against the foot of the bed. I shimmied sideways and watched her stroke her own thigh, until her palm rested over her pubis. My eyes were riveted on her hand, the sensation between my legs shifting from delectable to downright painful.

"When Manny was sucking at me, I imagined it was your mouth."

The magnetic catch broke off.

My eyes darted to her face. "You remember! You son of a bitch."

Terror distorted her features. "Just now. I swear. I didn't remember until now."

All the sexual energy converted instantly into anger. "Cut the crap, Helen. You remember every goddamn detail of that night."

I watched her hands flutter as if they were birds that suddenly had no place to nest. Finally they slunk into her jean pockets. "It's not what you think. I only remember some of what happened. Like Manny's head between my legs." Still testing my response, she bent her head coyly and moaned. "Ooo, she was good, Robbie."

I was sick of the game. Time to attack, I decided. "As good as your sister?"

Her face scrunched up in puzzlement. "What are you talking about? I'm an only child."

I crawled further out on the limb. "You made a comment about incest to Manny. When she found you pouring booze on Noreen."

Now she was the one backing away. Clearly flustered, she said, "Incest? Pouring . . ." Then her entire face altered. Her eyes widened, her skin paled. Her shock was no act. "Oh shit. I do remember." She crashed on the bed, her hands hanging limp between her legs. "Oh shit."

Watching her sit there, slumped and shaking her head in disbelief, I knew with absolute certainty that whatever sins Helen was guilty of, none of them included murder.

Finally she raised her head and looked at me. She seemed slightly ashamed. And horribly unsettled. "She's right. Man, it all just came back like that," she said, snapping her fingers for emphasis.

There was a knock on the door and I shouted, "We'll be out in a minute," then motioned for Helen to continue.

"When Manny bolted out of the house right after we . . . I guess I can't say made love . . . after we . . . fucked —"

The way she said the word made me cringe. Even now there was a glint of triumph in her eyes. Poor Manny was no match for this woman. Then again, I wasn't sure I was either.

"I was so pissed." Helen's animation was returning. "Noreen had everything I wanted. The house. A steady lover. I wanted some way to pay her back. I thought stealing Manny would be the best way to sting her. Besides, Noreen was such a horror to live with, in the long run I'd be doing Manny a favor. But she rejected me, and that was too much. That's when I really started drinking." She stared up at me with uncustomary earnestness. "I swear I don't remember much after that. What you said just now — about pouring the booze — is just a dim memory. Like a scene from a movie I watched half-asleep."

"Tell me what you do remember."

"Just what you said. Somehow I ended up in Noreen's kitchen and found her just as she was passing out. I can remember thinking, what a perfect threesome we were. Two drunks and an adulteress."

There was another knock on the door and K.T. peeked in. "Robin?" She looked concerned. "We're ready to eat now." I could almost feel heat rising from her flushed cheeks.

I crossed the room and kissed her mouth lightly. "We're almost done."

I closed the door behind her and stayed there, one hand braced on the jamb, my back toward Helen.

"Do you remember using the word *incest*?"

"For chrissakes, it's just an expression. Tell me you've never heard lesbians complain about how incestuous our community is. If Manny said I used the word, I probably did. I was monogamous for seven fucking years — with a woman that beat the shit out of me regularly. So now if I'm having a good time sleeping around, big deal. And if I sometimes happen to get a special kick out of seducing certain unavailable women, well, we're all grown-ups, now, aren't we Robin?"

I believed her, but strangely I didn't feel any relief. The fact that Helen was probably innocent of murder meant that the real killer was still outside of my reach. But there was something else. I knew exactly what she had hoped to accomplish by flinging that last barb. I was about to confront her on it when the door swung open under my hand.

"It's Thanksgiving, for heaven —" As Amy took in the scene, her expression shifted from mild annoyance to apprehension.

She stepped into the room and closed the door softly. In a voice so thin I could barely make out her words, she said to Helen, "You promised."

Helen wore a Cheshire cat grin I wanted to scratch off.

I watched the two of them, the tension in the room sucking me in like quicksand. "Get out, Helen," I said, not in the mood to mince words. Amy didn't argue. Neither did Helen. When the door closed again, I finally faced Amy.

"Robin, it was one time. Not even. I swear. Yesterday morning . . . right before you got sick. You interrupted us. Afterward, I felt so confused. What made it worse was coming home and finding you with Hassle. Shit. I was mortified. Later, when Carly came home and started raving about Helen and me having an affair, I felt like I was really losing it. I just wanted to run. I spent the night talking with Helen. Just talking. I don't even know why I —"

I interrupted. "Does Carly know?"

Her eyes were brimming. "Yes."

I closed my eyes and sighed. "Then that's it." I enfolded her in my arms, her slender body trembling against mine, and wondered if Thanksgiving would ever be simple again.

Chapter 12

From the bed I reached an arm out and lifted the edge of the blinds. Moonlight flickered over the treetops.

Thanksgiving dinner had been "tasteful." Good food. Stilted conversation. No one talked about what she was thinking or feeling, and eye contact occurred only once — when Carly asked me to pass the balsamic vinegar. K.T. tried to fill the silence by talking about her childhood in West Virginia. But by the time dessert was served, we had crashed into a conversational lull that threatened to engulf us like a black hole.

K.T. and I left a half-hour later. We remained silent even after we stomped into the cabin. I rolled my shoulders as if I could shrug off the night's events. But they clung to me like stale cigarette smoke.

I bustled around the fireplace, stacking enough wood in the black iron ring to last the entire winter, while K.T. slapped the couch pillows vehemently. Our combined efforts raised a mushroom cloud of dust, sawdust, and ash. I quickly learned there are few things less romantic than hacking with a new lover in front of a raging fireplace. I grabbed K.T.'s hand and hustled her up the stairs.

I wanted to make love, but when we lay down in bed she wiggled her butt against me in a tight spoon and asked me to turn off the light in a tone that said, "Don't argue." I complied, but the darkness made me edgy. I spun restlessly in bed, K.T. shifting with me reflexively in her sleep — first a leg wrapped around my calf, then an arm draped over my waist. No matter where I moved, she managed to maintain physical contact. And that's exactly what I craved.

With a light sweat beading up between us, I turned to face her. In the moonlight, with her steady breath soughing against my lips like a warm ocean breeze, she was more exquisite than ever before. Her lashes, a golden ocher, fluttered against well-defined cheeks. I traced the shape of her mouth with a fingertip.

Words — no, not words — emotions percolated inside my body. Julie Andrews on the mountaintop.

Anna dancing with the King. The entire cast of *Oklahoma!* warbling about beautiful mornings. Aching for K.T. in corny-musical mode, I tried to tell myself that it was just lust. Just lust that made my stomach fill with drunken hummingbirds. Just lust that made my heart beat just a little too fast.

Just lust.

I swept her curls away from her forehead and kissed her there, tears unexpectedly rushing to my eyes.

I can't do this again.

The words ricocheted in my head as my lips swept across the line of her jaw, obeying a will of their own. My mouth covered hers greedily. She stirred in her sleep, shaking her head as if dodging a mosquito.

"K.T." I whispered her name with surprising desperation. "Wake up. I need you."

A small frown skimmed her face. I licked the base of her neck and murmured hoarsely, "I want you, baby."

All of a sudden she was wide awake and kicking at me blindly. Startled, I threw a leg over her and tried to still her, crying her name over and over as she beat at me with her fists. "Get off of me, you son of a bitch!" she hollered.

I spun off and bolted for the light. When I flicked it on, K.T. was sitting upright, the blanket tucked tightly under arms, her eyes wide. They focused on me slowly, embarrassment replacing the fear. A rash the color of ripe strawberries blossomed on her chest and her eyes turned glassy.

"You all right?" I asked, and as the words left my mouth comprehension ignited in me like a brush fire. Shit. I moved toward her then halted abruptly as an almost imperceptible shudder flowed through her. Uneasily I asked, "Is it all right if I just hold you?"

The strain in my voice didn't go unnoticed. Her eyes flitted over my face, her eyebrows pressed together in concern. "I'm sorry, Robin. I didn't want —" She broke off with a forced laugh.

"Who was it, K.T.?" I made sure she could hear the certainty in my voice.

She averted her eyes. "It was a nightmare, that's all. Don't make such a big deal out of it." Still wrapped in the blanket, she shifted to the far edge of the bed and picked up her *Gone With the Wind* T-shirt from the floor. The fabric hung loosely from her narrow shoulders, making her look like a teenager at a pajama party. Except that her shoulders were hunched and her body shivering.

"It's so damn cold in here," she said suddenly. "Can't you turn up the heat?" She crossed to the dresser where she had unpacked her clothes, pulled out a pair of slouch socks and hopped into them, focusing on the task with obvious relief.

"K.T.?" I wanted to reach out to her, but the abyss was still too wide.

Ignoring me, she scuffed back to bed, swept the blankets around her again, and curled into a ball. "Let's go back to sleep," she said. "Make sure you turn out the light."

I crawled in next to her and held her so tightly I could feel the angle of her ribs under my palms. "Please, K.T. Don't shut me out like this."

Her breath grew ragged and my heart jerked in

response. Again I asked, in a voice so thin I wasn't sure she'd hear me, "Who was it, honey?"

Her words came with a tremor. "A friend of the family. I used to call him Uncle Potter. It happened only once, two months after my father died." She turned to face me. "Can you imagine how hard it was for my mother — a widow with seven kids and a father who spent half his days in the mine and the other half drunk as a fiddler's bitch? Potter's wife, Sara, was real fragile, but she did whatever she could to help my mom out. So did Potter."

She shook her head, her features revealing a sadness whose edges had been worn down by time. "I was pretty close to one of his daughters. Lurlene. Anyway, one day Potter tells my mom she needs a break. He offered to take me in for a couple of days."

Potter caught up with K.T. as she was returning from the outhouse a few nights later. "I don't remember much of what happened. Just the way his cheek was all bristly when he started to kiss me." She shimmied against me and said softly, "I was eight."

I stroked her wet cheek and waited for her to continue.

"When we got back to his house, Potter sent me back to Lurlene's room. Lurlene was sitting up in her bed, crying real quietly. As soon as I saw her face, I knew. I can't explain where I got my strength from, but I grabbed Lurlene off the bed. The two of us ran back to my house."

All at once, she sat up. "My mother was incredible. She decided there and then she had enough of Wizard's Clip. She took a poker from the fireplace, hiked over to Potter's and had it out with him. Sara never said a word, even when my mother said she was taking Lurlene. A week later, she handed her house keys to my grandfather and jammed us into my dad's battered pick-up truck."

The family moved into a cousin's house just a few miles outside of Charlottesville, Virginia.

"We invented new lives there," K.T. whispered, her damp, ice-cold limbs so entangled with mine I could feel her blood pulsing as if it were inside me. "My mother practically killed herself trying to make it up to me —" She stopped, waiting until her voice grew stronger. "She worked day and night at my cousin's bakery."

By the time K.T. entered high school, her mother was ready to launch a catering business. K.T. worked alongside her and in a few years their reputation had spread north to Washington, D.C. A highbrow inn in northern Virginia hired K.T. a few months later and her career was secured.

"So I guess I owe it all to Potter. We never saw him again, though we heard he was mule-headed about finding Lurlene. Two years after we moved, he died in a mine accident." Then the anger was back. "The day we found out he died, Lurlene came to me and said, 'He lived too long. I should've killed him myself.'"

All of a sudden K.T. flopped onto her back and stared up at me. "Robin, one of the Finnegan children started the fire that killed Noreen's parents. I'm sure of it."

There was such harsh certainty in her eyes that I wondered if she was right.

We didn't fall back asleep until almost five. I woke just two hours later and left K.T. in bed after a quick kiss.

K.T. had said that she could understand how an abused child could be desperate and angry enough to set fire to her family home and watch it burn without regret. How was it possible that someone could consciously kill a member of his or her own family? I had accidentally murdered my sister Carol and her death had plagued me almost every day of my life.

But I had loved Carol. I tried to remember if I had ever wanted to kill my father, whose deliberate silence had condemned me from the moment of the accident to the day he passed away — his tightened lips thin, cracked, and unrelenting.

No. I had wanted to kill myself.

The realization made me furious. I stomped into the den and plugged in my modem. I wanted to put this case behind me and get on with my life. I dialed an on-line database and accessed the criss-cross directory. I typed in the names of the couple who had adopted Daniel and Melanie Finnegan and began my search.

Andrew Van Eyck and his wife had remained at the same address for nearly twenty years before dying in 1975 within three months of each other.

Daniel, who had to be around eighteen years old at the time, remained in the family home for a short time. I pulled up a new Wilkes Barre address for him in 1976, then lost track of him the very next year. Melanie's name never appeared in the listing at all.

I ran a series of complex searches, but the trail for both children was stone cold. My best bet in such cases was to backtrack and gather additional data on the adoptive parents. A few phone calls and a mega on-line search tab later, I discovered that Andrew had served as pastor of the Central Presbyterian Church in a small town just outside Wilkes Barre for nearly nineteen years.

It was nearly seven in the morning when I logged off. By then, my vision was blurred and my wrists aching. Still, I was feeling a lot better. I knew just where I intended to go this afternoon. With luck, I'd have a lead on the Finnegan twins by nightfall.

Time for the masquerade. I checked my reflection in the hospital bathroom's stainless steel mirror.

Whadda doll, I sniveled silently.

I had teased my short-cropped dark brown locks into a hairdo suitable for an Avon lady. The one dressy outfit I had packed was more corporate than country, but I had tried to soften the appearance with a scarf draped over my shoulders and inexpertly tied around my neck. No matter how hard I tried, the damn thing looked more like an oversized tie than a fashionable *fichu*. I smacked my lips, sneering at the taste of lipstick and the promise I had guiltily made last night to Dean. Any case that could reduce me to hairspray, lipstick, and mascara was not worth my time. Unfortunately, it was too late to back out.

Dean was waiting in the hall outside his office. I checked my watch. I was five minutes late and he was already pacing like an expectant father. I straightened my navy tweed skirt and wiggled toward him. He glanced at me, frowned, studied his wristwatch, spat out a frustrated "Dammit," then bolted into his office.

With a start I realized that he hadn't recognized me.

I pushed the door open and blinked. Dean had exchanged the normal dirty-sock-gray fluorescent light fixture for halogen bulbs with maximum wattage. Unlike the rest of the hospital, which was painted the color of day-old grits, the office walls were whiter than Caribbean sand. His receptionist, clad in crisply ironed whites, stood up and questioned me with a voice that sounded mechanized.

The room was so dazzlingly sterilized it somehow felt dirty. My voice was a squeak as I gave my name. Dominique Inez, as the aluminum nameplate announced, was Dean's OFFICE MANAGER/ PATIENT COORDINATOR. Her breasts were conical and at least four sizes too large for her body. She wagged a finger under my nose as she led me into the inner office, muttering pointedly about promptness and loyalty and New York manners. I tried to slam the door in her face but she was too fast. Instead I glided into a leather director's chair and smiled daintily in Dean's direction.

He was perched on the edge of his desk, which was gunmetal gray and the size of a high-class coffin. A stethoscope jauntily tucked into the pocket of his white jacket, a blue cotton shirt neatly buttoned to his neck, his face so recently shaved I could almost smell the shaving cream — he was soap-opera perfect. He winked at me and started to say who I was, or at least who I was pretending to be, but broke off when he caught the warning in my eyes.

Opposite him, in a hunter-green leather sofa that had the sheen of butter, sat a young woman with raggedy, dirty blonde hair that hung down to her waist. I rose to shake her hand. She smiled shyly and offered me a limp, thin paw. Instead of the handshake I expected to give, I ended up tightly grasping her palm in mine, the blood in my veins stinging as her eyes filled. Shit, I thought. She's just a baby.

"It's good to meet you, Caroline," I said politely. Some damn maternal instinct I didn't even know I had rose up in me like indigestion. She was in such obvious distress I wanted to burble over her and cradle her in my arms. I swallowed hard and sat back down, my eyes still riveted to a face so young that its features were still rounded and not entirely defined.

"Caroline is doing very well, hon," Dean said. I glanced his way. A grin was pasted on his face like wallpaper over cracked plaster. It barely masked the strain of the past few days. "So's the baby. We're expecting any day now, aren't we?" He addressed Caroline, who barely nodded in response. "Do you have any questions for, uh," he hesitated, then continued, "either of us?"

Now that I was sitting here, with this child just a few feet away, the masquerade mutated into a nightmare. I can't do this, I realized with a sinking sensation. Once again, I was going to let Dean down.

Caroline shifted in her seat. She wore faded jeans, fashionably torn at the knees, and a tulip-littered maternity blouse that screamed hand-me-down. Her belly was large, but well cloaked. Right now she crossed her hands over her stomach like a woman twice her age and sighed. "She just kicked," she said, sounding surprised. It was the first time she had spoken and her voice nailed me. A shaky treble, it curled around me and sucked me in.

"Are you sure you want to give her up?" I asked impulsively. I felt Dean's glare before I saw it.

She zeroed in on me and nodded. Ignoring the heat spiking toward me from Dean's end of the room, I continued, "Why do you want to do this?"

The query made her pout and her eyebrows scrunch together. "I'm just fourteen. I'm not ready to be a mother."

Her statement, perfectly logical and honest, raised another question for me. "Where are your parents, honey?" I said, frightening myself by instinctively tagging on the word *honey*. Christ. It must be in the genes.

She turned to Dean, who didn't bother looking at me as he explained. "Her mother passed away during delivery, and her father died last year. She's been living with her aunt." Finally he made eye contact with me. "The woman's fifty-five. The two of them don't get along very well."

Got it.

"And the boy?" I asked him.

Caroline broke in. "Jason Boylston. He's real cute. A football star. In high school. He's good in science, too."

Great. I bet he also gets solid grades in Seduction 101.

I stared at her and said nothing. How the hell did I get myself into this stew?

"Sweetheart, maybe we should let Caroline ask us some questions." Dean's request sounded like a command. I bit my lip and scuffed my shoe against the chair leg.

"You like children?" Caroline piped up suddenly.

I couldn't meet her eyes. "Yes, I do."

Did I really? Kids always remind me first of my sister Carol, then the accident. I couldn't enumerate the times I had seen an adorable five-year-old girl and suddenly tasted ash on my tongue.

"Would you let her smoke cigarettes?"

My glance shot across the room. What kind of silly question was that? But Caroline's expression was dead serious. "At what age?" I asked.

She pondered a moment and then said defiantly, "Whenever she wanted to."

We gazed at each other and I suddenly felt as if I were on a witness stand. "No," I answered gravely. "I would not. Children need love *and* discipline."

She tilted her head at me, obviously weighing my response, then nodded. All of a sudden she blurted, "I want to be a nurse . . . that's what my mother was. I don't wanna drop out of school." One hand rubbed her belly thoughtfully. "She was a mistake, you know. But that doesn't mean she should suffer too. Right?"

It was my turn to bob my head.

We chatted a little longer, each second making the acid geyser in my throat a little more virulent. When I could barely breathe anymore, Dean's intercom crackled. The voice of Dominique, the dominatrix OFFICE MANAGER/PATIENT COORDINATOR, squealed from the box. "You're needed in the delivery room, Dr. Flynn."

Apparently satisfied with my performance, he said, "Well, we're finished here anyway. I'll be right out."

Caroline and I fell silent as Dean the Doctor clipped on his beeper, dialed his call-forwarding service, and grabbed a chart from the cabinet behind his desk. "Duty calls," he said lightly, then he kissed my cheek, whispered a heartfelt "Thank you" in my right ear, patted Caroline on the shoulder, and darted outside. I was left sitting alone with a vulnerable teenager and a horrible lie.

I cleared my throat, rose and crossed to the sofa. "Do you have a few more minutes?" I asked as I lowered myself next to her.

"Sure." Her smile was genuine. I had the sense she trusted me, which made the scenario so much worse.

"Promise me you'll listen to what I'm about to say, okay? Even if you get mad. Can you do that?"

Her smooth brow wrinkled with distrust. I wanted to kiss the furrows away but knew I couldn't. I took a deep breath, then said, "I'm not who you think I am. I'm a friend of Dean's — not his wife. Maggie, his wife, had a miscarriage recently and she was so depressed, she had to go away to be alone. But she and Dean want a child so badly, he asked me to meet you."

Her eyes narrowed further as I explained as much of the truth as I had to. At one point I feared that she was going to bolt away from me, but I pleaded with her to stay. We talked for an hour more, until Dominique kicked us out of the inner sanctum. By then, the truth had bonded us.

We retreated to the hospital cafeteria for jelly donuts and Yoo-Hoos, where Caroline somehow managed to wring out of me the fact that I was not only a private detective but also "Laurel Carter," author of countless *Harbor Romance* novels. Caroline was one of my biggest fans. She was pretty angry when I told her I didn't plan to write a sequel to *Love Conquest*, but we were able to make amends. By the time we parted she had decided Dean must be okay if the two of us were friends, but she made me promise to make sure he and Maggie were good parents to her baby. We shook hands firmly, the pact between us authoritative and unambiguous.

I walked her out to the parking lot and stared in amazement as she proceeded to unchain a three-speed bike. "You biked here?" I shouted at her bike. The temperature had risen, melting most of the snow, but many of the pine-shaded roads still glistened with unexpected patches of ice.

She lifted her bulky down coat over her butt and mounted the bike, her swollen belly just inches from the handlebars. "I live less than a mile from here," she said, as if that actually made sense.

"Where's your aunt?" I was turning shrill and didn't give a shit.

"Calm down, Robin. She's working. No big deal." She lifted a foot to a pedal and I dashed forward, jamming my toes against the front wheel.

"I'll drive you home." It was an order and she knew it.

Unexpectedly, she smiled. "Cool." She hopped down and waited for my next command.

I led her to my car, jammed the bike so that it was half inside and half dangling out the side window, and then pointed Caroline into the passenger seat. As I was starting the car, I heard her sniffle.

"Thanks." She gave me directions, then started playing distractedly with the glove compartment knob. "I really don't want anything to happen to the baby. If I had wanted that, I could've had an abortion. But I didn't." She flashed me a sideways glance. "Not that I think an abortion's sinful, or anything like that. It just wasn't for me. Besides, Jason's really smart. And his father's a lawyer." She patted her belly meaningfully. "The baby could end up being someone important, you know. We should at least give her a chance." She shifted toward me, then asked suddenly, "You're not interested in adopting, are you?"

I almost skidded off the road. "Not right now. I'm just learning how to be in a relationship."

"Is he a nice guy?"

All at once, the drive seemed way too long. Surely we had already passed the mile mark.

"Well?" she said impatiently.

Here goes . . . "*She's* wonderful," I said, taking a breath before continuing. "I'm gay."

The abrupt silence was unnerving. So was the way she fixated on the window crank. I made the turn into her driveway before she responded. "I never knew a lesbian before."

"Well, now you do." I shifted into park and waited.

She looked at me hard and I cringed. Now what?

"You could still adopt, couldn't you?"

I released my breath. "It's harder for us, but not impossible."

As she opened the door, she shook her head. "That's not right. You'd make a good mother."

So would Caroline, I thought. One day.

We exchanged phone numbers, shook hands, then laughed and hugged each other like old chums.

I headed home to change into real clothes, but as the hospital again came into view I made other plans. I marched through the entrance, waving to Roy the guard the way the nurse before me had, then proceeded in the direction of Dean's office. No one stopped me.

Before I reached his door, I made a sharp left. If I remembered correctly, the records office was just down the hall from the bathroom. A minute later I was tapping on the door like a lady searching for a potty. No one answered. I tried the knob.

The damn door was locked. I was appalled. After all, this was rural Pennsylvania, not New York City. Why did they need to lock doors here? I rummaged through my hardly-ever-used handbag for a lock pick. I made a selection from the kit my brother had given me and proceeded to jiggle the lock.

I heard the footsteps a second too late.

"What the hell are you doing?" A voice boomed at me from down the hall.

I pocketed the pick and whirled around. It was Dean. He was dressed now in surgical greens, a face mask dangling on his chest. "You scared the wits out of me," I said with welcome relief.

He stomped over to where I was standing. "Were you just trying to break into the records room?"

"Well — yes."

"Mind explaining why?" I didn't like his self-righteous tone. After all, I had just participated in a highly unethical charade at his behest. I had no compunction about reminding him of that awful ruse. He cocked his head at me and smirked. "You got me. So at least tell me why."

I explained my theory about Noreen's siblings. "If I'm right, then there's a chance one of my suspects is related to her. I'm hoping the hospital records will provide me with family histories."

Dean cupped his hands over his nose and rubbed his face wearily. "I can't let you in there, Robin. I've already pushed the rules of propriety way too far."

Principles can be so irritating. "Fine, Dean. Then you do it. You owe me. By the time Caroline and I said goodbye, she was ready to sign over her next five children to you."

His eyes lit up. "She agreed to sign the adoption papers?"

I nodded, victory just a cheap deadbolt away.

Five minutes later, Dean was inside the records room rifling through the designated files. While he was busy, I darted into the bathroom to scrub the makeup off my face. My skin smelled like Listerine by the time Dean exited from the room. Empty-handed.

"Sorry, Rob. There are no records on either Fred or Camilla. And the file on Douglas didn't provide any critical family information. I have to tell you I felt really cheap checking up on him like that. The guy's been a good friend to me."

"Does he ever talk about his family?"

"No." He faltered. "All I know is that his parents are no longer alive and they were never really close. He left home when he was just a teen-ager. Went to medical school down in Mexico. He paid his way by acting in stupid B movies." With a smirk, he added, "Teenage-werewolf type crap."

"No siblings?" I asked, wondering at the same time why Douglas had lied about his acting career.

"None that he's ever mentioned to me. But, look, he's no killer. Besides, your theory seems pretty far-fetched to me. I think you've got a lot more viable suspects, more than you can probably handle."

"Yeah. Well, maybe you're right."

I wanted to ask him about Maggie's background, but thought better of it. Instead I said, "Do you know if anyone in Telham drives a Bronco?"

"Hell, Robin, half of the community owns Broncos. Matter of fact," he said, hesitating for a split second, "that's what Noreen drove."

"Noreen?"

Goddamn it. I had never checked her garage.

"Thanks, Dean."

I hastily turned to leave but he stopped me with an impetuous shout. "Whoa! Man, that's it." He snapped his fingers. "I couldn't figure out why you wanted me to check on the DeLucas, but I just got it." He stared at me like I was Sherlock Holmes.

"What are you talking about, Dean?"

"The test results came in this morning. There was enough aconite in that sciatica tincture to kill a cow. You think Fred —"

"I don't know what I think," I said impatiently, heading down the hall.

He scrambled after me. "Will you call me as soon as you learn anything?"

"Dean, I don't have time to make pit stops to check in with you —"

"Just tell me — does this investigation have anything to do with Maggie's disappearance?"

I closed my mouth. But not soon enough. "I thought so. Look, I have too much at risk here." He scampered in front of me and walked backwards down the hall, talking at breakneck speed. "My wife. Caroline's baby. Our future." He patted his back pocket, then clucked his tongue. "Come back into my office. I'll give you the keys to my Audi. It has a cellular phone. Please."

He folded his hands together as if in prayer. I would have done anything then just to shut him up. I followed him into the office and exchanged keys, but not promises.

"Great, great. You'll call, right?"

"If I can."

"Can I do anything in the meantime? To help."

I said no, but changed my mind before I reached the door. "Can you find out from Douglas who ordered Noreen's cremation?"

He looked startled. "He wouldn't tell you?"

"No. He just said a family member. I have to find out if he's telling the truth. Call me if you find out."

I left him standing there open-mouthed, the blood of someone's newborn splattered across his body.

Chapter 13

Lousy drainage, I thought, as I parked the Audi in a puddle of greenish mud. Noreen's house was perched on a piece of land that sloped sharply down to the creek. The garage was discreetly located in the rear, at the end of a descending driveway that looked more like an overused bridle path. No wonder I had overlooked the garage earlier, I thought as I trudged through the mud, the sciatica again shooting pain up into my back. Nothing is as lovely as a walk in the woods after seven inches of snow have melted in a quick thaw.

I scanned the garage door and groaned. A goddamn electric door. I scrambled over bulbous tree roots, searching for another entrance. Since most of the houses in Telham are built on rock ledges, few have finished basements. But Noreen's house was perched high enough on the hill for the garage to be constructed on a lower level. I hoped that meant she also had a basement or usable crawl space.

I found what I was looking for around the corner from the garage. It would have taken me less than a minute to break into the basement if the lock hadn't already been broken. The rusted knob drooped in my hand as I pushed open the door, a rush of cold, dank air filling my nostrils. A string was looped into a metal clasp near the door. I tugged it once and a fluorescent light shuddered on. The basement was small and, not surprisingly, cluttered. Wooden skids circled the room and were stacked high with boxes, beach chairs, used appliances, and odd knickknacks that Noreen had probably picked up at garage sales.

My heels made sucking noises as I crossed the room to the door that led to the garage. I swung it open and flipped on the light switch. The basement smelled like fresh-turned earth, warm and musty, and a little too intense. Right under the garage door switch were seven or eight sacks of top soil, the top bag slashed diagonally along the center, the dark soil bursting through the cut like a chicken's innards. A shiny green tarp reared over the side of the sacks, the odd lumps underneath sculpting the thick plastic so that it resembled the tail of a giant lizard.

At last, I turned my gaze to the object in front of me. The Bronco was parked at a rakish angle, as if someone had backed into the garage at sports-car speed, then jammed on the brakes right before slamming into the cinder block walls. I circled the car cautiously, noting the fresh scratches on the fender and one distinct dent that recalled too vividly the jolt that had sent me off the road. I reached to open the driver's door. My hand paused mid-air. If there were fingerprints, I sure as hell didn't want to smudge them. I pulled off my pantyhose, which were pretty much reduced to rags anyway, wrapped a bit of it around my fingers and gingerly pulled the door toward me. I eyeballed the cabin, then cocked my head as an object locked in my crosshairs.

An envelope was stuck under the brake pedal. I grabbed it by the corner and shook the contents onto the driver's seat.

Then I just stared, confounded.

Three one-way plane tickets to Puerto Rico. For Manny, her mother, and her brother. I flipped through them. They had been purchased the same day I flew to Atlanta, the same day someone tried to run me off the road in *this* Bronco, the same day someone beat me to the airport and to Maggie's hotel.

The family's departure was scheduled for this Sunday.

My eyebrows pinched together. Why were the tickets here and not in the house? The most logical explanation was that they had inadvertently fallen out of a coat pocket or handbag. Unless they had been planted under the brake on purpose. Unless someone was eager to focus suspicion on Manny.

A rattle emanated from the direction of the basement. I flipped off the light-switch, darted to the far side of the Bronco and waited. The smell of the soil was heavy. I fingered the floor and found the edge of the tarp. A shiver ran through my limbs. What was hidden under that tarp anyway?

Just then, the sound repeated, followed by a shuffle. No question, someone was in the basement, heading my way. I inspected the walls near me for another exit. The only way out was by activating the electric garage door — hardly inconspicuous but nonetheless effective. I edged my way toward the switch. I was almost there when my right foot slipped on the slimy tarp. I clambered for balance, knocking over a metal watering can in the process. The response from the basement was immediate. As the lights switched on, I dove for cover.

Whoever had entered the room had crossed directly to the tool rack. As I draped the heavy green tarp over my head I glanced under the Bronco and saw the metallic head of a pick tapping against a jeaned ankle. I shimmied back and rammed into something that jiggled against the back of my thighs. If I just stayed where I was, huddling like a scared possum under the tarp, I was bound to be discovered. Peeking out, I located the single bulb hanging almost directly above the Bronco. I was a pretty mean pitcher when I was twelve, but over two decades had passed since I had sliced a ball under a batter's nose. Still, remembering how hot Randi Ellovitz had looked when she swung at one of my balls, I decided to take a shot. There was a clay pot pressing into my hip. I hefted it in my right hand, scanned the room one final time, and hurled the pot just as the figure reached the front of the Bronco.

The pot hit well enough, the bulb shattering

instantly, the clay pot itself smashing onto the van's hood. I bolted for the rear of the garage, colliding with countless unknown objects as I scrambled for the basement door. My hand was on the knob when I felt the sharp tip of the pick dig into the base of my neck. Immediately my hands went up in an "I give" gesture. Meanwhile I desperately tried to visualize a maneuver my tae kwon do teacher had demonstrated just last month.

Behind me there was a deep intake of breath, and then a growl. "Open the door slowly and step through."

The voice was Manny's.

Shit.

I kicked open the door with one mud-caked pump and spun around, my head barreling into Manny's diaphragm with a sickening thump. She fell backwards and I smashed my heel into the wrist wielding the pick. The light from the open basement door spilled over us as I dropped onto her mid-section, pinning her to the cold cement floor like a wrestler. She looked startled. And in more than a little pain. "You okay?" I asked, the question utterly insane, given the circumstances.

"Robin? Dammit, get off me."

I considered her request, then decided against it. I could still feel the unfaltering edge of the pick against my neck. The lady knew how to take care of herself, no question about that. "I found the tickets, Manny. Why just one way —you sick of the States?"

She flashed me the kind of look my cat Geeja does when I rub her hindquarters without first asking permission and said, "I have no idea what you're talking about," then bucked under me. I

227

braced myself and waited for her to wear herself out. When she spoke again, there was fire in her words. "This is *my* fucking house and *you're* trespassing." When I didn't respond, she gritted her teeth and snarled, "Girl, I coulda killed you with that son-of-a-bitchin' pick and it would have been justifiable self-defense." Her eyes folded back into mean slits.

She was really pissing me off now — especially since she was right. Even if I could prove she was Noreen's murderer, my actions would still be construed as breaking and entering. The nerves in my upper thigh protested as I raised myself off her. She slithered away until her back was braced by the Bronco.

I nodded at the van. "Noreen's Bronco forced me off the road two days ago. You can see the paint chips from my car on the bumper. And then, there are these." I flipped the tickets toward her.

She stared at them blankly. "Where'd you get these?" She shook the tickets at me quizzically, but I noticed that her hold on them was so tight she was white-knuckled.

I answered with a question of my own. "Why are you running away, Manny? Am I getting too close?"

She rolled her eyes and pursed her lips like someone who had just sucked lemon. "Christ, you're an idiot. Leave me the fuck alone."

The tickets disappeared into her jean pocket. Still, she sounded sincerely indignant. Manny Diaz was either a phenomenal liar or one fed-up woman. Unfortunately for me, I had no idea which characterization was accurate.

She raised the bottom of her crew-neck sweater and said, "Man, what the hell did you do to me? My stomach feels like it's collapsed on itself."

One palm vigorously rubbed her belly. She was lucky I had hit her that low. If I had followed my teacher's instructions to the tee I would have broken at least three ribs.

"Manny, I'm fed up with the lies. You can tell me what's really going down or you can tell Crowell. It's your call."

She raised herself with difficulty and shook her head in obvious disgust. "You are something," she said, her tone clearly implying that the "something" was, at best, akin to scum. "I told you what I know. As for the Bronco, I can't even drive the damn thing. It's a stick shift. You ever stop to think someone might have 'borrowed' the van to make me look like shit?"

"So someone broke in here and stole the van without your knowing it, is that what you're saying?"

"Real unlikely, huh, Sherlock? After all, this place is locked up like Fort Knox. Only a genius like you could figure out how to break in here, right?"

I could feel my resolve weakening. Too often I've let my personal likes and dislikes sway my judgment in a case. I liked Manny, but I didn't like the fact that so many roads ran to her door. I said, "I can't ignore the Bronco, Manny. Whoever tried to kill me was in that car. There may be fingerprints, fiber traces, some conclusive evidence too valuable to pass by. And I can't collect that by myself. I have to call in Crowell."

Manny's face twisted with anger. "You know,

229

you're just like the rest of them. Have you even stopped to consider other suspects? *I* could do a better job of investigating this than you *ever* could."

I looked at her and said, "Where would you start, Manny?"

She had my attention now and she knew it. Her smile shouted victory at me. "Noreen kept a file on almost everyone she ever met. I found one on the DeLucas a few months ago, right after the accident. Apparently, Mr. Naycha —"

"Naycha?"

"Yeah, isn't that how they say it in Brooklyn? *Naycha.* As in big trees and green gardens. Fred was a car thief in his rednecked youth. So maybe he's the one that took the Bronco for a joyride."

"Tell me something I don't know."

My response disappointed her. "You knew about his record and you still suspected me? Christ." She practically spat the words. "Well, don't ask me how, but Noreen found out and threatened to spread the word around. She didn't think it was in the interest of the community to hide the fact that he was an ex-con."

"She was blackmailing him?" I asked, suddenly remembering the three large bank withdrawals Jill had uncovered.

"No. She just didn't think his past should be kept a secret," Manny answered offhandedly. "A week after she confronted him, Camilla smashed her Cutlass into Noreen's old Beetle — that's what she used to drive when she was running errands around town. After that, it was war. I think the lawsuit was one of Noreen's greatest coups. The legal bills alone were draining the DeLucas' savings. Noreen was real proud of that." Her face tightened. "It wasn't the side of Noreen I loved."

"Where are the rest of these files?"

"Under your nose, detective." She bobbed her head toward the left. The light from the adjoining basement dimly lit the garage. I stared at her blankly, then followed the direction of her gaze. Cement walls, garden tools. Bingo! The file cabinets.

Without wasting another moment, I stormed toward the steel cases.

Manny cut me off just as my fingers locked on the handle of the top drawer. "Wait a minute." She reached into her pocket and pulled out a key ring. "Noreen's keys," she said with a smirk.

Irritated, I slammed my fist into the drawer. Both of us paused as it sputtered open on its own. The drawer was empty. "Is this a joke?" I snapped.

"No," Manny whispered, apparently dumbfounded. Could she really be that good an actress? Still fixated on the open drawer, she said, "Reen kept her files in here." She bent to the second drawer. She jerked on the handle, but it wouldn't budge. I eased the top drawer back, and the second one slid out so fast Manny stumbled backwards. It too was empty.

My heart was racing. "Did she have personal files in here as well?"

She looked at me openly. For the first time, I saw real fear in her eyes. "Her life was in here. Everything but her passport and her birth certificate."

"The stuff in the file under her bed?"

Instead of the rage I expected to see, Manny looked on the verge of tears. "This place makes my mother's apartment in Harlem look good. Did you find our vibrator, too? Or maybe you just wanted our love notes?"

The barb struck home. Suddenly I felt as sleazy as a Forty-Second Street pimp. "Manny," I started sheepishly, "did she keep her files on the adoption search in here?"

She glared at me. "Don't you already have everything you need?"

My stomach churned. Only one of us was going to leave this room with her self-respect intact. And it wasn't going to be me. In exchange, I planned to carry out at least one kernel of hard data.

I repeated my question. It wasn't even noon yet and I felt like collapsing.

Finally she said, "I suppose so. I never looked. All I know is what Noreen told me."

"You know anything else about your neighbors?"

"Look, I've told you enough." She kicked the drawer shut and walked away.

I yelled at her back. "You still haven't explained the plane tickets."

"And I don't plan to," she retorted without glancing back.

"Did you read the names?"

"Yeah," she snapped. "And the destination. Curious, ain't it? Maybe they're a parting gift from Noreen." Now she turned to face me, hands on her hips.

"One way?"

"Noreen liked her space."

She was playing with me now, and the game was getting old fast. "What made you come down here?" I asked.

"Dean Flynn's car is in my driveway. When I didn't find him upstairs, I thought he might be down here."

"So you decided to welcome him with a pickax?"

"Honey, this is still private property, despite what you think. And there's a murderer loose who seems to want to finger me. Remember where I come from — when in doubt, take the other guy out. That's how I survived seventeen years in the ghetto. And that's how I'll get through this."

I was ramming my head into a dead end here and I had other leads to follow. I passed her and headed for the basement door. She scuffled toward me and I spun around, ready to kick her nose half way to Philadelphia if I had to.

A finger wagged under my nose as she snarled, "Don't break into my house again. Next time, *if you're lucky*, I'll call the police."

I stomped out, caked mud chafing the skin between my toes. My feet were burning by the time I reached Dean's car. As I started it up, I noticed that my knuckles were turning blue from where I had hit the file cabinet. The motor turned over and I headed for the cabin.

I didn't fully realize how beat up I felt until I read my condition in K.T.'s eyes. She was sitting cross-legged by the fire, my laptop computer perched precariously on two couch pillows. A semicircle of recipe cards surrounded her. As soon as the door was flung open, she stood and crossed to me. Her full, ever-moist mouth opened wide and her eyebrows pressed together in concern. Quietly she asked, "Were you attacked?"

I groaned and stormed past her. How could I look into those eyes and explain that I had just broken into Manny's home and then mowed her down, using my head as a battering ram?

Upstairs I stripped and retreated to the shower. I was standing there, the hot water pounding on my head, when K.T. entered the bathroom. "Manny just called. She wants to know if you're planning on paying for the damage to the Bronco's hood. Do you know what she's talking about?"

I was angry with myself, angry enough to tell K.T. the truth. Scrubbing myself with soap that felt way too smooth on my skin, I blurted the details of my morning exploits.

K.T. laughed. I snapped the curtain to the side and stared at her. "What a wildcat you are," she said. "Good thing you have such a thick skull."

The woman amazed me. What would it take to chase her away? And did I really want her to go?

As a glint entered her eyes, I knew the answer was an unequivocal no. At least for the moment.

K.T. zeroed in on my breasts and playfully flicked an eyebrow up and down. "Mmmmm."

The sound was painfully arousing. I scanned the length of her, the way her full thighs and rounded butt pulled the fabric of her jeans taut, the way her loose T-shirt draped over her small, firm breasts. I wanted to pull her into the shower fully clothed and strip her with my teeth, pulling the damp layers away from that satin-soft skin. My hand lifted slightly and then halted.

What if she felt I was being too aggressive? I had already unknowingly triggered nightmares from her past. Would this act have a similar effect? I smiled awkwardly and slid the curtain back into position. Despite the hot water rushing over me, I felt chilled.

Less than a moment passed before the water turned off suddenly. I opened my eyes to find myself staring into K.T.'s face. Her cheeks were bright red. "What the hell was that about?"

I groped for a towel, found one on the rack, and stepped out. Burying my head into the damp terry cloth, I muttered, "I have no idea what you're talking about."

The towel whipped out of my hands. "Yes, you do. I could see exactly what you had in mind when you looked at me. You *wanted* me —and for the first time you stopped yourself, didn't you?"

Why the hell was she so damn insistent? I refused to look at her. Instead I grabbed another towel, wrapped it around me and marched into the bedroom.

"Why, Robin?" The change in her tone stopped me in my tracks. The anger had evaporated too fast. In its place was an inflection that was both mournful and resigned.

I tightened the towel around me and faced her. Fighting the impulse to shiver, I smiled at her. K.T. was leaning against the doorjamb, staring at me with a look so intent it made the smile wither on my lips instantly. I scrambled for a lie. "I just realized that there wasn't time, that's all. I'm already running behind schedule."

She frowned and said, "Yeah, right," then propelled herself toward the hallway.

My lie had just dug the foundation for an impenetrable barrier between us, the Berlin Wall that I always built in relationships to prevent my egress to intimacy. Isolation was so much safer. And so damn oppressive. I could feel the cement rushing into the void with each step she took away from me. I scrambled to the top of the steps and called her name. She didn't respond.

"I was afraid." My words snowballed down the stairs. By the time they hit her, I was trembling. Dammit. I wasn't ready for this.

She gazed up at me, swept her curls from her face with one hand that came to rest above her ear, as if she wasn't sure that she heard right. I felt more naked than I ever had in my life. I wanted to run into the bedroom and layer myself with thermals, wool sweaters, thick corduroys.

"Afraid of what?" she asked warily.

Here was my chance to bolt. But my feet wouldn't move. Her eyes captured me. No one had ever looked at me that way. They said: *Tell me the truth or lie. Either way, I'll know.* Her gaze was as penetrating as a deer's, and its depth as unsettling.

I lowered my eyes and said, "Of your past — and of mine."

Without looking up, I knew she was climbing toward me. And all I could think about was making love to her. Not tenderly. But with a hunger that shook me to my core. When she stood beside me and raised my face with a finger under my chin, I whispered hoarsely, "How will I know when it's too much?"

She blinked once and said, "I guess that's something we'll just have to find out together."

And with those words she led me to the bedroom.

Chapter 14

The drive to Wilkes Barre took just over an hour. I spent the whole time replaying our lovemaking. Something was happening to me I didn't fully understand. I had slept with several women and most of them I had loved. But I had never felt like this before. For the first time in my life, I realized with amazement, I was truly falling in love. And I was petrified.

I missed my turn and had to drive around the

block. The squeal of the tires against the road brought me back to the moment. I'd deal with my relationship later. I swung the car around hard and hit the parking marker. I scrambled out to make sure I hadn't scratched Dean's car. Relieved to see the silky paint job unblemished, I locked up and faced the church.

The building was Norman Rockwell perfect. The chalk-white steeples stretched up toward a sky that had turned periwinkle. Wrought iron gates were propped open against cement-cast planters. Three narrow steps led up to the entrance. I climbed them with growing agitation. A discreet brass plaque bore the name of the church: Central Presbyterian. The pastor was the Reverend Doctor William Boyle. I made a mental note of the name and headed inside.

A wood splinter jabbed my finger as I pushed open the rough-hewn doors. I cursed, then halted abruptly, my eyes scanning the shadows for witnesses. Of the few congregants scattered among the darkly gleaming pews, none seemed to note my presence. I took a deep breath and started searching for the pastor's office. As I entered a dimly lit corridor that smelled of Windex and ammonia, a few feet away a white-haired man wearing cloth overalls at least two sizes too large for his slight frame doggedly scrubbed a glass case bearing church announcements. He smiled at me, then returned to his work with a quick wink in my direction. I could tell from the wrinkles in his red, leathery skin that winking was undoubtedly one of his favorite pastimes. I marked him instantly as a source. I strode over and said, "Beautiful day, isn't it?" in a hushed tone. He ignored me. Mildly piqued, I repeated the question.

The answer came from behind me. "Certainly is. Just another reason for thanksgiving."

Turning, I came nose to nose with a heavyset man in his late fifties. "Adam's hard of hearing, aren't you?" he said, tapping the older man on the shoulder. He turned around and adjusted the hearing aid I hadn't noticed before.

"Hey, Reverend," Adam said, waving the Windex at us both.

"Don't say 'hey.' Remember?" The reverend lowered his chin and raised his eyebrows meaningfully. Although gentle, the rebuke was unmistakable.

"Sure enough," Adam said with another wink in my direction.

The reverend had already turned his attention to me. He extended a pudgy hand and peered at me through thick eyeglasses, his curiosity blatant. "I'm Doctor Boyle, and you are —"

"Rosemary Harris." Scary, how easy it was for me to lie.

"Well, Rosemary, I've not seen you here before. Are you interested in joining our humble congregation?"

The moment he said the word "humble," my distrust escalated. He was too self-conscious and his graciousness far too deliberate. I answered him warily. "Not exactly. I'm a lawyer. The former pastor —"

His shoulders snapped back into a military

posture and his left hand sliced through the air, cutting me off. "My office," he ordered abruptly. Dr. Boyle's slit of a mouth sank into his face like a stone into mud.

I glanced at Adam, who mugged for me the way a kindergartner might when his best friend's been caught in a prank. As I passed him, he muttered something under his breath. It wasn't until Dr. Boyle closed the office door behind me that the words sank in. "Make sure he doesn't take a ruler to your fingers." I was sure Adam was joking, but to be on the safe side I sat down in the tufted leather chair farthest from the reverend's desk and crossed my hands in my lap.

The room was small and sparsely decorated. Besides two chairs and a desk, there was one potted plant, two religious paintings in plain wood frames, and an umbrella stand. The office could have belonged to anyone, or no one.

Boyle eased himself into a hard-backed chair, his hands braced on the desk as if he were afraid someone might wheel the chair away from his butt without his knowing. He palmed his thin, dank gray hair back over his scalp, then steepled his hands with great deliberation. All of a sudden, I saw the reverend as a youth — the nerd everyone loved to tease. The image made me feel kindlier toward him.

"Okay, Miss Harris," he said in a no-nonsense tone, "before you say anything more, let me tell you that this congregation has changed quite a bit since the Reverend Van Eyck was in charge."

He was so defensive I had no choice but to attack. I leaned forward and asked, "How?"

241

"How, indeed," he replied ponderously. "Some sixteen years have gone by. I can assure you, I'm no Van Eyck." Boyle was an artful dodger, and the glint in his heavily lidded eyes told me that he was well aware of his skill. As I tried to decipher his answer, his features squirmed into an artificial smile. "And your mission here?"

I parried the question. "Van Eyck's legacy is a hard one to overcome, I suppose?" I hoped that the query was open-ended enough to trick him into disclosing what he apparently assumed I knew.

He pressed his fingertips together so tightly, his knuckles cracked. "I'd hardly call it a legacy."

I watched his eyelids flutter and wondered what the hell he was hiding. "Van Eyck was pastor here for *nineteen* years, Dr. Boyle," I said indignantly. "I imagine there are many individuals in your congregation right now who were just babies when he first joined the church."

He slapped the desk and jumped up, slamming the chair against the wall so hard that the windows rattled. "Just as I thought! I will not tolerate another scandal. Who sent you here?"

I started putting two and two together, and I didn't like the number I was arriving at. "Everything that's said in this room will remain confidential, Dr. Boyle. I assure you. Please sit down."

He stared at me with undisguised anger. "This is *my* church, Miss Harris. I do not need assurance from you. Now, are you going to tell me who has conjured up this latest revelation?"

Since he wasn't about to sit down, I stood up

and asked in my most lawyerly voice, "Just how many of these 'revelations' have you had, Dr. Boyle?"

An incisor tore into the corner of his lower lip as he considered his answer. "This, this," he sputtered, waving at me as if I were a roach that had just crawled into morning oatmeal, "this is outrageous. What good can you serve? The reverend died years ago, and my church has put his memory in its rightful place."

"Can you give me the names —"

"Child," he said, his eyes boring into mine like twin laser beams searching for cataracts to burn, "this church . . . all churches . . . are fighting for their lives right now. Do you have any idea of how this congregation has shrunk over the years? How can this —" He paused and whipped his hand around his head, in one gesture somehow compelling me to take in the cross hanging above his desk and the mesmerizing portrait of Mary holding an apple-cheeked baby Jesus. "How can this compete with what's out there? Yes, Reverend Van Eyck disgraced all of us. But I — we — still have so much to offer. Tell your client to let the devil lie. No good will come from pursuing the evils of one's past. Tell him to come to me, face to face, and we will exorcise the demons together."

Boyle was so roused it seemed he had almost forgotten my presence. I could hear the hiss of the radiator as he stared at the cross with a rhapsodic intensity that both disturbed and moved me. Whether I agreed with him or not, I couldn't doubt his sincerity.

I cleared my throat, then said, "I will relay your message, but first please answer one question."

Smoothing his hair again, he nodded, his back still toward me.

"Did he sexually abuse Daniel and Melanie as well?"

He spun around, his jowls flushed and his eyebrows angled up in an expression that pleaded with me to leave. "I will not talk of these things. The Reverend Van Eyck has met his Maker. May he, and his sins, rest in peace." With those words, he flipped the back of a hand at me three times, letting me know that it was time to go.

I went eagerly. If Reverend Boyle did not want to speak ill of the dead, I had a feeling someone else would. I scampered through the halls searching for Adam. After I had circled the building twice, I gave up and headed outside.

Adam was leaning on the trunk of a car, smoking a cigarette. I waved and received a thumbs-up gesture that made me laugh. He pulled the cigarette from between his lips with his thumb and forefinger and hollered, "See you still got your fingers. You're a lucky gal."

I walked over to him, "I gather you're no fan of Dr. Boyle's."

He inclined his head and studied his cigarette, then said quietly, "You're wrong there. I've been a Deacon in this church nearly thirty-two years. Reverend Boyle's the best thing that ever happened to this place." He pointed the unlit end of the butt at the building with a look of genuine tenderness. "He's a good man, Dr. Boyle, a tad too self-righteous, maybe, but there's worse sins. All I know is Boyle is just what we needed. I seen him wipe a baby's behind when her mama was too sick to stand. And I seen him shimmy under a car to help fix an axle when Old Jimmy Dale's car slid into a ditch. No, Boyle's done right by us. He's just a bit sensitive about certain matters, you know." Adam's eyes were light gray and belonged on the face of a man thirty years younger. Now they smiled at me and waited for me to make the next move.

"You know I was asking about the Reverend Van Eyck?"

His eyes were riveted to my mouth as I spoke. Their gleam disappeared as he abruptly spat at the ground. "Don't call him no reverend. The man played a part, that's all, but he weren't no pastor, I can tell you that."

"So the stories are true?"

"Well, I can't say yes or no to that without knowing the stories, can I?"

We stared at each other for a solid minute. Adam might have been hard of hearing, but he had twenty-twenty vision. He pulled on the cigarette hard with his lips, expelling a cloud of smoke that made my eyes tear. His gaze never wavered. Finally, I gave in. I've been in this business long enough now to know that there are some people to whom I cannot lie effectively. Adam was one of them, and it made me respect him that much more. "I'm trying to find out what happened to Rev — Van Eyck's children."

"You're talking about Danny and Mel?" he asked.

I nodded.

"Hell." His expression turned as arid as a riverbank in late August. "I'm as guilty as the rest —"

Before I asked him for an explanation, he tapped a finger on my lips. The dry skin smelled vaguely medicinal. "You gotta learn to hush up every now and then if you want to hear someone." To underscore the point, Adam lowered his hearing aid with a self-deprecating smirk and said, "We all blamed the kids themselves. They were adoptees, you know? So we was sure they just came from bad blood. There was no way *our* pastor could be responsible for them."

His laugh made my flesh creep.

Adam noted my silence with a single raised eyebrow. "I like a smart learner." He heeled the cigarette into the pavement, then stooped down, picked it up carefully and stuffed it into a side pocket. A whiff of burnt tobacco sailed over me.

"Danny was a handful right off. Mel was real quiet. Six months later, the reverse was true. The twins must have been around nine or ten when he first came here —" Adam scratched behind his ear lazily. I couldn't tell if he was adjusting the hearing aid or just grazing in his hair. "By the time they was teens, they was strictly forbidden company. Something about them made me want to either slap them silly or run like fire in the opposite direction. It wasn't till after the Van Eycks died that anyone came forward with the truth."

He stopped suddenly, scanning me with renewed interest. "You aren't one of their siblings, heh? A man came by last August looking for them, just like you. Said he was a private eye hired by a family member. A sister, if I recall right."

"George Morris?"

"Wouldn't know his name. He didn't get around to me. Instead, he got old tightwad Benita Welch. Man was lucky if he found out how much a beer cost in town."

I explained my role in the investigation and saw his assessment of me change right before my eyes. "No fooling?" he said. "That's mighty courageous work for a woman, don't you think?"

I stepped around the question. "How'd the reverend die?"

"Hit-and-run. They never found the driver. When the truth starting coming out about Van Eyck, folks just figured he got what was due him."

A shiver rolled through me. "And his wife?"

"She just shriveled up after that. Lasted a few months. No one was surprised by that. She weren't ever real healthy."

"What happened to the kids?"

Adam was alert enough to sense the change in my tone. Suddenly, he was all business. "Danny left town first chance he could. Don't know what happened to him. Kid was a loner. Only time I ever seen him smile was when he was around younger kids, or prowling around antique stores. Strange habit for a kid, but that was Danny. Always in his own world. Sharp as the point of my penknife, and just as cold. Mel was another story. She had a chance. She was kind of plain, but she had lots of spirit. Used to run down the church aisles whenever Van Eyck stepped up to the pulpit. Didn't make much sense then, but it does now."

"Where is she?" I asked.

His face darkened again, just as the sun disappeared. I glanced up at the sky. Storm clouds had rolled in. Adam followed my gaze and said quietly, "A big one's coming in. If I were you, I'd buy myself a couple of gallons of water and head home."

"Where is she?" My voice was louder than I intended.

"Last I heard? Spruce Hill. They locked her up when she was seventeen."

I was surprised to hear myself gasp. "The sanitarium?"

"Poor girl's mad as a rabid dog."

Hospitals give me the willies. There was no word for what Spruce Hill gave me. The grounds were immaculate. Trees lined both sides of the road, their limbs meeting above my head in a graceful canopy. The central building bore a magnificent stone face, lush ivy creeping over the boulders in defiance of the recent cold snap. Everything was so clean, so *organized*, I wanted to scream. The realization that such a scream might propel others to shut me up in this perfect domain made the horror all the worse.

I had already given my name and pretext for visiting to five indistinguishable officials. Each of them had held so tightly to some absurd rule of propriety, I wondered if they had chosen to be the keepers of the mad solely out of fear that they would have otherwise gone mad themselves. The last keeper had informed me that, yes, Melanie Van Eyck was still a patient, but, no, a visit could not be allowed without prior clearance by the appropriate authorities. I had tortured the man long enough to find out that Melanie was probably in the "day" room, playing solitaire. Disturbing such a critical activity was strictly out of the question.

I don't take no for an answer if I can lie, pretend, steal or sneak my way around it. This time, I had used a combination of tactics. The end result was that I was now wearing a visitor badge that someone named Agnes Lipshin had dumped into the waiting-room garbage pail. Twenty minutes of subterfuge had carried me from the swinging mahogany doors of the unrestricted Spruce Hills into the smudged-blue corridors that were its true center.

I felt like Alice stumbling through the looking glass. Gone were the pristine peach walls and polished wood rails, the brass pedestal ashtrays, the gallery of impressionist art highlighted with halogen spots, the piped-in Mozart. Instead, the walls muttered at me: a harsh male laugh, the discordant murmurs of conversations that knew no privacy, and a clanging piano that cried out for hands that could caress rather than cudgel the keys.

I was standing a few doors away from the day room. Now that I was this close to finding Noreen's sister, my nerve was failing me. In the distance a metal door slammed, releasing a gaggle of goose bumps along my arms. I spun around, suddenly ravenous for the artificial peace of the public Spruce Hills. Only after breathing deep, my palms braced against a wall, did my resolve return. I rushed back down the corridor and glanced inside the day room — a gymnasium-like space in which games, books, a battered piano and a nineteen-inch television had been tossed like bread crumbs into a public square populated by denatured pigeons.

The air stank of perspiration, sour milk, and popcorn. Close to thirty individuals were scattered throughout the room, each thoroughly engaged in his or her own tortured world. A man my age was seated at the piano, his shoulder-length brown hair whipping the air as he slammed his fingers against the same few keys over and over. To my left an elderly woman who reminded me of my own mother lay on the floor, fastidiously fingerpainting an uncanny self-portrait. It was like entering a twilight zone version of a kindergarten class. The only attendant in sight was parked in a tattered recliner, intent on watching *Oprah.*

I had no trouble skirting him. I positioned myself next to a pillar and scanned the room. Just then someone tugged at my jacket. I turned around, ready to bolt if I had to.

"Hi ya, honey." It was the fingerpainter. She was a good foot shorter than me, but she had the voice of a six-foot-four trucker. "Didn't think I noticed you, huh, Agnes? Not much escapes these eyes," she said, gesturing with a paint-smeared hand to pupils that were ringed with a milky white substance. Her pale skin was fiercely freckled with age marks, but amazingly free of wrinkles. As a matter of fact, her flesh seemed so smooth and supple that my hand ached to touch her cheek. She smiled coyly, a smile that belied her years, then all at once she lashed her finger across my cheek. I could smell the paint even before I saw her green-tipped finger prime for another attack. I stepped back and she cackled. " 'Fraid of a little waterpaint, honey?"

Impulsively, I reached for the plastic jar in her left hand and dabbed my index finger in the inky liquid. "Not if you aren't, grandma," I replied, wagging my finger at her in warning.

She roared. "Oooh, Agnes, you're a sly one." I snapped my head toward the attendant's chair. He hadn't heard. Or didn't care to hear. "Who are you here to see?" she asked, taking the paint back from me with a goodhearted chuckle.

"Melanie Van Eyck."

"Ah, yes. I know Melanie well," she said with such lucidity that I found myself wondering how she had ended up here. As if she read my thoughts, she blurted, "This is the dumpster, Agnes, that's what this place is. Some people would rather buy a new television than try to fix the one they got. So they dump the old and forget it ever existed. Here, they do that to people. My daughter hasn't visited me in two years." She shook her head, lips pursed, eyes still gleaming at me mischievously. "But I'm better off than her." She pointed her chin toward the barred window. I followed her gaze and shivered.

The fingerpainter disappeared as I focused on Melanie. She was perched on the windowsill, a deck of cards spread in front of her. She was ten, maybe twenty pounds heavier than Noreen, but in many other ways, her mirror image. Even from across the room, I could see how her pale blue eyes resembled Noreen's. Somehow, despite her size, she was a delicate woman. Her light brown hair was pulled

251

back into a loose knot and her pale skin seemed damp. She wore the same sea-foam green, Spruce Hills-stamped gown as the fingerpainter. I glanced around. Most of the other patients were clad in conventional clothes. Excluding the fingerpainter I had dubbed grandma, the gowned patients seemed the most withdrawn, the most defeated. Maybe grandma would end up that way as well, I speculated with sadness.

I turned my attention back to Melanie. She had gathered up the cards and was now shuffling them with the facility of a cardsharp. I approached her hesitantly. She didn't look up, even when I was near enough to smell the sour scent rising from her skin. I stood there silently, watching her surprisingly long fingers flip through the deck, snapping cards into place, seven across. On her first deal, she hit the ace of hearts. The smallest of smiles flickered across her face as she slapped the card down onto the sill.

"Good start," I ventured.

She didn't respond verbally or physically. I had the sense that she was used to having her space invaded. I decided to take a different tack. "Do you mind if I watch while you play?"

Her hand paused in midair and I felt my throat catch. Slowly she raised her eyes to mine, then she read my name tag. "Are you going to give me a test?" she asked in a voice that sounded eerily like Noreen's, except much younger. Judging from her voice alone, I'd have guessed her age as fifteen, sixteen tops. From my investigation, I knew she was actually a few years older than I.

I shook my head and sat down on the sill, just

beyond the ace of hearts. "Would you mind talking with me?"

She laughed — a bitter, croaking sound that made my blood boil. What the hell had John Finnegan and Andrew Van Eyck done to her as a child? "Everybody talks, talks, talks," she said in a singsong manner.

I stared at her hard, until our eyes locked. "Melanie, listen to me carefully. I need your help."

She looked puzzled. Her hands caressed the cards absentmindedly as she weighed my words. Then, unexpectedly, her eyes opened wide and filled with fear. "Uh-oh. Danny's in trouble again. I told him not to hurt anyone, but he wouldn't listen."

A fever swept over me. "Melanie, what did Danny do?"

"Never tell. Never tell." She repeated the words over and over, like a well-trained bird. With a sharp glance in my direction, she returned to the cards. I backed off until she had gone through the entire deck twice. When she was out of moves, her eyes flooded. "Danny didn't want to hurt mommy. He loved her. That was the bad part," she said through her tears.

I leaned closer, my pulse pounding so loudly in my ears I could hardly hear myself speak. "The fire wasn't an accident, Melanie, was it?" I whispered.

Her head snapped up, then swiveled toward the attendant. "Don't tell. Shhh." She put her finger on my mouth. I fought the urge to kiss her hand, to cradle her in my arms.

How had K.T. survived the horror of her youth? How had I?

I grasped her hand and said, "Don't worry. This is just between us. Danny started the fire, didn't he?"

Her face opened up like a sky spilling its weight after a relentless heat wave. "You know!" She almost smiled.

"Yes. But I don't know why. Can you tell me?" She glanced down at our hands. She was sweating profusely. I squeezed her palm tighter. "Danny said you could tell me. It's okay now."

Her eyes sought mine with greedy surprise. "You know Danny?"

I nodded.

"He's going to come for me any day now. He promised." She swept the cards to the floor, shimmied toward me, then pressed her mouth to my ear. "First, he's going to take care of Andrew."

The reverend. Her stepfather.

I whispered back. "The way he took care of your father?"

Instantly, her arms circled my neck and she was sobbing horribly. I peeked over her shoulder and saw the attendant finally rousing himself. I had to get out of there quick. But Melanie was clinging to me now. I pressed my palms against her arms and pulled away, then I kissed her cheek.

"Everything's going to be okay soon, Mel. I promise." I cursed myself for lying as I made a beeline for the door.

Chapter 15

I veered onto the shoulder, suddenly grateful for the cellular phone that Dean had installed in his car. My heart was still racing when K.T. finally answered.

"I'm closing in, K.T." I shouted into the phone, not giving her a second to speak. "The trace won't be easy, but it's not impossible. Obviously, Daniel's changed his name. But I think he's someone I already know. I wonder . . ."

D for Douglas. I felt my heart skip.

"Jill can do some of the data search. I may need

to stay here a day or two. I'll canvas the neighborhood Daniel lived in before he disappeared. If that doesn't work —"

"If you'll shut up for a minute, you may be interested in hearing what I have to say!" K.T. was agitated, I realized a little too late.

"Sorry. What's up?"

The problem was that I wasn't really sorry. I wanted to get off the phone and race over to city hall and the county courthouse. Right now, I needed access to public records: voter registration rolls, car registration records —

K.T.'s voice crackled into my ear. "Someone named Lisa called here looking for you."

Lisa? Who the hell —

"Maggie contacted her this morning."

Shit. Maggie's sponsor at Alcoholics Anonymous. "What did she say?"

"Finally I have your attention." K.T. sighed. "Where are you?"

"K.T.! What did Lisa say?"

"You first."

I gritted my teeth and answered her.

"God. The reception's so clear."

"We can rhapsodize over modern electronics some other day. What did —"

"Lisa say?" She finished the question for me. "Maggie's in Pennsylvania. She told Lisa that she's out of cash and can't use any of her credit cards anymore. She asked Lisa for a loan."

So much for confidentiality. I wondered what had compelled Lisa to contact me.

"Did she tell Lisa why she was running?"

"Not that I know of. To tell you the truth, Robin,

she was so nervous it scared me. When you talked about the case, it was distantly intriguing. A puzzle to be solved. But hearing this woman's panic . . . brrr. It gave me the shivers."

K.T.'s words worried me. Maybe she wouldn't be able to handle the pressures of being with a private detective. I had never thought about how my work might affect someone else. When I spoke again, I felt edgy. "Anything else?"

"Yeah, plenty. Lisa said to tell you that Maggie seemed drunk. She also wanted to make it clear that the only reason she called you at all was because she's afraid that the stress of covering for Maggie would send her off the edge herself."

"Did she actually say the word 'covering'?"

K.T. hesitated. "I'm pretty sure. Why?"

Something was troubling me, but I couldn't put a finger on it. I deflected K.T.'s question and started to ask one of my own, but she stopped me. "Let me finish. The two of them plan to rendezvous sometime tonight. Maggie's supposed to call back with the details between seven and eight."

It was nearly half past four now. I slapped the dashboard impatiently as K.T. continued to talk. "One last thing. Jill Zimmerman called you. She said you need to contact the office pronto. It's urgent."

"Damn. I'm hanging up, K.T."

I barely registered her goodbye as I disconnected. A second later, as Jill picked up the line, K.T.'s parting words sank in: "I'm frightened for you, honey."

I covered my burning eyes with a damp palm and barked into the phone. "What's up, padre?" My tone was a hell of a lot more cavalier than I felt.

"Listen, John Wayne redux, I'm solving this whole stupid case for you, so act like a mensch for a minute, okay?"

Despite my mood, I laughed. "I love you, Jill, you know that?" I surprised us both. Why had I said that?

She grumbled an abashed retort, then got back to business. "I'll spare you the details of my impeccable investigation and give you the bottom line: George Morris died of a cardiac arrest. While driving. Guess where?"

"Canadensis?"

"Bingo. Route three-ninety, to be exact. But you were close enough. And now, for the ten-thousand-dollar prize, can you name the coroner on record?"

I held my breath. Jill tick-tocked in my ear gleefully. For her, it was a lark. But I knew these people. "If it was Canadensis, it had to be Douglas Marks."

Faint applause trickled over the phone. "Bravo, detective. You win the prize."

I wasn't as sure as Jill. "Did Morris have a prior heart condition?" I asked.

"Not yet confirmed, oh captain mine. But it will be, have no fear. Dougie boy is quickly climbing the charts in my book."

Jill was feeling cocky. Still, I couldn't shake that gnawing feeling in the pit of my stomach.

I glanced at the clock and quickly updated Jill. Then I started the car up. "I'm heading back to Canadensis now," I said to explain the sudden jolt in our connection. I pulled into the road. There was something perverse about driving and talking on the telephone. "Maybe Doug and Danny are one and the same," I said, fumbling for the headlight switch. After all, if Doug really did have acting experience —

"I don't get it," Jill persisted. "Why do you assume that Daniel's the murderer?"

"Too many connections. Van Eyck's suspicious death. Morris's adoption search. His sudden death. The ransacking of Noreen's sister's apartment. Besides, we already know he's capable of murder."

"Just don't jump to conclusions too fast, Rob," Jill said, sounding increasingly unsure herself. "You said you noticed a resemblance between Maggie and Noreen. How do you know she isn't involved in this? Maybe she and Dougie were, you know, bot-a-boom-bot-a-bing, and Noreen caught on. Then again, I'm not sure Fred is out of the picture either. And Manny —"

A deer darted across the road and I had to brake suddenly to miss it. "Look, Jill, I'm not good at rubbing my belly and patting my head at the same time. I'll catch up with you later."

With the telephone back in the cradle at last, I floored the pedal and headed for Telham Village.

After twenty minutes of watching my headlights illuminate one evergreen after another, I found myself again trying to sort through the events of this too-long day, starting with the role play exercise in Dean's office. That's when I remembered. I had asked him to press Doug for the name of the person who had authorized Noreen's cremation. I grabbed the phone and tried to dial Dean. After three wrong numbers, I called K.T. at the cabin. Her voice was shaky. "What's wrong?" I asked right away, forgetting to even say hello.

"There's another storm coming."

I wasn't sure if she was being evasive or metaphorical. And I didn't have time to find out. I explained the situation and asked her to contact Dean.

"He's here. Hold on."

"How come you're there?" I asked him when he took the receiver from K.T..

"I tried calling the cellular phone a few times and I couldn't get you. I started to worry, so I stopped by the cabin. K.T. filled me in on what's happening," he said. Then in a lighter tone, "You're a lucky woman to be coming home to her."

I didn't appreciate his comment on my domestic life, but I let it fly for now. "Have you talked to Douglas yet?"

"I tried to, but his assistant told me Doug's out of town for the day. From what Michael said, I gathered the decision was pretty impromptu. He should be back early tomorrow. Why?"

I breathed a sigh of relief. "You sure?"

Now he was worried. "Why? Robin, what's wrong?"

"I can't go into the details now, but let me just say I don't think you should mention Noreen's cremation to him. At least, not yet."

The phone line went dead for a moment. "Christ. You suspect him, don't you? Not Doug, for heaven's sake. It doesn't make any sense. Manny had the most to gain. And Fred—"

I cut him off. I was sick of speculation. The case was muddy enough without everyone poking in a stick and stirring up more dirt. I repeated my warning.

"When are you coming back?" he blurted.

I steered around a pit in the road, swerving a little too far into the oncoming traffic lane. "I'm on my way home now. Why?" If I didn't focus on my driving soon, I'd never make it back to the cabin.

"I need my car tonight, if it's possible. Will you be back by five-thirty?"

I checked the time, cursing myself for agreeing to exchange cars. What I didn't need now was more pressure. I clenched the wheel hard and said, "Six-thirty at the latest. If you let me get off this damn phone."

"Great."

A light rain had started and I knew the snow wasn't far behind. I stretched my neck to one side until it cracked, then floored the gas.

The twin blue spruce trees that mark the entrance to Telham shivered in the headlights' glare. As the branches shuddered in the intermittent wind, a thin coat of frost cracked and floated to the ground. Even with the heater on, I was freezing. Yet the car interior was anything but cold.

My internal alarm had not stopped buzzing. With unsettling conviction, I knew this case was reaching critical mass. Something was about to break. I was getting too close, learning too much. What bothered me most, though, was the nagging suspicion that I had missed something. Whoever was behind Noreen's death was extraordinarily clever. He — or she — had deflected my investigation over and over. I had a sinking feeling that Manny was meant to be the fall guy. The problem was, she was just too easy to suspect. The more I thought of it, the more disturbed I became about the airline tickets I found on the floor of the Bronco. If Manny was in fact the murderer, she would have been gone a long time ago. If the tickets were in fact a ruse, it might mean the killer was getting jittery and a little sloppy.

It was just a matter of time before he'd strike again. And I had to be *numero uno* on his hit list, especially if my hunch about Daniel Finnegan was correct.

I slowed the car as I approached Douglas Marks' empty driveway. His house was dark. I found myself braking. Where had he disappeared to for the day? Could he have tracked me to Wilkes Barre? I mentally retraced my route. Had any cars followed me too closely? I remembered the sound of a car revving up just as I pulled away from the Central Presbyterian Church. If he had tailed me —

I cupped a palm over my mouth as anxiety bit down on my intestines. Without hesitating I cut my headlights and eased the car forward till it slumped onto the shoulder of the road, next to a stand of broad pines. Wherever Douglas was now, there was one thing I knew for sure — he wasn't home.

I retrieved my pick case from the knapsack in the back seat and slipped outside. My eyelashes flicked against the snow. If it kept up at this strange, halting pace, by morning we'd have less than an inch. I thought of K.T. back at the cabin, recalled how her skin flushed after a long bath. I envisioned the way shadows danced along the pine beams lining the ceiling of the living room, the logs hissing and cracking in the stone fireplace. Tonight was perfect for snuggling up on the couch, our bare legs entwined, her soft burnt sienna hair turning coppery in the fire's glow. I wanted to taste her again, make love to her as slowly as the drift of a snowflake in a night without wind.

But she was at the cabin with Dean and I was standing here, a slender pick in my hand, breaking into my neighbor's home. The lock gave easily — three quick flicks of the wrist and I was in. My eyes had already adjusted to the dark. Still, remembering the array of antiques cluttering this room, I searched my pocket for a penlight. The beam cut across the floor, leading me toward the rear hall. I stumbled only once, just as I entered Douglas' office. My right foot caught on the edge of the spinning wheel I had admired less than a week ago. So much had changed since then.

The office was located at the rear of the house. There was only one window in this room and memory told me that it overlooked a thick grove of oak and ash trees. I risked flipping on the overhead light, confident that my presence would be detected only by nosy raccoons and other nocturnal carnivores, then proceeded to search the desk.

The first thing that struck me were the research books lining the shelf above his desk. The assorted tomes on botany and ballistics no longer appeared innocuous to me. I pored through the contents of each desk drawer. Other than a pedantic paper on heart disease, I found nothing of even the faintest interest. Obviously, I was looking in the wrong place.

I retraced my steps, found the central hall, then climbed the stairs to the second floor. I cracked open a door and jerked backward as a light shot into my eyes. I flattened myself against the wall, heart pounding. It took a few seconds for my mind to register the after-image. I lowered the penlight and reentered the room. A large oval mirror hung on the opposite wall. I located the night table, then flicked on a lamp, grimacing as a reddish glow filled the room. The mirror was gilded, antique in design. The bed itself was king-sized, with red velvet and gold-tasseled ropes draped over the walnut canopy. The only furniture in the room besides the bed and night tables was a similarly ornate fainting couch angled so that it faced an incongruously modern armoire.

Instinct made me cross the room. I was just about to open the armoire's doors when I heard a creak behind me. I held my breath and listened with every cell in my body. Only after a full minute had passed did I continue with my search.

I slid the door open and felt my jaw drop. The armoire was actually an entertainment center — that is, if you deemed porn entertainment. The central compartment held a television and VCR combination unit. But what made my blood pump was the contents of the top shelves. I fingered the first book. *Spread Eagles.* The title was disturbingly accurate. I rotated the book, trying to discern just what part of a woman's anatomy the center spread depicted. When I figured it out, I snapped the book tight and glanced over to the titles printed on the spines of Douglas' impressive videotape collection. *Ride Her High!* I slipped the case out. The plastic jacket was yellowed and cracking from age. I started to return it to its place on the shelf, then stopped abruptly, my eye drawn to the front cover.

The photograph had to be at least a decade old, but the face on the bare-chested male was unmistakable. Douglas Marks was one of the film's stars. At last, the reticence about his acting career made sense.

So Douglas Marks used to be Doug Adonis, porn star. What did that prove? Nothing, I tried to convince myself as I finished rummaging through the bedroom.

Down the hall were two other bedrooms. Both were country-inn perfect. I wasn't surprised. In the past few years, I've come to learn that most of us move in more than one world. So often, the public persona reflects little of the passions, fears, and impulses that seethe under the skin.

What attracted me and repulsed me about my work was that it plunged right into the churning bloodstream of the shadow world.

As I opened drawers and closet doors, searched under beds and directed the penlight toward bookshelves, sounds of movement just outside the house rattled my nerves. I knew Doug could come home any minute. And a glance at my watch told me that I was almost late for Maggie's call. But I was intent on finishing my search. I had one last room to inspect. The knob resisted me. I smiled as I whipped out another pick.

Once inside I changed my assessment. The interior was more a walk-in closet than a full-sized room. A yellow light bathed the contents. On the right-hand wall was a gun cabinet. I moved aside an air mattress and jerked open the bottom drawer. I heard the bullets rattle before I saw them.

My fingertips and scalp were tingling, and the gurgle in my stomach echoed in my ears. I forced myself to stop and take ten slow breaths. I had to keep myself sharp and steady now. With measured calm, I scrutinized the rest of the closet. On a shelf on the rear wall, next to a twelve-pack of paper towels, I discovered a collection of antique binoculars. I held one in my hands and closed my eyes. Could Douglas be Daniel Finnegan? If so, Doug possessed not only motive and the medical knowledge necessary to take Noreen down, but also the ideal position for covering up his involvement in the death.

An alarm sounded downstairs and I jumped backward. Shit. Reflexively, I reached for the revolver resting in the bottom drawer of the gun cabinet. As soon as it was in my hand, my body broke out in a cold sweat. I hadn't held a gun since my sister Carol's death. My partner Tony had repeatedly admonished me that firearms provided a critical line of defense in our profession. I had taken tae kwon do instead.

Now I checked the gun to confirm that it was loaded. The bullet blurred as a drop of sweat rolled into my right eye. I wiped my forehead with the back of one hand, abruptly noticing that the buzzing had stopped and a voice was booming up the stairs.

Carol's face swam before me, her open mouth brimming with bright red blood. I can't handle this, I thought, prepared to drop the gun back in the drawer. Then I recognized the voice. Dean. All at once the only image before me was K.T.'s face, the way she looked in the morning as the sunlight gently swept her face.

I rushed out of the closet and clambered downstairs, shouting Dean's name. He just kept speaking, rushing over my words. I ran toward the sound, realization dawning on me as I neared the source.

Dammit. I screeched to a halt near Douglas's desk, the gun pointing at a son-of-a-bitching answering machine. Dean had already hung up. I put the gun down, flicked on the desk lamp, then searched for the "play" button. My finger hesitated for a nanosecond. Dean's call might be urgent. I pressed the button, wondering if he had seen his car in the driveway and was trying to warn me that Douglas was nearing home.

Glancing over my shoulder nervously, I listened to the tape whir into place. That's when I noticed the medical bag discreetly tucked behind an overstuffed armchair. I scurried over, snapped the flap, and began rummaging through the contents. My blood ran cold as I scanned the notes Douglas had hastily scribbled onto a legal pad.

Dean was Noreen's brother. And he was the one who had ordered her cremation.

There was a long buzz, then Dean's voice banged into the room. "Hey, Mr. Adonis, it's Dean. When you get home tomorrow morning, call me right away. I'm going to need your help to solve a little problem I've run up against. I'll explain later. Call me at the seven-eight-nine-one number. If I don't answer the first time, keep trying until you reach me. The calls will be forwarded to wherever I am, so don't give

267

up. You'll understand the urgency when you call. 'Bye."

There was a mechanical clack and then silence.

From the number he left, I gathered he had left K.T. alone. I breathed half a sigh of relief.

I was shaking as I dialed the number. It rang eight times before I heard a click. I waited for the bastard to pick up, but the ringing resumed. As I was setting the phone down, I heard a faint ringing in the distance. I cocked my head and listened. The ringing ceased as soon as I hung up. I dialed the number again and the ringing resumed. I ran a hand through my hair and stared at the doorway, fear finally riding a tidal wave through my limbs. Dean's car was out there. It was his cellular phone that was ringing.

Atlanta. Dean hadn't answered until the ninth ring. He could have had his damn calls forwarded to a phone booth at the airport. Or a cellular phone in a rented car. Or any goddamn place he chose.

The truth finally cracked through my defenses.

Chapter 16

I crashed Dean's car into the mail box post outside the cabin. I punched the gears into reverse, then punched them again into drive. I almost drove through the screened-in porch. The driveway was empty, I noted dully as I leaped out of the car.

My consciousness kept trying to warn me. *The driveway is empty.* Blindly, numbly, I raced up the steps. Only after I kicked in the front door and heard my cry shriek through the vacant rooms did I realize that I had Douglas's gun cemented to my right hand. I couldn't remember taking it. And I

269

couldn't put the damn thing down. I screamed K.T.'s name once, like a woman gone irretrievably and gratefully insane, then I searched through the house. There was no trace of them. No clue telling me where he might have taken her.

I will not lose you, a voice shrieked inside my head.

I ran into the den and rifled through my files, the gun still plastered to my hand. I found what I was looking for and grabbed the phone. As I listened to the line ring, I closed my eyes. Another refrain was swelling inside me. The Yiddish words my father had flung at me in disgust. *You are the Angel of death.*

"Carol!" I sobbed into the phone.

"Uh, no. This is Lisa." The voice was so unnaturally calm it tugged me back to the moment. I told her what I had discovered about Dean.

Lisa gasped.

"I was so afraid of this."

I screamed into the phone. "You were afraid of *this. This?* Don't tell me you suspected Dean."

Lisa didn't hear the threat in my words. Or she chose to ignore it. "I knew he had beaten Maggie in the past," she said quietly. "Enough so that she lost one baby. Believe me, I know what that's like. We talked a lot about what it was like to be battered, but she couldn't leave him. That's why I was so proud of her when she decided to go through with the abortion without Dean's permission. When he found out, he hurt her real bad. But he didn't kill her. So when you came to me — it just doesn't make sense that he'd murder Noreen."

I tried to interrupt, but she was hell-bent on

purging herself. "I figured Maggie had finally wised up and left him. I guess I was wrong. I told your friend that when I called a little while ago."

"You spoke to K.T.?" I was sputtering with rage.

"Well, yes. I told her Maggie wanted me to meet her at the abandoned Regal Park Inn. Your friend said that she'd go there in my place. What a relief that was —"

I never heard the rest of her sentence. I was already halfway to the front door.

Twenty minutes, I kept repeating to myself. Under normal conditions, the drive would take twenty minutes. But not tonight. I'd fly if I could. The engine roared, then shrieked as I hit the gas before I'd even shifted into drive.

I shuddered as I recalled Douglas's notes. I slammed the gas pedal to the floor so hard, the car skidded onto the shoulder with a jolt.

Calm down. Those two words became my new mantra. Then another one joined in: Think.

Calm down. Think.

Dean would want K.T.'s murder to look like an accident. That was his modus operandi. He wouldn't use a gun. Or a knife. His weapons were subtler, cagier. A syringe! That's what he'd use. But what about Maggie — and Lisa? I cracked a window, desperate for air. And then it dawned on me exactly what he planned to do.

The road disappeared as the tears broke through. I cursed myself over and over until my vision cleared. Not now, you moron. *Calm down. Think.*

He wants to trap Maggie. Setting a trap takes time. And time is just what I need.

I was on his cocky, sly heels. I slapped the wheel

with both hands, veering sharply across the road, then angling back, the smell of burnt rubber seeping into the car, smothering the scent of pine trees, of wet, delicious country air. He had already ordered that calls be forwarded to his car phone. What did that mean? He planned to come back for me. For his car. But he didn't intend to run, the phone call to Douglas told me that much. Instead, he was hoping — no — concocting another coverup, one that would include at least two more murders. K.T. and me.

I was whipping around curves with a fierceness as if some dark, defeated part of me wanted to lose control, to wrap Dean's car and my own body around the trunk of an unyielding, snow-kissed tree. Anything was better than losing again, than waking up tomorrow morning knowing that it had happened once more.

Why had I let that woman in? I felt as if razor blades were cutting through my throat. But I couldn't cry. Not yet. My teeth clamped down on my bottom lip and a spurt of blood oozed over my tongue, burning into my taste buds. My stomach heaved, past horrors rising on the tide of bile.

Calm down. Think.

Dean must have broken into Noreen's garage right after I phoned him about my plans to fly to Atlanta. I shivered, remembering the way the Bronco ran me off the road. He had wanted me to link the vehicle with Manny, find the airline tickets. Accuse the mourning lover. He practically pleaded me to do just that when I'd cut him off earlier today. Fred must have been his second choice. And Douglas too close for comfort. The man had spun me around his finger and manipulated my every move.

Damn! He must have followed me to Atlanta, hoping I'd lead him straight to Maggie. How terrified he must have been to realize that I had discovered another one of his siblings. Suddenly desperate to find out just how involved Ellen was in the investigation, he must have resorted to searching her house.

Then I remembered Caroline, how I pleaded with her to let Dean and Maggie adopt her as-yet-unborn child.

"What an asshole!" I exclaimed out loud.

With me out of the picture, Dean might still get his way. I steadied my hands and took the last turn with nerves of tightly coiled steel. This time, you bastard, you'll lose.

I cut my lights and shifted into neutral. I knew this park as well as Dean did. Maybe better. Carly, Amy, and I had spent many summer days exploring the rickety ruins of the former Regal Park Inn. Once an exclusive refuge for the oh-so-rich, the place had gone bankrupt in the eighties. Since then, its occupants had been small, furry mammals, none of which would ever make it to the shoulders of some Upper East Side matron.

By shifting into neutral, I could glide down the snow-covered road with hardly a sound. Dean wasn't expecting me and I had no intention of announcing my arrival. As the car skidded downhill, I scanned the grounds. A full moon, slipping in and out of night clouds, illuminated the snow. The wind had ceased entirely by now, and the landscape around me glowed with an eerie, deceptively peaceful smoke-blue light. For a split second, I felt as if I were embalmed in one of those plastic-domed

273

doodads that tourists bring home for their kids. Except the snowflakes were real and a killer was about to strike.

I turned the car off and waited a moment, my hot breath fogging the windows. I removed my jacket and used its sleeve to clear the window. It was no use. I unlocked the door, opened it a crack, then paused. The gun was on the seat next to me. There was no way I could use it, yet I found my fingers closing around it, a new kind of horror driving me. I stepped outside. By now, my pulse rate was off the charts. I wanted to dart into the center of the road and scream Dean's name at the top of my lungs. Instead I searched for my rented car. Finally I found it parked off the road, tucked between two massive rhododendrons. The windshield was already dusted with snow. I continued to scan the terrain methodically, but Maggie's car was nowhere to be seen.

Panic gripped me. What if she hadn't arrived yet and Dean was hiding out in the inn, waiting for her car to edge through the old stone gate at the top of the hill? Right now, he could be watching me, waiting for my next move. The other alternative was worse. K.T. was already dead and Dean had escaped in Maggie's vehicle.

I started marching in the direction of the park's entrance, then stopped abruptly. Over the stone wall that circled the grounds I caught a glint of moonlight reflecting off a maroon car roof. It was completely clear of snow. Maggie must have arrived minutes before me. Now I barreled toward the inn, my palm sweating against the gun metal. Somewhere deep inside me, a voice was screaming for me to drop the gun. I couldn't listen. K.T. was inside that inn and she was waiting for me.

The back door was warped and hung limply from rusted hinges. I sidled in and held my breath. Voices trailed toward me from the west wing. The former ballroom. I closed my eyes and pictured the way it had looked last summer. A cavernous, octagonal room with a gaping hole in the ceiling that a stained glass skylight once spanned. Only fragments of glass remained. Verdigris onion-shaped sconces were fastened to a copper railing that ran along each wall. Off to one side, sinking like the Titanic, was an abandoned piano, one thin leg cracked, the others ready to give in. Plaster columns circled the room. There were two exits — one of them blocked by a wooden plank nailed over the outside.

I took one step forward. Dean's voice carried better than the others. Its harsh tone — so unlike any I had ever heard flow from that honied, lying tongue — froze me in its tracks. The words made my flesh blister. He was ordering someone to shoot.

I scrambled toward the ballroom. Flattening myself against the door frame, I glanced inside. Moonlight crashed through the broken skylight, spilling strange, frenzied shapes of violent blue-red over the tiled floor. The colors, flickering with snowflakes, made the scene hard to decipher at first.

A second or two elapsed before I saw Maggie, a small handgun quaking in her pale palms. I leaned into the room and squinted. Dean was smart. The gun was small. Twenty-two caliber at most. The typical "woman's" gun. She was shaking her head back and forth, slowly, numbly. A crumbling plaster column blocked my view of her target. But I knew

275

the eyes staring down at that barrel had to be K.T., There was a growl off to my left. I backed off and looked down for an instant. My hand was raised, my finger braced on the trigger. The growl repeated, low, threatening. It had to be Dean. I squatted and started to spin in the room, then stopped myself. Dammit.

Tony was right. My guilt over Carol's death had prevented me from learning how to handle a gun. And now it was holding me back from saving K.T. Waves of nausea swept over me as I leaned against the doorjamb again.

Then Dean bellowed. "I'm losing patience, Maggie." His voice came from the right!

Maggie's gun was leveled at *him*.

I lowered myself again and entered the room slowly. Dean's taunting rebuke buried the sound of my movement. "Shoot. Go ahead." He paused. "See. You can't do it, Maggie. You can't. Know why? You still *need* me. For God's sake, we'll just end up killing each other."

His words didn't make sense until I found him standing close to one of the exit doors, a revolver steady in his clasped hands.

"All I want you to do is shoot *her*," Dean said, bobbing his head to indicate direction. "A stranger, someone who could harm us both."

My head snapped to the left. K.T. was braced against the wall farthest from me, her wrists tied to one of the sconces with a yellow tie. My heart collapsed. The growling had come from her. My hand tightened around the gun's grip.

From my current position, I could no longer see

Maggie. I had to sidle forward again until all three of them were in sight. With two, no, three guns in the hands of unstable players, I couldn't take any risks.

"Maggie. Listen to me." Dean's tone had turned patronizing, disturbingly calm. When I finally got Maggie back in sight, I understood why. She was swaying slightly. For chrissakes, she was drunk!

I was so close to Dean now, I could see his teeth when he smirked. "I've done this all for you and me. I've arranged for us to adopt a baby, honey. A baby!"

That's when the first bullet rang out, the report exploding like a firecracker in a garbage can. Dean had rolled toward the exit. I scrambled toward the nearest column and pressed myself against it like a lover. I wasn't sure where Maggie had gone, but I knew that K.T. was still stranded out there, exposed and vulnerable. None of us moved for what seemed forever, then I heard Maggie simpering.

Dean snaked toward the column next to mine. I edged backward, watching the glint in his eyes. All of a sudden, there was a thump and the discordant sound of plucked piano strings echoed throughout the ballroom. For some reason, the heinous notes made my eyes brim.

Calm down. Think.

Maggie had either fallen or climbed around the collapsed piano. Dean was seeking cover so that he could exchange fire. I had a clear shot at him as he dragged himself forward, using his elbows as levers. I lifted the gun and aimed. He was wearing the same blue shirt he'd worn earlier, when we met with Caroline. I lowered the gun. There was no way I could shoot. I remembered him ladling hot cider for me, the gentle way he had ministered to me at Carly's and Amy's place —

The son of a bitch had broken into Amy's lab and tainted her preparations.

Just then there was a muted spitting sound, then a fierce hiss. Dean had fired his revolver using a silencer.

"Dean!" Maggie wailed, apparently unhurt. "Just tell me why. Please. How could you kill your own sister?"

"You know why, Maggie," he replied, almost pleasantly. "She would have ruined me. Us. Once you told her about . . . that incident between us and she started having nightmares about the fire, I knew it was just a matter of time before she remembered. I couldn't afford to have people prying into my past. You know that, sweetheart. Still, I waited."

All the time he was talking, he was positioning himself for another shot. Now he raised himself so that his back leaned against the column, then he checked the revolver, blew on the barrel like a little boy playing cowboys and Indians, and took aim again.

"But she was family. It's not right —"

Dean lowered the gun and snapped. "Right? What's *right*? You think my father and foster father were *right*?" He took a deep breath, rubbed the gun barrel with an index finger, then said quietly, "Noreen shouldn't have threatened me." He lined Maggie up in his sight. "I never did figure out if you were on the extension that night. But it's okay, baby. I took care of her. And you helped me. You know you did. I would never have known Amy was preparing another elixir for Noreen if you hadn't made such a big deal about picking it up for her. You were the one that planted the seed." His grin widened.

From the opposite side of the room came a muffled sob. She was a sitting duck for him. Sooner or later, he would hit her and another death would be on my head — and then another. I mirrored Dean's movement, slinking down the column till I was in a tight squat.

Another shot rang out. The bullet pinged a few feet above Dean's head. Either Maggie was extremely lucky, or she was far less drunk than I assumed.

A new voice broke in. "You should run." It was K.T. From the way she slurred, I could imagine the way her mouth must have looked, bloodied no doubt by the back of Dean's fist.

Dean's eyes narrowed as he shifted the gun in a new direction. Blindly, wildly, my pulse hammering in my ears, Carol's blood-splattered howl echoing distantly, I pulled the trigger. He jerked backward, a spray of blood ripping against my face. I froze. The gun was fire in my hands, the bizarre moonlight room a dark smoky inferno swallowing everything and everyone I had ever loved. Someone was screaming out Carol's name again and again. With a start, I recognized the voice as my own.

By then, Dean had recovered from the shock. The bullet had pierced his upper thigh. He struggled to straighten himself, the barrel of his revolver pointing at the bull's-eye that was my head. I still couldn't move. Not to drop the gun. Not to save my life.

Shoot, Dean, I whispered somewhere deep inside. Shoot.

When the explosion came, I didn't flinch.

Maggie was racing across the room, squeezing the trigger in an unseeing rage. Dean whipped around to face her, training the gun on her this time. There was no time to think, to mourn, to fear. I aimed and fired, recoiling as Dean's body lifted and smashed against the column, the left side of his chest a scarlet hole. Maggie and K.T. cried out, their strangled voices winging around my head like wild birds.

When I finally lowered the gun, I realized that Maggie had raised hers and that the still hot barrel was slipping between her lips. I bolted across the hall, hurling my arms toward her as she squeezed the trigger one last time.

The gun clanked as I barreled into Maggie and we tumbled to the floor, limbs entwined. She had run out of bullets.

Across the room K.T. slumped against the wall, her head raised toward me, her eyes finding mine despite the dark, despite the bizarrely painted, twisted shadows falling from the broken skylight. I lifted Maggie gently and steered her toward K.T., my arm cradled around her shoulders. I didn't let go until I was just a few feet from K.T. and heard her mouth my name. A single glance at her swollen, bloody lips told me more than I wanted to know. My fingers felt like lead as I fumbled to untie the knot. Our bodies were pressed together, K.T.'s head burrowing into my neck like a cat's, nuzzling me with a sound that was half purr, half moan.

Finally her wrists were free and she collapsed into my arms. I kissed the tip of her ear, her damp, tangled hair. Crying now, sobbing out loud, at last out of control, I howled, "I love you," over and over.

When we finally parted, the snow from the skylight had already wiped its hand over the battle's scars and Dean's body lay still beneath a cold and lacy pink-stained veil.

The fur tickled my palm as I searched for just the right spot to press. There was no mistaking when I found it. Instantly flowing from the stuffed bear's belly were the sweet notes of the theme song from *God Bless the Beasts and the Children*. I smiled and continued down the hospital corridor, grateful for a moment alone.

During the past three weeks the only time K.T. and I were separated was when Sheriff Crowell had insisted on questioning us one at a time. Other than that, we spent every minute in each other's arms, soothing each other when the nightmares struck, making love when we were strong enough for the healing to start.

With Dean dead, a lot of questions would have to remain unanswered. But Crowell rose to the occasion. I suppose having firebrands like Jill and Tony prodding him ten times a day helped.

From what they've told me, Crowell arranged for the body of George Morris to be exhumed. A few days later, the coroner replacing the still-at-large Douglas Marks revised the cause of death. With Maggie filling in some of the gaps, Crowell learned that Dean had readily agreed to a second interview with the private investigator Noreen had hired to find her siblings. As Morris had quizzed Dean about his sister Melanie's strange ravings, Dean prepared a deadly salad of mixed greens, radish, and monkshood leaves. Maggie never questioned Dean about the investigator's death. It was only months later, after her abortion, that she finally opened up to Noreen and told her about Dean's violent streak and her suspicions about the strange salad Dean had forbidden her to eat.

Then, just a few days before Noreen died, Maggie found Dean using a pestle to grind down something that looked like a dried radish. Terrified that her husband planned to kill her in retaliation for the abortion, Maggie contacted Noreen and asked for her help. That's when Noreen told her the whole truth about Dean's past. Maggie began plotting her escape right away.

On the Saturday before Thanksgiving, Dean's mood shifted drastically. He seemed suddenly euphoric, rambling on about how he wanted the two of them to adopt Caroline's baby. Unable to decipher her husband's sudden good humor and in increasing fear for her life, Maggie went on an alcoholic binge. In desperation, Maggie fled to Noreen's house early Sunday morning, while Dean was still at the hospital. As soon as she saw Noreen's body, she realized what had happened. She stole Noreen's shoulder bag and drove directly to Atlanta, hoping that Ellen might be willing to help her prove Dean's guilt.

I'm still hoping that they don't press charges against her. In my opinion, the woman has suffered enough.

No one's been able to confirm that it was Dean who ran me off the road with Noreen's Bronco, but the facts point that way. Jill did finally track down the airline agent who sold a ticket to Atlanta to a somewhat frazzled individual who said his name was Fred DeLuca.

Crowell spent at least eight hours grilling poor Fred, who had to prove not only that he had never left Pennsylvania but that he also had a legitimate explanation for the large bank withdrawals made in the preceding months. It took a shoebox of receipts, credit card statements, and lawyer's bills to prove that most of the money had gone to the lawyer representing the DeLucas in the lawsuit Noreen had filed. The other money went to repairing Camilla's car, installing a new heating unit in the greenhouse, and purchasing lumber for the two-car garage they planned to build.

Jill and Tony helped Fred by unearthing the fact that Dean had rented a Cadillac with a cellular phone from the Hertz desk in the Atlanta airport. It's Tony's guess that Dean probably paid a homeless woman to quiz the Hotel Nikko's front desk clerk.

Working together, Jill and I also succeeded in locating the last Finnegan child. John Junior had been adopted by a family in San Francisco, where he still lives. We've talked twice on the phone and, to my relief, the man seems to be a fine, caring person. Suspecting his brother's role in the fire from the start, he had confided in his father's best friend on the police force. The friend had convinced John to keep quiet for the sake of the surviving family members. With a quiet sigh, John had admitted to me that he'd had nightmares ever since. The second time we talked he told me he was planning to fly out to visit Melanie.

When all the facts were in, Crowell concluded that Dean had been a little too sly and a little too eager to cover his tracks. He went so far out of his way to point the investigation at other suspects that he ultimately succeeded in trapping himself in a whirlpool his own hand had stirred up.

No charges were brought against me. Even Crowell admitted it was a clear case of self-defense. The sentence I imposed on myself was a lot more ambiguous.

There was some good news. Carly and Amy have decided to renew their commitment at a spectacular anniversary celebration scheduled for May. Manny held a very small but poignant memorial service for Noreen just a few days ago. I understand Manny plans to sell the house and use the money to move her family back to Puerto Rico permanently.

The best news just came in this morning. Caroline gave birth to a healthy baby girl just two days ago, way past her due date. K.T. and I have spent quite a bit of time with her. So have Dinah and Beth. It won't be long now before they finalize the adoption.

I nodded at the green-eyed cutie humming Christmas carols while she trimmed the tree standing near the nurse's station. It was great having one of our own watching over Caroline. I shifted the teddy bear to my left arm and pushed open the door. K.T. was by my side instantly, cooing at me as if we'd been separated days instead of less than one hour. What scared me most was that I didn't mind.

I did the usual kissing round. K.T. first, then Beth, Dinah, and finally Caroline. As I was bending over to plant one on her forehead I finally saw the baby. Scrubbed pink and wrinkled like a balloon that had only been half-filled, she scrunched her face at me and burped.

"Here," Caroline said, stretching the baby toward me. "It's time you held her."

For what seemed the two-hundredth time, I refused.

Dinah bellowed from the other side of the bed. "For heaven's sake, Rob. She belched in your face. What more do you want?"

I raised my eyes to hers. It was good to have my family here. Then I felt K.T.'s palm in the small of my back. "It's okay, honey," she whispered in a voice meant only for me. "You won't hurt her."

My pulse racing, I reached for the limp, squiggling body that had just days ago been safely sheltered in her mother's warm folds.

At last she was in my arms, arms that somehow knew how to cradle this tiny, talcum-scented body, knew how to circle her, soothe her. She burped again.

I let the back of a finger drift over her so-smooth chin, my eyes brimming as my lips curled up in an unbearable grin. "Hi there, Carol," I whispered. "Welcome home."

A few of the publications of
THE NAIAD PRESS, INC.
P.O. Box 10543 • Tallahassee, Florida 32302
Phone (904) 539-5965
Toll-Free Order Number: 1-800-533-1973
Mail orders welcome. Please include 15% postage.
Write or call for our free catalog which also features an
incredible selection of lesbian videos.

FORTY LOVE by Diana Simmonds. 240 pp. Joyous, heart-
warming romance. ISBN 1-56280-171-6 $11.95

IN THE MOOD by Robbi Sommers. 112 pp. The queen of
erotic tension! ISBN 1-56280-172-4 11.95

SWIMMING CAT COVE by Lauren Douglas. 192 pp. 2nd
Allison O'Neil Mystery. ISBN 1-56280-168-6 11.95

THE LOVING LESBIAN by Claire McNab and Sharon Gedan.
240 pp. Explore the experiences that make lesbian love unique.
ISBN 1-56280-169-4 14.95

COURTED by Celia Cohen. 160 pp. Sparkling romantic
encounter. ISBN 1-56280-166-X 11.95

SEASONS OF THE HEART by Jackie Calhoun. 240 pp. Romance
through the years. ISBN 1-56280-167-8 11.95

K. C. BOMBER by Janet McClellan. 208 pp. 1st Tru North
mystery. ISBN 1-56280-157-0 11.95

LAST RITES by Tracey Richardson. 192 pp. 1st Stevie Houston
mystery. ISBN 1-56280-164-3 11.95

EMBRACE IN MOTION by Karin Kallmaker. 256 pp. A whirlwind
love affair. ISBN 1-56280-165-1 11.95

HOT CHECK by Peggy J. Herring. 192 pp. Will workaholic Alice
fall for guitarist Ricky? ISBN 1-56280-163-5 11.95

OLD TIES by Saxon Bennett. 176 pp. Can Cleo surrender to a
passionate new love? ISBN 1-56280-159-7 11.95

LOVE ON THE LINE by Laura DeHart Young. 176 pp. Will Stef win Kay's
heart? ISBN 1-56280-162-7 $11.95

DEVIL'S LEG CROSSING by Kaye Davis. 192 pp. 1st Maris Middleton
mystery. ISBN 1-56280-158-9 11.95

COSTA BRAVA by Marta Balletbo Coll. 144 pp. Read the book,
see the movie! ISBN 1-56280-153-8 11.95

MEETING MAGDALENE & OTHER STORIES by
Marilyn Freeman. 144 pp. Read the book, see the movie!
        ISBN 1-56280-170-8 11.95

SECOND FIDDLE by Kate Calloway. 208 pp. P.I. Cassidy James'
second case.   ISBN 1-56280-169-6 11.95

LAUREL by Isabel Miller. 128 pp. By the author of the beloved
Patience and Sarah.   ISBN 1-56280-146-5 10.95

LOVE OR MONEY by Jackie Calhoun. 240 pp. The romance of
real life.   ISBN 1-56280-147-3 10.95

SMOKE AND MIRRORS by Pat Welch. 224 pp. 5th Helen Black
Mystery.   ISBN 1-56280-143-0 10.95

DANCING IN THE DARK edited by Barbara Grier & Christine
Cassidy. 272 pp. Erotic love stories by Naiad Press authors.
        ISBN 1-56280-144-9 14.95

TIME AND TIME AGAIN by Catherine Ennis. 176 pp. Passionate
love affair.   ISBN 1-56280-145-7 10.95

PAXTON COURT by Diane Salvatore. 256 pp. Erotic and wickedly
funny contemporary tale about the business of learning to live
together.   ISBN 1-56280-114-7 10.95

INNER CIRCLE by Claire McNab. 208 pp. 8th Carol Ashton
Mystery.   ISBN 1-56280-135-X 10.95

LESBIAN SEX: AN ORAL HISTORY by Susan Johnson.
240 pp. Need we say more? ISBN 1-56280-142-2 14.95

BABY, IT'S COLD by Jaye Maiman. 256 pp. 5th Robin Miller
Mystery.   ISBN 1-56280-141-4 19.95

WILD THINGS by Karin Kallmaker. 240 pp. By the undisputed
mistress of lesbian romance. ISBN 1-56280-139-2 10.95

THE GIRL NEXT DOOR by Mindy Kaplan. 208 pp. Just what
you'd expect.   ISBN 1-56280-140-6 11.95

NOW AND THEN by Penny Hayes. 240 pp. Romance on the
westward journey.   ISBN 1-56280-121-X 11.95

HEART ON FIRE by Diana Simmonds. 176 pp. The romantic and
erotic rival of *Curious Wine.* ISBN 1-56280-152-X 11.95

DEATH AT LAVENDER BAY by Lauren Wright Douglas. 208 pp.
1st Allison O'Neil Mystery. ISBN 1-56280-085-X 11.95

YES I SAID YES I WILL by Judith McDaniel. 272 pp. Hot
romance by famous author. ISBN 1-56280-138-4 11.95

FORBIDDEN FIRES by Margaret C. Anderson. Edited by Mathilda
Hills. 176 pp. Famous author's "unpublished" Lesbian romance.
        ISBN 1-56280-123-6 21.95

SIDE TRACKS by Teresa Stores. 160 pp. Gender-bending
Lesbians on the road.   ISBN 1-56280-122-8 10.95

HOODED MURDER by Annette Van Dyke. 176 pp. 1st Jessie
Batelle Mystery. ISBN 1-56280-134-1 10.95

WILDWOOD FLOWERS by Julia Watts. 208 pp. Hilarious and
heart-warming tale of true love. ISBN 1-56280-127-9 10.95

NEVER SAY NEVER by Linda Hill. 224 pp. Rule #1: Never get involved
with . . . ISBN 1-56280-126-0 10.95

THE SEARCH by Melanie McAllester. 240 pp. Exciting top cop
Tenny Mendoza case. ISBN 1-56280-150-3 10.95

THE WISH LIST by Saxon Bennett. 192 pp. Romance through
the years. ISBN 1-56280-125-2 10.95

FIRST IMPRESSIONS by Kate Calloway. 208 pp. P.I. Cassidy
James' first case. ISBN 1-56280-133-3 10.95

OUT OF THE NIGHT by Kris Bruyer. 192 pp. Spine-tingling
thriller. ISBN 1-56280-120-1 10.95

NORTHERN BLUE by Tracey Richardson. 224 pp. Police recruits
Miki & Miranda — passion in the line of fire. ISBN 1-56280-118-X 10.95

LOVE'S HARVEST by Peggy J. Herring. 176 pp. by the author of
Once More With Feeling. ISBN 1-56280-117-1 10.95

THE COLOR OF WINTER by Lisa Shapiro. 208 pp. Romantic
love beyond your wildest dreams. ISBN 1-56280-116-3 10.95

FAMILY SECRETS by Laura DeHart Young. 208 pp. Enthralling
romance and suspense. ISBN 1-56280-119-8 10.95

INLAND PASSAGE by Jane Rule. 288 pp. Tales exploring conventional & unconventional relationships. ISBN 0-930044-56-8 10.95

DOUBLE BLUFF by Claire McNab. 208 pp. 7th Carol Ashton
Mystery. ISBN 1-56280-096-5 10.95

BAR GIRLS by Lauran Hoffman. 176 pp. See the movie, read
the book! ISBN 1-56280-115-5 10.95

THE FIRST TIME EVER edited by Barbara Grier & Christine
Cassidy. 272 pp. Love stories by Naiad Press authors.
ISBN 1-56280-086-8 14.95

MISS PETTIBONE AND MISS McGRAW by Brenda Weathers.
208 pp. A charming ghostly love story. ISBN 1-56280-151-1 10.95

CHANGES by Jackie Calhoun. 208 pp. Involved romance and
relationships. ISBN 1-56280-083-3 10.95

FAIR PLAY by Rose Beecham. 256 pp. 3rd Amanda Valentine
Mystery. ISBN 1-56280-081-7 10.95

PAYBACK by Celia Cohen. 176 pp. A gripping thriller of romance,
revenge and betrayal. ISBN 1-56280-084-1 10.95

THE BEACH AFFAIR by Barbara Johnson. 224 pp. Sizzling
summer romance/mystery/intrigue. ISBN 1-56280-090-6 10.95

GETTING THERE by Robbi Sommers. 192 pp. Nobody does it
like Robbi!   ISBN 1-56280-099-X   10.95

FINAL CUT by Lisa Haddock. 208 pp. 2nd Carmen Ramirez
Mystery.   ISBN 1-56280-088-4   10.95

FLASHPOINT by Katherine V. Forrest. 256 pp. A Lesbian
blockbuster!   ISBN 1-56280-079-5   11.95

CLAIRE OF THE MOON by Nicole Conn. Audio Book —Read
by Marianne Hyatt.   ISBN 1-56280-113-9   16.95

FOR LOVE AND FOR LIFE: INTIMATE PORTRAITS OF
LESBIAN COUPLES by Susan Johnson. 224 pp.
                                               ISBN 1-56280-091-4   14.95

DEVOTION by Mindy Kaplan. 192 pp. See the movie — read
the book!   ISBN 1-56280-093-0   10.95

SOMEONE TO WATCH by Jaye Maiman. 272 pp. 4th Robin
Miller Mystery.   ISBN 1-56280-095-7   10.95

GREENER THAN GRASS by Jennifer Fulton. 208 pp. A young
woman — a stranger in her bed.   ISBN 1-56280-092-2   10.95

TRAVELS WITH DIANA HUNTER by Regine Sands. Erotic
lesbian romp. Audio Book (2 cassettes)   ISBN 1-56280-107-4   16.95

CABIN FEVER by Carol Schmidt. 256 pp. Sizzling suspense
and passion.   ISBN 1-56280-089-1   10.95

THERE WILL BE NO GOODBYES by Laura DeHart Young. 192
pp. Romantic love, strength, and friendship.   ISBN 1-56280-103-1   10.95

FAULTLINE by Sheila Ortiz Taylor. 144 pp. Joyous comic
lesbian novel.   ISBN 1-56280-108-2   9.95

OPEN HOUSE by Pat Welch. 176 pp. 4th Helen Black Mystery.
                                               ISBN 1-56280-102-3   10.95

ONCE MORE WITH FEELING by Peggy J. Herring. 240 pp.
Lighthearted, loving romantic adventure.   ISBN 1-56280-089-2   11.95

FOREVER by Evelyn Kennedy. 224 pp. Passionate romance — love
overcoming all obstacles.   ISBN 1-56280-094-9   10.95

WHISPERS by Kris Bruyer. 176 pp. Romantic ghost story
                                               ISBN 1-56280-082-5   10.95

NIGHT SONGS by Penny Mickelbury. 224 pp. 2nd Gianna Maglione
Mystery.   ISBN 1-56280-097-3   10.95

GETTING TO THE POINT by Teresa Stores. 256 pp. Classic
southern Lesbian novel.   ISBN 1-56280-100-7   10.95

PAINTED MOON by Karin Kallmaker. 224 pp. Delicious
Kallmaker romance.   ISBN 1-56280-075-2   11.95

THE MYSTERIOUS NAIAD edited by Katherine V. Forrest &
Barbara Grier. 320 pp. Love stories by Naiad Press authors.
                                               ISBN 1-56280-074-4   14.95

DAUGHTERS OF A CORAL DAWN by Katherine V. Forrest. 240 pp. Tenth Anniversay Edition. ISBN 1-56280-104-X 11.95

BODY GUARD by Claire McNab. 208 pp. 6th Carol Ashton Mystery. ISBN 1-56280-073-6 11.95

CACTUS LOVE by Lee Lynch. 192 pp. Stories by the beloved storyteller. ISBN 1-56280-071-X 9.95

SECOND GUESS by Rose Beecham. 216 pp. 2nd Amanda Valentine Mystery. ISBN 1-56280-069-8 9.95

A RAGE OF MAIDENS by Lauren Wright Douglas. 240 pp. 6th Caitlin Reece Mystery. ISBN 1-56280-068-X 10.95

TRIPLE EXPOSURE by Jackie Calhoun. 224 pp. Romantic drama involving many characters. ISBN 1-56280-067-1 10.95

UP, UP AND AWAY by Catherine Ennis. 192 pp. Delightful romance. ISBN 1-56280-065-5 11.95

PERSONAL ADS by Robbi Sommers. 176 pp. Sizzling short stories. ISBN 1-56280-059-0 11.95

CROSSWORDS by Penny Sumner. 256 pp. 2nd Victoria Cross Mystery. ISBN 1-56280-064-7 9.95

SWEET CHERRY WINE by Carol Schmidt. 224 pp. A novel of suspense. ISBN 1-56280-063-9 9.95

CERTAIN SMILES by Dorothy Tell. 160 pp. Erotic short stories. ISBN 1-56280-066-3 9.95

EDITED OUT by Lisa Haddock. 224 pp. 1st Carmen Ramirez Mystery. ISBN 1-56280-077-9 9.95

WEDNESDAY NIGHTS by Camarin Grae. 288 pp. Sexy adventure. ISBN 1-56280-060-4 10.95

SMOKEY O by Celia Cohen. 176 pp. Relationships on the playing field. ISBN 1-56280-057-4 9.95

KATHLEEN O'DONALD by Penny Hayes. 256 pp. Rose and Kathleen find each other and employment in 1909 NYC. ISBN 1-56280-070-1 9.95

STAYING HOME by Elisabeth Nonas. 256 pp. Molly and Alix want a baby . . . or do they? ISBN 1-56280-076-0 10.95

TRUE LOVE by Jennifer Fulton. 240 pp. Six lesbians searching for love in all the "right" places. ISBN 1-56280-035-3 10.95

KEEPING SECRETS by Penny Mickelbury. 208 pp. 1st Gianna Maglione Mystery. ISBN 1-56280-052-3 9.95

THE ROMANTIC NAIAD edited by Katherine V. Forrest & Barbara Grier. 336 pp. Love stories by Naiad Press authors. ISBN 1-56280-054-X 14.95

UNDER MY SKIN by Jaye Maiman. 336 pp. 3rd Robin Miller Mystery. ISBN 1-56280-049-3. 10.95

CAR POOL by Karin Kallmaker. 272pp. Lesbians on wheels
and then some!   ISBN 1-56280-048-5   10.95

NOT TELLING MOTHER: STORIES FROM A LIFE by Diane
Salvatore. 176 pp. Her 3rd novel.   ISBN 1-56280-044-2   9.95

GOBLIN MARKET by Lauren Wright Douglas. 240pp. 5th Caitlin
Reece Mystery.   ISBN 1-56280-047-7   10.95

LONG GOODBYES by Nikki Baker. 256 pp. 3rd Virginia Kelly
Mystery.   ISBN 1-56280-042-6   9.95

FRIENDS AND LOVERS by Jackie Calhoun. 224 pp. Mid-
western Lesbian lives and loves.   ISBN 1-56280-041-8   11.95

BEHIND CLOSED DOORS by Robbi Sommers. 192 pp. Hot,
erotic short stories.   ISBN 1-56280-039-6   11.95

CLAIRE OF THE MOON by Nicole Conn. 192 pp. See the
movie — read the book!   ISBN 1-56280-038-8   10.95

SILENT HEART by Claire McNab. 192 pp. Exotic Lesbian
romance.   ISBN 1-56280-036-1   11.95

THE SPY IN QUESTION by Amanda Kyle Williams. 256 pp.
4th Madison McGuire Mystery.   ISBN 1-56280-037-X   9.95

SAVING GRACE by Jennifer Fulton. 240 pp. Adventure and
romantic entanglement.   ISBN 1-56280-051-5   10.95

CURIOUS WINE by Katherine V. Forrest. 176 pp. Tenth Anniversary Edition. The most popular contemporary Lesbian love story.
                                        ISBN 1-56280-053-1   11.95
     Audio Book (2 cassettes)   ISBN 1-56280-105-8   16.95

CHAUTAUQUA by Catherine Ennis. 192 pp. Exciting, romantic
adventure.   ISBN 1-56280-032-9   9.95

A PROPER BURIAL by Pat Welch. 192 pp. 3rd Helen Black
Mystery.   ISBN 1-56280-033-7   9.95

SILVERLAKE HEAT: A Novel of Suspense by Carol Schmidt.
240 pp. Rhonda is as hot as Laney's dreams.   ISBN 1-56280-031-0   9.95

LOVE, ZENA BETH by Diane Salvatore. 224 pp. The most talked
about lesbian novel of the nineties!   ISBN 1-56280-030-2   10.95

A DOORYARD FULL OF FLOWERS by Isabel Miller. 160 pp.
Stories incl. 2 sequels to *Patience and Sarah.*   ISBN 1-56280-029-9   9.95

MURDER BY TRADITION by Katherine V. Forrest. 288 pp. 4th
Kate Delafield Mystery.   ISBN 1-56280-002-7   11.95

THE EROTIC NAIAD edited by Katherine V. Forrest & Barbara
Grier. 224 pp. Love stories by Naiad Press authors.
                                        ISBN 1-56280-026-4   14.95

DEAD CERTAIN by Claire McNab. 224 pp. 5th Carol Ashton
Mystery.   ISBN 1-56280-027-2   10.95

CRAZY FOR LOVING by Jaye Maiman. 320 pp. 2nd Robin Miller
Mystery.   ISBN 1-56280-025-6   10.95

STONEHURST by Barbara Johnson. 176 pp. Passionate regency
romance.   ISBN 1-56280-024-8   9.95

INTRODUCING AMANDA VALENTINE by Rose Beecham.
256 pp. 1st Amanda Valentine Mystery.   ISBN 1-56280-021-3   10.95

UNCERTAIN COMPANIONS by Robbi Sommers. 204 pp.
Steamy, erotic novel.   ISBN 1-56280-017-5   11.95

A TIGER'S HEART by Lauren W. Douglas. 240 pp. 4th Caitlin
Reece Mystery.   ISBN 1-56280-018-3   9.95

PAPERBACK ROMANCE by Karin Kallmaker. 256 pp. A
delicious romance.   ISBN 1-56280-019-1   10.95

THE LAVENDER HOUSE MURDER by Nikki Baker. 224 pp.
2nd Virginia Kelly Mystery.   ISBN 1-56280-012-4   9.95

PASSION BAY by Jennifer Fulton. 224 pp. Passionate romance,
virgin beaches, tropical skies.   ISBN 1-56280-028-0   10.95

STICKS AND STONES by Jackie Calhoun. 208 pp. Contemporary
lesbian lives and loves.   ISBN 1-56280-020-5   9.95
Audio Book (2 cassettes)   ISBN 1-56280-106-6   16.95

UNDER THE SOUTHERN CROSS by Claire McNab. 192 pp.
Romantic nights Down Under.   ISBN 1-56280-011-6   11.95

GRASSY FLATS by Penny Hayes. 256 pp. Lesbian romance in
the '30s.   ISBN 1-56280-010-8   9.95

A SINGULAR SPY by Amanda K. Williams. 192 pp. 3rd
Madison McGuire Mystery.   ISBN 1-56280-008-6   8.95

THE END OF APRIL by Penny Sumner. 240 pp. 1st Victoria
Cross Mystery.   ISBN 1-56280-007-8   8.95

KISS AND TELL by Robbi Sommers. 192 pp. Scorching stories
by the author of *Pleasures.*   ISBN 1-56280-005-1   11.95

STILL WATERS by Pat Welch. 208 pp. 2nd Helen Black Mystery.
                                            ISBN 0-941483-97-5   9.95

TO LOVE AGAIN by Evelyn Kennedy. 208 pp. Wildly romantic
love story.   ISBN 0-941483-85-1   11.95

IN THE GAME by Nikki Baker. 192 pp. 1st Virginia Kelly
Mystery.   ISBN 1-56280-004-3   9.95

STRANDED by Camarin Grae. 320 pp. Entertaining, riveting
adventure.   ISBN 0-941483-99-1   9.95

THE DAUGHTERS OF ARTEMIS by Lauren Wright Douglas.
240 pp. 3rd Caitlin Reece Mystery.   ISBN 0-941483-95-9   9.95

CLEARWATER by Catherine Ennis. 176 pp. Romantic secrets
of a small Louisiana town.   ISBN 0-941483-65-7   8.95

THE HALLELUJAH MURDERS by Dorothy Tell. 176 pp. 2nd
Poppy Dillworth Mystery.   ISBN 0-941483-88-6   8.95

SECOND CHANCE by Jackie Calhoun. 256 pp. Contemporary
Lesbian lives and loves.   ISBN 0-941483-93-2   9.95

BENEDICTION by Diane Salvatore. 272 pp. Striking, contem-
porary romantic novel.   ISBN 0-941483-90-8   11.95

TOUCHWOOD by Karin Kallmaker. 240 pp. Loving, May/
December romance.   ISBN 0-941483-76-2   11.95

COP OUT by Claire McNab. 208 pp. 4th Carol Ashton Mystery.
                                                  ISBN 0-941483-84-3   10.95

THE BEVERLY MALIBU by Katherine V. Forrest. 288 pp. 3rd
Kate Delafield Mystery.   ISBN 0-941483-48-7   11.95

THE PROVIDENCE FILE by Amanda Kyle Williams. 256 pp.
2nd Madison McGuire Mystery.   ISBN 0-941483-92-4   8.95

I LEFT MY HEART by Jaye Maiman. 320 pp. 1st Robin Miller
Mystery.   ISBN 0-941483-72-X   10.95

THE PRICE OF SALT by Patricia Highsmith (writing as Claire
Morgan). 288 pp. Classic lesbian novel, first issued in 1952 . . .
acknowledged by its author under her own, very famous, name.
                                                  ISBN 1-56280-003-5   10.95

SIDE BY SIDE by Isabel Miller. 256 pp. From beloved author of
Patience and Sarah.   ISBN 0-941483-77-0   10.95

STAYING POWER: LONG TERM LESBIAN COUPLES by
Susan E. Johnson. 352 pp. Joys of coupledom. ISBN 0-941-483-75-4   14.95

SLICK by Camarin Grae. 304 pp. Exotic, erotic adventure.
                                                  ISBN 0-941483-74-6   9.95

NINTH LIFE by Lauren Wright Douglas. 256 pp. 2nd Caitlin
Reece Mystery.   iSBN 0-941483-50-9   9.95

PLAYERS by Robbi Sommers. 192 pp. Sizzling, erotic novel.
                                                  ISBN 0-941483-73-8   9.95

MURDER AT RED ROOK RANCH by Dorothy Tell. 224 pp.
1st Poppy Dillworth Mystery.   ISBN 0-941483-80-0   8.95

A ROOM FULL OF WOMEN by Elisabeth Nonas. 256 pp.
Contemporary Lesbian lives.   ISBN 0-941483-69-X   9.95

THEME FOR DIVERSE INSTRUMENTS by Jane Rule. 208 pp.
Powerful romantic lesbian stories.   ISBN 0-941483-63-0   8.95

CLUB 12 by Amanda Kyle Williams. 288 pp. Espionage thriller
featuring a lesbian agent!   ISBN 0-941483-64-9   9.95

DEATH DOWN UNDER by Claire McNab. 240 pp. 3rd Carol
Ashton Mystery.   ISBN 0-941483-39-8   10.95

MONTANA FEATHERS by Penny Hayes. 256 pp. Vivian and
Elizabeth find love in frontier Montana.   ISBN 0-941483-61-4   9.95

LIFESTYLES by Jackie Calhoun. 224 pp. Contemporary Lesbian
lives and loves.   ISBN 0-941483-57-6   10.95

MURDER BY THE BOOK by Pat Welch. 256 pp. 1st Helen
Black Mystery.   ISBN 0-941483-59-2   9.95

THERE'S SOMETHING I'VE BEEN MEANING TO TELL YOU
Ed. by Loralee MacPike. 288 pp. Gay men and lesbians coming out
to their children.   ISBN 0-941483-44-4   9.95

LIFTING BELLY by Gertrude Stein. Ed. by Rebecca Mark. 104 pp.
Erotic poetry.   ISBN 0-941483-51-7   10.95

AFTER THE FIRE by Jane Rule. 256 pp. Warm, human novel by
this incomparable author.   ISBN 0-941483-45-2   8.95

PLEASURES by Robbi Sommers. 204 pp. Unprecedented
eroticism.   ISBN 0-941483-49-5   11.95

EDGEWISE by Camarin Grae. 372 pp. Spellbinding
adventure.   ISBN 0-941483-19-3   9.95

FATAL REUNION by Claire McNab. 224 pp. 2nd Carol Ashton
Mystery.   ISBN 0-941483-40-1   10.95

IN EVERY PORT by Karin Kallmaker. 228 pp. Jessica's sexy,
adventuresome travels.   ISBN 0-941483-37-7   10.95

OF LOVE AND GLORY by Evelyn Kennedy. 192 pp. Exciting
WWII romance.   ISBN 0-941483-32-0   10.95

CLICKING STONES by Nancy Tyler Glenn. 288 pp. Love
transcending time.   ISBN 0-941483-31-2   9.95

SOUTH OF THE LINE by Catherine Ennis. 216 pp. Civil War
adventure.   ISBN 0-941483-29-0   8.95

WOMAN PLUS WOMAN by Dolores Klaich. 300 pp. Supurb
Lesbian overview.   ISBN 0-941483-28-2   9.95

THE FINER GRAIN by Denise Ohio. 216 pp. Brilliant young
college lesbian novel.   ISBN 0-941483-11-8   8.95

BEFORE STONEWALL: THE MAKING OF A GAY AND
LESBIAN COMMUNITY by Andrea Weiss & Greta Schiller.
96 pp., 25 illus.   ISBN 0-941483-20-7   7.95

OSTEN'S BAY by Zenobia N. Vole. 204 pp. Sizzling adventure
romance set on Bonaire.   ISBN 0-941483-15-0   8.95

These are just a few of the many Naiad Press titles — we are the oldest and
largest lesbian/feminist publishing company in the world. We also offer an
enormous selection of lesbian video products. Please request a complete
catalog. We offer personal service; we encourage and welcome direct mail
orders from individuals who have limited access to bookstores carrying our
publications.